AURIC

BOOKS BY TIM FRANKOVICH

Heart of Fire
Until All Curses Are Lifted
Until All Bonds Are Broken
Until All the Gods Return
Until All the Stars Fall

Dragontek Lore
Viridia
Incarnadine
Auric

AURIC

DRAGONTEK LORE, BOOK 3

by Tim Frankovich

Dedicated to the memory
of David Wolverton

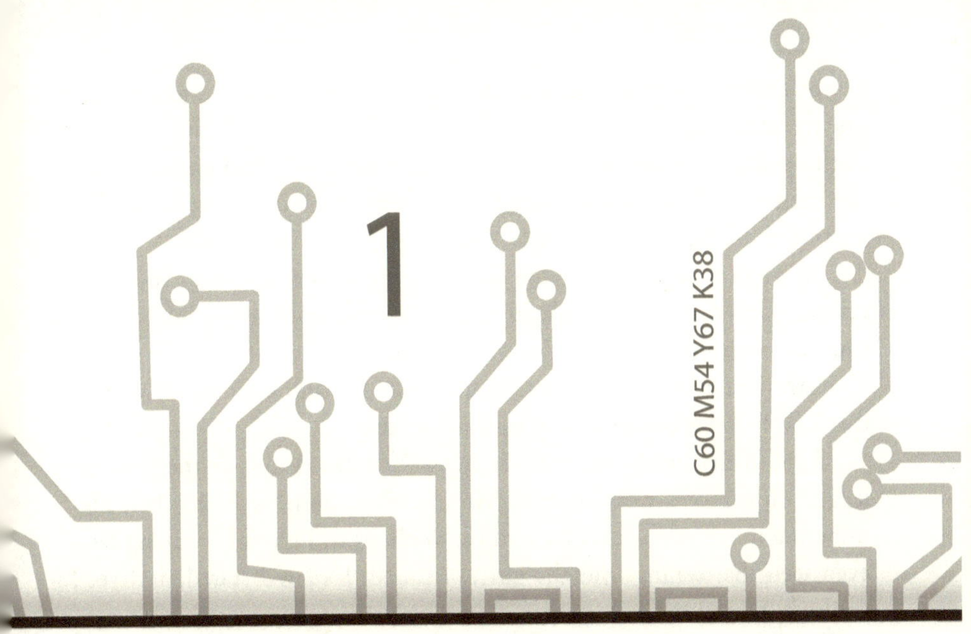

Everything I thought I knew turned out to be wrong.

Okay, maybe not everything. Just… some of the fundamental beliefs everyone in The Circle grew up believing. Things like: "the dragons who rule the six cities are immortal." We proved that one wrong when we killed the blue dragon. And then there's "draconics are all evil creatures whose sole purpose in life is to enforce the dragons' will." I had trouble letting go of that one, but Protogonus Blue, the draconic who joined our rebel band, had gone a long way to disproving it. "The skies belong to the dragons." Ha. I proved that wrong when I flew Loden's wing device. Except, of course, the red dragon, Incarnadine, would have eaten me if he'd caught me, and I barely escaped. So maybe they kind of did still own the skies.

But one of the other fundamental beliefs we all shared was: "all humans live in one of the six cities of The Circle, ruled by the dragons." After I crashed Loden's flying wing, the Sky Claimer, into the side of the mountain, I discovered… that one wasn't true either.

I woke up once or twice in the days following the crash, but not to full consciousness. I remember pain, feeling cold, hearing two voices discussing me, one male and one female, but nothing else. I drifted in dreams, or nothing at all. Pure sleep, I suppose.

When I finally did wake up, I thought at first I was in our cave leading to Loden's workshop. My eye focused on a rock ceiling. Then I remembered:

I only had one eye now. And that one was probably cybernetic, just like the one the draconic ripped out of my face. For a few minutes, I could think of nothing else. How much of me was even human now? I had no idea. Until the moment it happened, I would have sworn that my eyes were just like anyone else's. But if they weren't… what else?

As these thoughts drove me down, I finally took notice of the rocky ceiling. Our cave didn't look anything like this one. It was higher and rougher, with spikes of stone hanging down. Where was I?

"Are you awake?" The voice was female, but not someone I knew. I think I'd heard it before during my half-waking.

I rolled my head, which made my neck ache. A girl sat there, cross-legged on top of a wooden crate. An electric lantern sat beside her, illuminating much of the cave around us. Without it, I guess I wouldn't have even seen that ceiling. But the girl… I stared. I knew I stared, and yet I couldn't stop myself.

I didn't stare at her because she looked around my age, or because she was overly beautiful. In fact, she was average… but different from anyone I'd ever known. Her skin looked both pale and weathered, as if she spent a lot of time outside, but not in direct sunlight. Her mousey brown hair hung around her face, but didn't reach her shoulders. She wore warm-looking clothes in very dull colors that covered everything except her head. Not a hint of any of the primary colors showed anywhere. At some point, I realized I had been right to be cold earlier, because it was freezing in this cave! I clutched the blankets spread over my body.

But no, I stared because of her face, so unlike every other face I knew, except for the orphan Lovat. She did not have a chromark, the facial tattoo showing which dragon owned her. How was that possible? How could she be that old and not have one?

"Your face," I croaked. Was that my voice? I sounded horrible.

"Water it is," she said. She uncrossed her legs and hopped down from the crate. She picked something up from below my line of sight and approached my bed. I guess it was a cot. I hadn't been able to analyze that just yet. The girl held out a squeeze bottle over my face. I opened my mouth, and she poured water down my throat. I swallowed and felt a little better. The girl had green eyes, natural green, not the contact lenses or alterations I'd seen so often growing up in Viridia.

I needed to move, but everything felt sluggish, like my body didn't want to listen to my brain. I mentally sought out my cybernetic implant and triggered a bit of a boost into my arms. Immediately, I felt stronger. I pushed myself into sitting up, noticing some serious pain from my left hand. I didn't seem able to flex my wrist. I fought for balance. My brain wanted to throw me back down.

"Whoa," she said. "I didn't expect you to be able to do that just yet."

I blinked—does it still count as blinking if you only have one eye? I wasn't trying to wink at her—and looked around. The cave wasn't huge, but it was much larger than ours. Passages led off in at least three different directions that I could see from the limited light.

"Where are we?" I asked.

"In a cave in the mountains," the girl answered. "At least you didn't start with 'who am I?' So do you know who you are?"

I turned back to her. "I'm Beryl."

"Good meeting, Beryl. I'm Lainey."

Her voice sounded a little huskier than most girls I knew, and her accent unlike anything I'd ever heard. She pronounced her long vowels deeper and more distinct.

I gestured and she handed me the water bottle. After a few more swallows, I felt better about speaking. "Where are you from, Lainey?"

"Around." She studied me for a moment, then moved behind the crate, heading toward one of the passages. "Let me get my father to check you out."

Her father. Good to know I hadn't imagined the male voice I'd heard earlier. And yet, it disturbed me a little. I could imagine one person living out here in the mountains alone, maybe an orphan like Lovat, who made her way up to find shelter. But a family? Even just two people made it more complicated. The dragons flew around the mountains quite often, or so it was said. How could people stay hidden from them?

While I waited, I tested the rest of my body. Nothing major appeared to be broken, but everything still ached, especially my left hand and wrist. I knew I was lucky to be alive. Lucky, or… Loden. I couldn't help but wonder what other cybernetic enhancements had been done to my body all those years ago. I swung my legs over the side of the cot. Only then did I notice I wore similar clothing to the girl, much thicker and warmer than my usual. Even so, I shivered. I couldn't know how high in the mountains we might be, but it was cold. I didn't think I had crashed very high, but they could have carried me higher. Or I might not be remembering right. My thoughts did seem a little fuzzy.

I lifted my left hand and looked at it. Heavy bandages covered the whole thing, and the wrist appeared to be splinted. Maybe something was broken, after all. And if it was broken, then maybe it was normal.

"You can probably take that off in a day or two," an older male voice said. I looked up as Lainey followed her father back into my cave. A lanky-looking man, he wore the same kind of warm clothing in drab colors. More importantly, he also lacked a chromark of any kind. A grown man this old? Impossible. He rubbed a bit of gray scruff on his chin as he looked me over. "You've had a good recovery time, so it shouldn't be much longer for the wrist."

"How long have I been here?" I wanted to know.

He glanced at Lainey. "It's been what? Almost two weeks?"

"Two weeks!" I exclaimed. "I can't, I mean, I need—" I started to stand up. Spots swam in front of my eye and I almost fell forward onto my face

"Whoa, whoa, whoa." Lainey's father hurried forward and caught me. "Don't rush it, boy. Your body hasn't been up and about for a long time."

"Too long," I moaned. "I need to get back. My friends…"

"You'll see them in time. Lay back now. Let your body finish healing."

I didn't have the strength to resist. He helped me lay back on the cot and pulled the blankets back over me.

"You've been through a lot," Lainey said from behind him. "It's okay to rest."

My eye did feel heavy, and my thoughts were scattered and fuzzy again. Maybe I did need more rest. But I had so many questions. None of this made sense.

"What city are you from?" I mumbled.

My brain fought to stay awake long enough to hear his answer. He hesitated, glanced at Lainey, then looked back down at me. "Son," he said, "we're not from any of your cities."

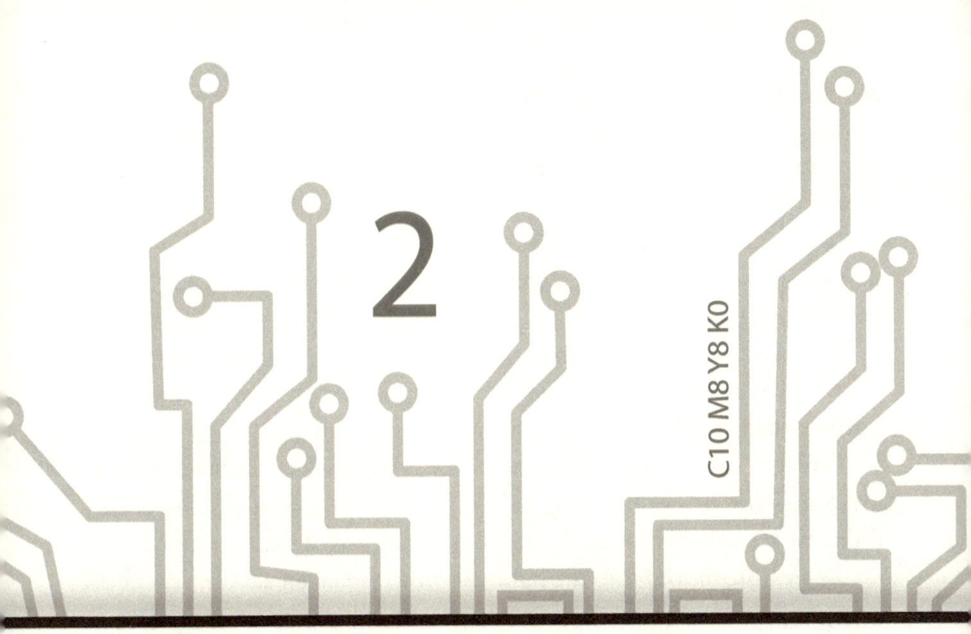

2

I had no concept of how long I slept after that. When I woke again, neither Lainey nor her father were in sight. This time, a handful of candles gave meager light to the room. I shifted on the cot and noticed significantly less pain than the last time. A good sign, but also worrying. How long had I been out this time?

With slow and careful movements, I sat up. My brain didn't rebel too much, and I managed not to lose my balance. The splint was gone from my left wrist. I flexed it a few times. Some soreness, but not too bad.

A sudden need to relieve myself pushed other thoughts aside. I swung my legs over the side of the cot, took a deep breath, and stood up. I wavered, but sent a small boost to my legs to keep me up. I took a couple of practice steps. Yes, I could walk. I looked about, my need growing stronger. No light came from any of the passages, so I had no idea which one might lead outside. I picked up one of the candles and started toward one of the other passage entrances. Not the one Lainey's father had come through. I needed some quick privacy.

The ground turned out to be quite uneven, not at all like the smooth floor of our own cave back at the Achromatic Asylum. In some places, spikes rose up from the floor toward the ones hanging from the ceiling. A couple of them actually connected, including a pillar no more than an inch or two in width. My brain told me this must be a natural cave without any enhancements. I reached the entrance to the passage and tried to look down it with just the candle. I could barely see two or three feet ahead of me. I took a few more steps and spotted a hole in the ground where it met the wall. That would have to do.

My immediate need satisfied, I pulled my pants back up. As I picked up the candle again, I heard a growl from a few feet away. It sounded like a cat… a very big cat.

I backed away, holding the candle in front of me, for what little light it gave. Two pinpricks of light appeared, far closer than I'd like. "H-hello," I called, then coughed. My mouth and lips were dry.

My foot struck a rock outcropping and I stumbled. I dropped the candle. Somehow, it kept burning, so I left it there and moved further back. I didn't have much light near the cot, but a little was better than none.

A creature moved into the light cast from the fallen candle. My initial thought about a cat turned out to be right, except it was like no cat I'd ever seen. This thing stood over three feet tall. Muscles bulged from its legs and back. I could barely make out some kind of dark pattern on its whitish fur. It snarled at me, revealing two longer fangs hanging down from its top jaw. Aside from the draconics, I could not imagine anything more terrifying.

I needed a weapon. I might be able to fight this thing with my cybernetic strength, but I didn't relish the idea of getting clawed and bitten while I did. My eye darted around as I took another step back. Nothing looked feasible. I was almost ready to just grab the blanket off my cot and hope I could tangle it up, when an idea finally occurred to me.

I stepped to my right and grasped the narrow stone pillar. Keeping my eyes on the cat, I triggered a boost into my arms, as much as I could. Then I yanked on the pillar. To my delight, a three-foot segment snapped loose into my hands. I had a weapon, of sorts.

"Come on, cat," I whispered, all I could manage with the dryness. I waved the stone staff at it.

The cat moved closer. I couldn't back away much more. The ground was too rough to move about without looking. If I fell, that thing would be on me in a second.

I swung my improvised weapon, hoping to scare it back. The cat batted at it with an enormous paw. I smacked the ground to make a sound.

And my stone staff broke in two. Fewmets.

Growling, the cat crouched down on its powerful front legs. It was going to spring at me, and I couldn't do anything to stop it. I held my one-foot piece of rock in front of me. Maybe I could get lucky and impale it as it mangled me.

"Hey!" Lainey's shout echoed through the cave. The cat's eyes flickered off to my right. I risked a quick look and saw Lainey holding a long rod of some kind at her shoulder, aimed at the cat.

"This is going to be really loud," she said.

A cacophonous explosion reverberated through the cave. I dropped my weapon and slapped my hands over my ears. The echo persisted for several moments. I blinked and shook my head. The cat lay still on the ground, bleeding from a hole in its chest.

Lainey walked past me and nudged it with the rod. "Dead. That's crazy. One of these shouldn't be this high in the mountains. Even the wildlife is crazy around your valley."

I staggered back beside the cot and tried to grasp what had happened. The rod must be some kind of projectile weapon, but nothing like anything I'd ever seen in The Circle. Strong enough to kill a creature of that size? It might even work against draconics. I needed one of those.

Lainey's father appeared. "What in the world was that?" he demanded.

Lainey turned on an electric lantern and held it over the cat's body. "Mountain lion of some kind," she said. "Saber tooth."

"That shouldn't be this high in the mountains."

"That's what I said!"

He strode over and bent over the cat. "Female. It might have a cub or two back there somewhere." He glanced at me. "Was it trying to attack you?"

I nodded.

He got to his feet. "Probably a cub then. Can't think of any other reason it would come after a human."

"I'll find it," Lainey suggested.

"Take care of him first," he said, pointing at me. "Then you can go cub hunting."

Lainey grinned. She set her weapon and the lantern on the crate, then looked me over. "I'm not sure you should even be up yet," she observed. Her father nodded and left the room again.

"I need to…" I swallowed and licked my dry lips. "I need to get back to my friends."

"As soon as you're able to make that kind of trip, you're welcome to," she replied. She walked over to me and took my arm. "Sit down for now. You need food and water."

That I could agree with. I let her guide me to sit on the cot. She reached behind the crate and found another water bottle, which she tossed to me. I surprised myself by catching it. While I drank, she found some kind of grain bars. I looked one over and took a bite. Dry, but substantial at least. I ate the whole thing and reached for another.

"Good. You've got an appetite."

I took another bite and considered my next moves. Part of me wanted to lie back down and get some more rest. But if I had been missing for two weeks, I didn't have time to rest. I needed to get back to my friends. Everyone must think me dead, devoured by the red dragon.

"Where did your father go?" I asked around bites.

"He's busy." She climbed onto the crate again and watched me.

"Are we… is this cave near Caesious?" I drank some more water.

"Is that the blue city?"

I almost choked, but nodded.

"We're not too far from it. But you're not from there, are you?" She tapped her forehead over her eye, tracing where a chromark would be.

"No. I'm originally from Viridia." I finished the bar. "But you. Your dad said you're not from any of the cities. What did he mean?"

"We're not from anywhere in your valley."

"Valley?"

"You know." She made a swoop with her hand. "The space between mountains. A valley?"

"I know what a valley is. I've just never heard anyone call The Circle that."

"You call it a circle?"

"The Circle." I stared at her. "How do you not know this?"

She shrugged. "Told you. We're not from your valley."

"You're from… outside The Circle?"

Lainey nodded.

"I, I didn't know anyone lived out there."

She gave a short giggle. "Of course people live out there. Did you think your six cities made up the whole world?"

"I don't know," I answered, irritated. "It's all I've ever known. The dragons have ruled us for a thousand years. We don't get to see what's outside."

"Oh. Right. The dragons." She cocked her head. "You had one chasing you."

"You saw that?"

She nodded. "You flew into that big tower, and then the dragon hit it. Then you flew into the mountains and…"

"Crash."

"Yep."

I closed my eye and lowered my head. "Did you see anything that happened down in the city after that?"

"Yeah, it was pretty cool."

"Cool?" I had no idea what she meant.

"Yeah." She swooped her hand through the air. "After the red dragon smashed into the tower, there was all kinds of fire and things breaking. And then…" She drew it out, and swooped her other hand in. "Then the black dragon showed up out of nowhere! And he smashed into the red dragon, who was still on the tower!" She threw her arms up. "The whole tower came down!"

"The dragons fought?"

"Oh yeah. Big fight up in the air after the tower fell. They tore into each other."

"Did, did they both survive?"

She shrugged. "They flew away in different directions, so I guess so."

The dragons fought each other. And I missed it. Even so… this was amazing! Somehow, despite all our stupid mistakes, our plans were working! The dragons were still mad at each other and fighting. I guess when the red dragon destroyed the peace conference, it didn't go over well. What could we do to take advantage of this? And how badly injured were the two dragons who fought? Might there be a way to finish them off?

In only a few moments, I'd gone from terrified of a big cat to wondering if I could kill another dragon. My life was crazy.

3

I looked up to see Lainey studying me. "You seem pretty excited about the dragon fight," she observed. "I thought you were all servants of the dragons down there."

"Not by choice," I answered. "And some of us are trying to fight back. We killed the blue dragon."

"You what?"

"We killed Caesious, the blue dragon. That's what started all this."

"Dad!" Lainey yelled up the passage. "You need to hear this!" She looked back at me. "He's got to hear this."

Lainey's father came tromping down the passage and entered the light. "What's going on?"

Lainey gestured at me. "They killed the blue dragon. That's why we haven't seen it lately."

"What are you talking about?" He looked at me, eyebrows narrowed. It suddenly occurred to me that I knew nothing about these people. Yes, we'd killed a dragon, but what did that mean to Lainey and her father? Who were they, really? Maybe I shouldn't be bragging so much.

"Well?" he asked.

"I'm… I need to know more about you," I said lamely. "Who are you people?"

"I'm Carl Roberts and this is Lainey."

"That's not what I meant. You said you're from outside The Circle. Why are you here?"

He rubbed his beard. "Honestly, we're here to find out what's happening down in your… Circle. We're interested in everything we can find out about your society."

"Why?"

"That's a little more complicated. I'm sure you have things you don't want to talk about, so let's start with what we have. I've told you a little. Now you tell me a little."

I frowned. "A little" barely defined what he'd told me. But if I played along, maybe I could learn more. "All right. My friends and I killed the blue dragon and started a war. Did you build the tower over the Blasted Lands?"

"Did we build the what over the what?" He blinked.

"The Blasted Lands. That's what we call the area on the east side of The Circle," I explained. "There used to be a city. Now it's just destroyed. But I saw a tower in the mountains overlooking it. Did you build it?"

"No." Roberts dug around and found a short stool. He took a seat. "And before you ask, I don't know who did. My turn. How did you kill the dragon?"

Since I had already claimed the killing, I guess it didn't hurt to give some details. "We lured him out in the middle of nowhere and then ran a train into him. Sort of."

"And that killed it?" He tilted his head and lowered one eyebrow.

"The train had kind of a giant sword mounted on the front," I admitted.

"Now that's cool," Lainey said. There was that word again. Maybe she used it the same way we used "hue"?

"Do the dragons ever come to your land?" I asked. "I know they fly around the mountains, but do they fly over them?"

"As far as I know," Roberts answered, "none of the dragons of your valley have ever left it. That's part of why we're here to study it. Your whole… setup down there is very different from what we know."

"And what do you know?"

"We're—" Lainey began.

"The rest of the world is run very differently," her father interrupted. "That's all you need to know right now."

"Then maybe I don't need to tell you anything else." I glared at him. And then I worried. If I didn't tell them what they wanted to know, they might try to keep me here. I still didn't know how to get out of this cave, let alone where in the mountains we were located. The dark cavern suddenly felt a whole lot more menacing.

"We're not your enemies," Roberts said.

"How do I know that?" I got to my feet and prepared to boost my legs. At the very least, I could run past him and check out the passage he'd entered through.

"Do you see marks on our faces? We're not from any of your cities. We don't care about your politics or whatever."

"We're all humans," Lainey said. "We should be on the same side."

"You'd think that," I answered, "but I've fought enough other humans to know it isn't always true."

"But you're not exactly human yourself, are you?" Roberts asked.

"What do you mean?"

"Your missing eye." He pointed at my face. "You have a socket there for some kind of artificial eye. Mechanical, I guess? I've never seen anything like it. And you survived a crash that no one has any business surviving. There's more to you than meets the eye." He chuckled. "Literally, I guess."

"I'm still human!" I protested. "But... I've got enhancements, I guess you could say. Enough that when I want to leave, you won't be able to stop me."

"When you're feeling well enough to leave, you're welcome to go." He pointed back at the passage. "That's the way out right there. We're pretty high up in the mountains, but you should be able to work your way down. Especially if you have... enhancements."

"Where are we, related to the cities?" I glanced at the passage. The ceiling here was high enough that I could probably jump over the both of them and run down it, if I so chose.

"About halfway between the blue and black."

Good. I wouldn't have to get near any of the cities. I could cut across the open land and head back to the Asylum. It would take a few days of walking, but wasn't as bad as I had thought it might be.

Mister Roberts sighed and ran a hand through his hair. "Look, we mean you no harm. We don't want to stop you, although... I can't help but wonder why you wanted to start a war."

"We killed one dragon." I looked at the passage again, then back at the two of them. "But we can't do it again. They're too powerful. We started a war to try to get them to kill each other."

"Makes sense. And how's that going?"

"Lainey just told me the red and black got in a big fight." I gestured toward her. "So I guess we're doing all right."

"Uh-huh."

"But why kill the dragons in the first place?" Lainey burst out.

"If you've never lived under their rule, you can't understand." I pointed at my chromark. "See this? We all have them. We're marked as the dragons' property. We're slaves. We mean nothing to them." I clenched my fists, then released my left hand. Still a little too sore for that. "They want to be worshipped as gods, and they have soldiers and draconics and, and..." I took a breath. "I hate them."

Roberts nodded. "I can see that." He pushed off his knees and got to his feet. "Well, like I said, when you're feeling up to it, you're free to go. We won't stop you. Sounds like you have things to do."

"I'm ready now," I said, swallowing.

He shook his head. "No, you're not. Don't be foolish. Another day or two of rest and maybe you can do it. Maybe."

I wavered.

"One more day won't change much."

"But... my friends probably think I'm dead."

"I'm sure they do. But one more day won't change that."

I guess he had a point. Even so...

"I should go with him," Lainey said.

Her father turned toward her, eyes wide. "What?"

"We want to know what's going on down there, right?" Lainey kept her eyes on me. "I should go with him, check things out myself."

"Absolutely not!"

"Think about it, Dad. With his group, I don't have to worry about the tattoo thing. And I'll be able to fit in with whatever they're up to. Maybe even help a little bit."

"No." Roberts made a cutting gesture. "It's ridiculously dangerous."

"It kind of is," I agreed.

"How else are we going to learn?" she argued. "I'll take the rifle. Even that is forbidden technology down there, from what we've seen."

"What's a rifle?" I asked. I'm guessing she meant the projectile weapon she'd used against the big cat.

She pointed at me while watching her father.

"And what will you do when the dragons discover their little rebellion?" he demanded. "When they show up breathing fire and everything to burn it all down?"

I wanted to argue that wouldn't happen, but I couldn't. It could happen. It most likely would happen, someday. Every day was a gamble with our team. With each new task we undertook, whatever it might be, we risked being discovered. And once discovered… we'd become another lesson to subsequent generations, just like the Blasted Lands.

Tiredness dragged at my bones. I sat down on the cot again.

"Let's talk in the other room," Lainey suggested. Her dad looked ready to argue some more, but he glanced at me and nodded.

"Get some more rest," Lainey told me. "One way or another, you'll be on your way back in a day or two."

They left, taking the electric lantern with them. At least they left me the candles. I sighed and stretched back out on the cot. None of this made any sense. But I supposed I could get a little more sleep, as long as I had the cot and everything.

I started to doze off when the light returned. Lainey walked past me and kept going. "Gonna find me a cub," she said.

Are all girls crazy, or just the ones I meet?

When I woke this time, Lainey sat on the crate again, but wasn't watching me. Instead, she focused on a large white ball of fur resting on her crossed legs. She scratched at it with a gloved hand.

"You found one," I said, pulling myself up.

"Yeah, only one," she answered. "Try not to make any sudden moves. You'll frighten her."

"Her mom terrified me. Seems only fair."

Lainey scowled. "Animals are only acting on instinct. They're not evil, like humans sometimes."

"The dragons are evil," I countered.

"I guess so. But they're not exactly animals, are they? They're intelligent creatures, like us."

I stood and only wavered a little bit. My strength was returning. I stepped closer and looked at the kitten in her lap. A little larger than a house cat, its fur was brighter than its mother's, but covered in dark spots. As I leaned over, it lifted its head and looked at me. Its mouth opened in a little hiss. Though its teeth weren't anywhere near its mother's, I could tell which two would someday grow out of the mouth.

"That's closer to the size cat I'm used to," I observed.

"She'll get a lot bigger," Lainey said, "as you saw."

I glanced back where the dead mother still lay. "You aren't going to keep it, are you?"

"Why not? If I take good care of it, it'll take care of me."

I shook my head, and picked up a bottle of water. "What did your father decide?"

"I'm going with you."

I swallowed the water and wiped my mouth with the back of my hand. "Really? He agreed to that?"

"He saw reason." She smiled and lifted the cub with both hands. "Glacier here and I will escort you back to your friends."

"Oh, the cat's coming too?" I chuckled. Well, why not? "Wait… you named it Glacier? Isn't that like a big mountain of ice?"

"I think it works. She's white, after all." She tickled the cub under its chin, eliciting a yowl of pleasure.

"How long was I asleep this time?" I had no sense of the passage of time in the cave.

Lainey shrugged and lowered the cub back into her lap. "Long enough. I found Glacier, brought her back, got some sleep myself, and came in here to wait for you."

"What time of day is it?"

"Early morning. You thinking of leaving soon?"

"As soon as possible." I set down the empty bottle. "I'll just gather up my things here… Oh wait, I don't have any things. What happened to my old clothes, anyway?"

"Burned them. After your wreck, they had more holes in them than could be repaired."

Of course they did. Again, I wondered how bad the wreck had been, and whether this was another one of those things I shouldn't have survived. "And the, uh, wreckage of my flying… thing?"

"Not much left of it." She looked up from the cub. "We can go look at it on our way down, but we'd get closer to the blue city. Did you want to try to recover something from it?"

"No, I suppose not." I sighed. The Sky Claimer had been glorious, if only for a short time. I would miss it.

Lainey scrambled down from the crate and offered me the cub. "Here, hold her while I go gather my things."

"What? I don't—" She dumped the cub in my arms and left the room. "I'm not a cat person," I called after her.

I looked down at the white ball of fur in my arms. Glacier looked up at me and yawned. Those two teeth looked more distinct every time I saw them. "You're heavier than I expected," I told her, sitting down on my cot. "But I guess that makes sense. You're going to grow up pretty big if you're going to be anything like your mother."

I was talking to a kitten. Wow. I needed to get back home. Still, I had to admit the little thing was cute. It might grow up into a killing machine, but maybe that was a good thing. I mean, if Lainey could control it.

I tried tickling it under the chin, like Lainey did. In return, it bit my finger. "Ow! Thanks a lot!" I sucked on my finger. At least my fingers were ordinary, or bled ordinary, anyway.

Lainey returned a few minutes later. She grabbed some things from the crate and stuffed them into a large backpack. Her rifle hung over her shoulder on a thick strap. "Caedan's going to love that thing," I muttered.

"What was that?"

"Just thinking about one of my friends." I held up the cat. "What are you going to do with her?"

"Watch," she said. She slung a length of cloth over her head and one shoulder, and shaped it into a kind of carrying sling. I handed Glacier to her, and she carefully placed the kitten into the sling. It snuggled up next to her and mewed.

"Here's a coat for you." Lainey offered me a warm garment. "It's much colder outside."

I struggled into the sleeves and pulled it in place. "You should let me carry the pack," I suggested. I would feel pretty foolish walking around while this girl carried everything by herself.

She narrowed an eyebrow at me. "You're still recovering."

"I'm stronger than I look."

Her eyes wandered to the broken stone pillar. "I guess you'd have to be." She handed me the backpack.

I almost regretted my offer. The thing was heavy. "What did you pack in here? Rocks?"

"Do you need me to carry it after all?"

"No, I got it." I slung the pack onto my back, but not without effort. The pack reached from the back of my head all the way down to my butt. You could fit almost anything in that thing.

Lainey jerked her head toward the passage. "This way."

She held up the lantern with one hand while keeping the other on the cub. We made our way down a twisting passage until it opened up into another room, somewhat smaller than the one I'd been sleeping in. Pale sunlight streamed in from a short passage leading to an exit on the far side. The temperature felt significantly colder. Lainey's father sat at an improvised desk near one wall. He got up as we entered.

"Did you pack enough ammo?" he asked her.

"I packed all that we brought," she answered. No wonder the pack felt so heavy.

He shook his head. "I'm still not completely comfortable with this. And now you're taking the cub too? You'll have to hunt for it, you know. It's going to want meat."

"We will too," Lainey said. "I'm not living off these protein bars."

Roberts snorted. "I guess not." He turned to me. "Beryl, I'm trusting you with the greatest treasure I've ever held. You can't possibly know how this feels."

I swallowed. "No, I can't, sir. I'm not a father. But I promise you, I'll do everything in my power to protect her."

"I'm the one with the rifle," Lainey pointed out.

"And if you haven't figured it out yet, Beryl has some… enhancements. He doesn't need a rifle."

Maybe not. But I wouldn't mind having one.

"I'm a little unclear on some things," I said. "Are you just taking me home and then heading back? Or sticking around to see what we're doing?"

"That's going to be up to her," Roberts answered. "She'll evaluate the situation and decide for herself when to return."

He clearly trusted her. I wondered what had changed his mind about her coming at all.

"I still want to know more about where you're from," I admitted.

"And we want to know more about where you're from," he said. "As Lainey sees fit, she can tell you more."

I nodded. I guess that made it fair.

Lainey gave her father a kiss on the cheek and a side-hug. The kitten prevented anything more intimate. Roberts whispered something to her and then stepped back.

Lainey gestured to me and led the way out into the sunlight. I blinked and shivered, even with the coat. A chill wind stung my hands and face. I stuck my hands in my coat pockets and looked around.

We stood on the side of a mountain, higher than I'd imagined. The Circle lay stretched out before me in a way I'd never seen, even while flying the Sky Claimer. Mountains towered to either side, circling around as far as the eye could reach. The landscape below appeared flat, even though I knew much of it consisted of hills. I could see patterns to the farmlands. And in the distance to my left, I saw the sun reflecting from the city of Caesious. I turned right and could just make out Atramentous, though it didn't shine quite as much. Too much black, I suppose.

"How does that sight make you feel?" Lainey asked.

"Small. Very, very small."

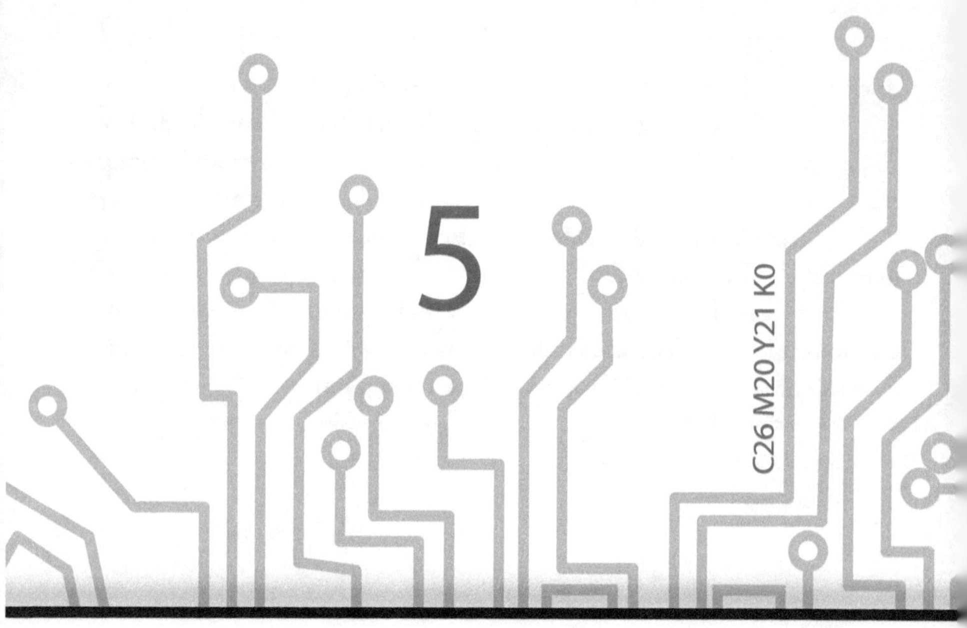

"You have to watch your step!" Lainey warned. She started walking to the right, following a trail I couldn't make out.

"How long will it take us to get down?" I asked. The trail almost immediately shifted into a decline, requiring careful balance.

She glanced back at me. "Off the mountains? Probably all day, at the least."

My heart sank. An entire day of this? I might be boosting my legs by lunchtime, just to keep up. Maybe I should have stayed in bed another day. But then I thought about my friends. They had to assume I was dead, right? How would they react when I walked into camp, alive and well? And missing an eye. And escorted by a girl carrying a cat and a powerful projectile weapon. This could be interesting, to say the least.

If anyone still believed in me, it would be Bice. He always believed, even without evidence. And maybe Rick. When I disappeared into Viridia's lair, he scoured the city looking for me. How could I have a truer friend? Sure, it bothered me that Kelly preferred him over me now, but I could get past that. Someday.

My mind wandered past the faces of my other friends: Caedan, Lovat, Don, even Peri. Only after all the others did I think about Olive. What had happened with her after the events in Incarnadine? Did Kelly or someone else get her back home to Viridia? Did she still believe she had been part of a Viridian Guard operation? Or had they been forced to reveal the truth to her after my disappearance?

"This next part is steep," Lainey called back.

The last part wasn't? I soon realized she was right. I had to lean back as we descended a steeper slope. In some places, I had to clamber with all four limbs just to keep from falling down on top of my guide.

"Don't even think about falling on me." How did she know I was thinking about that?

"Can't help it," I said. "I'm not used to this."

"It gets better."

By "better," she meant a slight lessening of the steepness. We entered a place where the trail went under an overhanging rock for at least a good half an hour. For most of the way, I could reach up and steady myself with a hand on the ceiling. It did help, but my ankles and calves were already getting sore from the unusual use of the muscles. I sent a tiny boost into my legs to help.

The shoes they had provided for me were a hair too large for my feet. Over the next couple of hours, I saw how much of a problem that could be. My toes wanted to slide down within the shoe with every step. By the time we stopped for a mid-morning break, I could already feel the blisters forming on my smallest toes.

I took off my shoe and felt around with my fingers. I winced. "I think my toes hate you," I announced.

"They'll hate me more by the end of the day," Lainey answered without looking up. She paid much more attention to that cat than to me. "But I guess that means you have normal toes, then?"

"Of course I have normal toes. What does that mean?"

She shrugged. "Dad said you had enhancements. You obviously had an artificial eye of some kind. I don't know what else you have."

I took a drink of water. "Are you asking? Is that how this works?"

She looked up, brow wrinkled. "How what works?"

"You're coming with me to learn, right? Well, I want to learn too. We have technology differences, so how about we start there."

"Okay. Tell me about your... 'enhancements.'"

"First you tell me about your rifle," I shot back.

Her head went back. "The rifle? What's so special about that?"

"We don't have them."

She stared, then looked down into The Circle below. "You mean to tell me that in all those cities, with electricity and trains and everything, and whatever it is they did to you, that nobody has guns?"

I rubbed my foot again. "Maybe it's weird to you, but you have to understand one thing: the dragons have controlled our technology."

"What's that mean?"

"They rule everything. So when it comes to science, they only allow research into areas that will benefit them. Projectile weapons would help humans, not dragons, so they're out." I paused. "Except short range stuff that doesn't kill, I suppose. Caedan has a projectile weapon that launches a kind of electrical shock."

"No guns," she repeated. "Wow. That's crazy. Guns were invented hundreds of years ago, long before trains or electricity."

"So what does it do?"

"Oh. Right." She picked up the rifle from where she'd set it down. "How do I explain this? You pull this trigger right here, and it ignites a charge inside that launches the bullet. The bullet is basically a big chunk of lead shaped as a, uh, projectile." She held one up for me. It was long and pointed. I could see how one of those flying through the air could do some damage. One shot had killed the big cat, after all.

"Your turn," she said, putting the rifle away.

I wasn't completely satisfied with the explanation, but some of my other friends would probably understand it better than I could. "All right," I said. "Around ten—no, eleven—years ago, I was in a horrible accident. I should have died. My parents did die. But a friend who worked for the dragons saved me. He's an absolute genius. He put a cybernetic implant in my brain." I tapped the back of my head. "With it, I can send boosts to my arms, legs, whatever, to give me extra strength and speed. Without it, I wouldn't even be able to walk."

"And the eye?"

"Oh, that. Yeah, I didn't even know about that until a draconic ripped my eye out." I felt the scar around the empty eye socket. "I guess I was even more damaged than I remember."

"You should ask him about it when you get back, then."

"I can't. He's dead."

"Oh." Lainey bent over the cat again. I guess she didn't want to deal with the topic of death. I didn't blame her. Loden's death still hurt, even months later.

I shivered and pulled my shoes back on. Sitting still made me realize how cold the air still was up here. Lainey stood up. "We should get moving again if we're going to make it down by the end of the day." She picked up the rifle and slung it over her shoulder. Glacier grumbled at the motion.

We started out again, continuing our steep descent. At times, the trail disappeared completely, and we scrambled over whatever terrain happened to be in our way until Lainey found another way down. We walked, crawled, hung over ledges and dropped: whatever it took. By mid-afternoon, I found myself sending a boost to my limbs every twenty or thirty minutes. Lainey at least had the decency to look tired herself, but she pressed on.

As twilight began, we realized we weren't going to reach the bottom before nightfall. We'd made significant progress, and could probably hit more level ground in another couple of hours, but it would soon be too dark to be safe. Instead, we sought out a hollow in the rocks where we could spend the night.

I dropped the pack and found a place to sit. "At least it's not cold any more," I pointed out. I stripped off my outer coat before turning my attention to my poor toes.

"It is summer here, right?" Lainey asked. She set Glacier down on his feet and removed his carrier before taking off her own coat. The cat wandered around the hollow, examining all the ridges and gaps.

"Yeah, somewhere around the middle of summer by now."

"And summer is warm, yes?"

"Of course it is." I suppressed my irritation at her obvious questions. I guess my questions sounded just as obvious to her. "All of The Circle has the same climate, pretty much." I paused. "Well, except for Incarnadine and Amaranth, apparently. It's colder there than everywhere else."

She stretched before taking a seat. "Those are the red dragons, right?"

"Yeah. It doesn't make much sense, does it? Fire dragons, living where it's cold."

"Maybe their fire makes them too hot and they like the cold."

Huh. Maybe. Even so, it didn't make sense for other reasons. The climate shouldn't be so different in that one area of The Circle. Someday, I hoped someone figured that out. The Circle seemed full of mysteries, now that I considered it. I wondered if anyone, anywhere, understood it all.

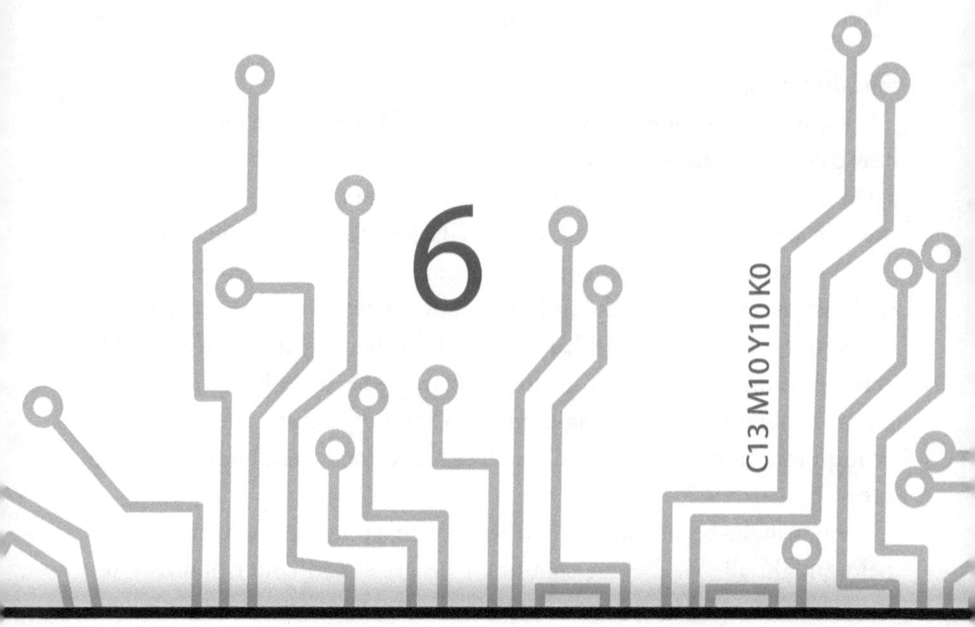

I didn't sleep very well on the rocks. Not only could I not get comfortable, my toes ached. I comforted myself with the knowledge that in just a few days, I'd be sleeping back at the Achromatic Asylum. Sure, it wasn't fancy, but at least I could sleep inside with blankets and a pillow. Also, Glacier woke us both several times during the night with complaints. I didn't know whether she was hungry or something else; I rolled over and let Lainey handle it. Did I mention I'm not a cat person?

After a meager breakfast, we set out again. I almost couldn't bear to put my shoes back on. I tried an extra layer of socks to see if it helped. At least we wouldn't be walking at a descending angle for much longer.

Sure enough, after about an hour and a half, the ground started to level out. We saw more and more grass. When we finally reached a large enough patch, I dropped the backpack and stretched out in it. "I never in my life thought I'd be so glad to see grass," I announced, looking up at the sky.

Lainey set Glacier down and then joined me. The cub moved about the grass cautiously at first. I rolled over to watch. This was probably her first time to even see this kind of plant life. After wandering around a bit, the cub began batting at some of the taller blades of grass. It yowled and attacked an especially tall clump of weeds.

I chuckled and rolled back. I let myself relax, feeling tension I didn't even know was there drain out of my back muscles.

"This is nice," Lainey said.

"Is it like this outside the mountains?" I asked.

"Parts of it. I've spent too much of my life inside a city, though."

"I understand that." Once we escaped Viridia and I learned what life was like outside the city, I never wanted to go back. Even if we killed all the dragons, I don't think I'd want to live in a city again.

After a while, Lainey sat up and looked at the position of the sun. "Which direction do we need to go now?"

I sat up as well. "Let's see. If we're between the blue and black cities, then we need to head mostly east and a little north. That'll send us north of Viridia, where our, uh, base camp is located."

"Base camp, huh? Cool." She got up onto her knees. "Glacier! Come back here, girl."

The cub had wandered pretty far. Lainey chased it down and brought it back. "You sure you want to try to keep up with that thing?" I asked. "The bigger it gets, the more wandering it's going to want to do."

"I'll teach her loyalty," Lainey promised. "She's still young. While she's dependent on me for food, she'll grow more attached."

"If you say so." I had little experience with pets of any kind, least of all cats.

We gathered up our gear and set out again. My toes still hurt, but at least now I could walk without having to lean back all the time. The Circle's gently rolling hills and flat plains never looked more appealing. Now that we were off the mountains, the temperature grew warmer. Even without the outer coats, the clothes we wore started to feel excessively hot.

"Do we have any other clothes?" I asked, wiping the sweat from my brow. At this point, I'd even prefer the clothes I'd worn in the crash, holes and all.

"Oh, right. Let me get into the pack."

I set the enormous backpack down and Lainey opened one of the many zippers. She pulled out one set of clothes and set it aside, then pulled out another which she tossed to me. "These were my dad's, but they should fit you well enough."

I looked them over. The shirt, unfortunately, was a dark green, but made of a lighter material than I usually wore. The pants, more of a tan, also felt lighter. They looked comfortable. I glanced around. We were in a flat area, with no trees or anything else nearby. "Maybe we could, um…"

"You face that way, and I'll face this way," Lainey said, pointing. "Don't turn around until I tell you. Simple."

"Right." I turned around and pulled off the heavy shirt. I breathed a sigh of relief as the cool air hit my bare skin. I almost didn't want to put the new shirt on, but that might make things awkward. I pulled it on, then bent down to untie and remove the shoes. As I did, I caught a brief glimpse of bare white legs behind me. I lifted my eye up in a hurry and made sure to keep my focus in the right direction. But my mind couldn't help but wander. They were nice legs.

I stripped off my extra pair of socks, and the heavy pants. Once I got the lighter pants and shoes back on, I waited. A few moments later, Lainey said, "Okay, let's pack this up." I picked up my discarded clothes and turned around.

Lainey wore a tan shirt and shorts that came down to just above the knee. She was much thinner than I'd thought, but of course she would be. She'd shed a pretty thick outfit. I probably looked a lot thinner too. Except she'd probably seen me in my torn clothes, which they took off… Anyway…

She smiled. "This does feel a lot better. I don't know why we didn't start the day out like this."

I didn't know what to say. Together, we stuffed the cold weather clothes into the backpack. I questioned the need to keep them, but I guess Lainey would need them when she went back. Already, the thought of her leaving bothered me. She was pleasant to be around. Sure, she wasn't flirting with me all the time like Olive, but at least I didn't have to hide my feelings like I did with Kelly.

"Early lunch?" Lainey suggested.

"Rowr," said Glacier.

We both laughed. "She'll be wanting fresh meat soon," Lainey observed as we got out our dried food. "There are animals around here, aren't there?"

"Um, yeah, I suppose." I looked around. "I mean, farmers raise cattle, sheep, goats."

"What about deer?"

"Deer?"

"You know, venison?"

"I don't know what you're talking about."

She scrunched up her eyebrows. "This place is so weird."

"If you say so."

Around an hour later, we saw a flock of goats wandering, spread out over a couple of hills. I didn't see anyone else around. This particular flock had probably been abandoned due to the war. Before I could comment on it, Lainey had lifted her rifle, aimed, and pulled the trigger. A loud explosion echoed across the hills and one of the goats fell over. The others panicked and ran in every direction.

"Are you crazy?" I exclaimed. "Somebody will hear that!"

Lainey lowered the rifle. "I told you we'd need some fresh meat."

"People around here aren't used to that noise. Someone is bound to come looking."

"I thought you all lived in the cities."

"Most people do, but there are farmers scattered around." I scanned the horizon in every direction. "And there's a war on, in case you forgot. There could be bands of soldiers anywhere."

"Then why are we just marching around out in the open?" She slung the rifle back over her shoulder.

"There's a difference between a couple of people out for a walk and someone setting off explosions."

She glanced around now, actually looking a bit nervous herself. "But we'll be okay, right? I've got the rifle, and you've got your cyber-thingy. Right?"

I took a deep breath. "I told your dad I'd protect you. Just… don't shoot that thing again unless you have to."

Lainey nodded, then led the way to the fallen goat. I tried not to react when I saw the goat up close. The shot had almost taken off its head. If we had just a handful of those weapons, we could make a huge difference. We could probably kill draconics with them!

Lainey took a knife from her belt. Much to the interest of the cub, she worked on skinning the goat and cutting out the worthwhile meat. Or at least I assumed that's what she was doing. I'd never seen anyone do it before and didn't know what to think. After a few minutes, I dropped the backpack and made my way to the top of the highest hill nearby where I could watch in all directions.

I tested the focus on my remaining eye. Since I could zoom, I knew it had to be cybernetic like my missing one. It gave me a strange feeling every time I thought about it. Still, I had these abilities and should make good use of them. Loden would want that.

I scanned multiple directions as far as my zoom could reach. I was about to head down to join Lainey again, when I caught movement to the south. Several figures were moving this direction. I zoomed in on them and saw three men dressed in black… and a towering draconic striding beside them.

7

"Gotta move!" I yelled to Lainey as I raced down the hill to her.

She looked up, holding a bloody knife. "I'm not done yet."

"No time. We've got a draconic and soldiers heading our way. We need to get out of here!" I grabbed up the backpack and pulled it on.

Seeing I was in earnest, Lainey finished up her work with quick and efficient movements. She cleaned the knife and put it away, wrapped up the meat she'd cut up so far, and stashed it in the pack. She picked Glacier up from where she was chewing on one of the goat's femurs. The cat yowled in complaint.

"Unless we all want to be food, we need to hurry," I urged.

Lainey paused. "Food? Do the draconics eat people?"

"What? No. I don't think so. It's just an expression. Let's go!"

She shook her head and joined me. We hurried over the hill and moved as fast as we could. I kept looking back to see if we'd been spotted. The enemy came in our direction, but they didn't seem to be moving faster than before. Maybe we'd get away without being noticed.

But then I saw a sudden motion from one of the soldiers. An instant later, all four of them were running. The draconic soon outdistanced the humans and bounded toward us at an alarming rate. This one had exceptionally long arms and used them while running, becoming almost a four-legged creature.

"They've seen us!" I gasped.

"What should we do?"

Time to keep my promise. "I'm going to pick you up and run."

"No offense, but I think I'm in better shape for running than you are."

I looked back again. The draconic would be on us in moments. No time to argue. I channeled boosts into both arms and legs. I grabbed Lainey, yanking her up off her feet. With one arm under her knees, and the other around her shoulders, I ran. The cybernetic boost gave me speed far beyond what I could normally maintain. The chasing draconic fell behind further and further with each second I kept moving.

"All right, I'm impressed," Lainey said after a few minutes. "How long can you keep this up?"

"Not sure," I gasped.

"You said you sent boosts into your body parts. Can you keep doing that? Is there a limit?"

"Hard to talk." I sucked in another breath. "While running."

"Sorry. I'll wait."

I didn't stop until I was completely sure the draconic wouldn't catch up to us. I changed direction a few times, crossed over two sets of railroad tracks (or maybe the same one twice), and ended up moving back in the direction I'd been wanting to go. All in all, I probably cut a full hour out of our walking time… assuming I didn't need to use that hour sleeping to recover.

I set Lainey on her feet, pulled the backpack off, and collapsed. As the boosts faded, sore muscles took over, and my blistered toes complained bitterly. I stretched out on the side of a hill and lay still. I'm not sure I could have gotten up if I'd needed to. Ordinarily, that kind of exertion would leave me tired, but not this tired. My body must not be fully recovered from the crash. And I guess I hadn't had any exercise for two weeks or more.

"I guess this answers my questions," Lainey observed from somewhere nearby. I opened my eye a bit to see her standing over me, hands on hips. She must have set the cub down right away.

"Yeah. I can do better, though."

"Uh-huh." I heard her moving around. "I don't see any sign of pursuit. Pretty sure you lost them. Which city were they from?"

"Atramentous. Black." My chest rose and fell as I struggled to regain my breath.

"What would have happened if they caught us?"

"You don't want to know."

I heard her move closer. "I do, actually. I want to understand everything."

I opened my eye to find her crouching beside me, arms resting on her knees. "Give me a second." I took a few more deep breaths, and then yawned for some reason. "I guess… it depends. You have no chromark. That makes you suspicious and strange. They'll want to find out why. You'd probably be taken back to the city and tortured until you tell them everything."

"Pleasant. What about you?"

"I have a green chromark, and Viridia is allied with Atramentous," I explained. "But… I'm far from where I should be, and I'm in the company of a girl without a mark. I'd be in just as much trouble, even more so once they found out about my abilities."

"Why is that?"

"My cyb implants are illegal fortek—forbidden technology, reserved for the dragons and their servants. Plus, Loden was ahead of all of them. I know the green dragon especially wants to know how my tech works." I thought of my encounters with draconics from the other cities. "I guess they all do, really."

"That makes you pretty important, doesn't it?"

I shrugged, but it probably looked weird while lying on the ground. "I dunno. I'm just trying to change things." My eyelid drooped. Lying down might not have been the best idea. Sleep chased me as intently as the draconic had been.

Lainey sat back on the earth. "Someone as important as you crashes into the mountains, and it just happens to be right where Dad and I were watching. The fates were with us all."

"The what?" I mumbled.

Lainey said something else, but I couldn't make it out. Sleep caught me.

Something nibbled at my ear, and I jerked awake. I rolled to the opposite side and pulled myself up. Glacier yowled in protest. Stupid cat.

"Don't go getting a taste for human flesh," I grumbled. I sat up and looked for Lainey.

I spotted her coming down from another hill not far away. She carried something in her arms. I couldn't tell what it was until she got close.

"Apples!" she announced. "Most of them weren't ripe yet, but I found a few."

She sat on the ground, letting her burden down. She tossed one to me. Glacier wandered over and sniffed the apples, then looked up at Lainey. "You can try some," Lainey said. "I'll cut one up for you."

To my surprise, the cub liked the taste and ate a good bit of one of the apples. I ate one myself while I tried to figure out how long I'd been out. Judging by the sun's position, it couldn't be too long.

"You were asleep for about half an hour," Lainey said, cutting another piece of apple for the cub. "I figured you needed it."

"Yeah, I usually don't crash that bad. Sorry."

"It's not a problem. I'm not in a hurry."

I got to my feet. "But I am. I really want to get back."

She looked up at me with eyebrows raised. "You're good to walk?"

I took a few steps. "I should be fine now." And if I wasn't, I'd boost myself a little here and there to keep going. I'd been gone for way too long.

The rest of the day passed without incident. The warm afternoon sun made all of us a little lethargic, I think, despite my determination to keep going. By the time it began to set, I was more than ready to sleep again.

"How long will it take to get there?" Lainey asked.

"I'm not entirely sure," I admitted. "The last time I traveled this far was with our four-wheelers. I'm guessing at least two more days."

"Do you think it's safe to make a fire?"

I hesitated. "Ordinarily, I'd say yes. We're far from the cities now. Anyone who sees it would likely think we're farmers or herdsmen. But now, with the patrol we've already seen? I don't know. Maybe the war is heating up."

She took the electric lantern out of the pack. "Then this will have to do when we need a little light. The batteries should be good for a couple more evenings. Can't cook with it, though."

"We'll survive. You found apples today, after all. Better than the dried stuff any day."

Lainey agreed, but pulled some of the dried stuff out anyway. We munched on a small supper, then prepared for sleep. No sleeping bags, but our warm clothes from earlier did just as well to give us something cushier than the ground. Much nicer than the rocks from the night before.

I rolled over and thought I would fall right asleep, but my brain kept replaying events from the last couple of days. It wasn't providing any new insight on anything, just rehearsing as if it wanted to be sure the memories were solid. Stupid brain. I needed sleep.

I heard murmurings from behind me. I rolled over again. In the dark, I could just make out Lainey's body facing away from me. She must have been talking to the cat. Her arm moved, as if petting it. I tried to lean closer without making any noise, trying to make out her words.

"…Chroma… he's nice… kind of odd, but nice all the same… maybe… one… What… think, Glacier?"

Embarrassed, I rolled back away. I firmly ordered my brain to shut up, focused on my breathing, and slipped off to sleep.

In the morning, I felt more refreshed than I had since waking up in the cave. Being home in The Circle, even out in the middle of nowhere, did a lot for my mood. Lainey's mood didn't seem to alter much, regardless of circumstances. I hadn't figured her out much yet, but nothing seemed to faze her very much. I wasn't sure if it made her brave or ignorant or both.

As we prepared for the day, she loaned me a razor and a mirror. I couldn't remember the last time I'd shaved. Maybe back at Marcus's house in Incarnadine? I did a reasonable job of cleaning my face up; my facial hair didn't grow very fast. I wondered if it was genetic, or if the cyb implants affected that too. I remembered my father growing a beard at least once. My mother didn't like it, so it didn't last very long.

We talked a lot during this day's walking. I didn't learn much more about Lainey, but I think she learned a lot more about me. Without meaning to, I gave her a complete picture of life in The Circle, or at least life in Viridia. Since almost everything sounded strange to her, I guessed her own life had been very different, though she didn't give away very much. Even so, I caught glimpses every now and then of something… bad. Her eyes would take on a kind of hollow look while she stared off in the distance without seeing anything. Then she'd snap out of it and ask another question to deflect.

We spent another night outside, this time finding a little more shelter in a small patch of pine trees. By this time, we were much more comfortable with each other's presence. As I drifted off that night, I thought no more of my traveling companion than I would Rick or Kelly. And, if I admitted it, Lainey's conversations were much more engaging than Olive's.

I had hoped to reach the Asylum on the next day, but we ran into multiple delays. Patrols from both Viridia and Atramentous crossed our path on multiple occasions. I'd never seen so many of them out in the open like this. It was like they were looking for something. I dreaded the answer to what that might be.

In the mid-morning of the fourth day since leaving the mountains, we crossed the railroad track from Viridia and drew near my home: the Achromatic Asylum, as Kelly named it. We didn't run into anyone as we approached. When I spotted home from a distance, I pointed it out. Lainey was suitably impressed with our camouflage from above.

"But it's now very obvious from here," she pointed out. "If any of those patrols get this close, they're going to see it."

I nodded. I should talk with Don about that possibility. Maybe we could build some hills of our own to block the view.

"Not to mention the wheel tracks leading to it," Lainey added. I looked where she was pointing and winced. We'd been using the four-wheelers too much in the same place. A clear set of tracks stretched dozens of yards long and led into the Asylum.

Regardless, it was home. I sped up as we approached, and Lainey jogged to keep up with me. I decided to skip past the outer areas and head straight for the cave and workshop. The people I most wanted to see would most likely be there, anyway. I didn't want to waste time talking to the priest or draconic, assuming they were still here.

Someone called to us as I reached the cave entrance, but I ignored it. Lainey followed me without question. It did occur to me that I was trusting her more than any of our other newer recruits, but it was too late to turn back now.

I burst into the workshop, looking from side to side, expecting to see Bice, at the least, possibly Rick and Kelly… But only one person sat at a table, looking over one of Loden's journals. A woman I didn't recognize looked up at me with a puzzled expression through her glasses.

"Who are you?" I exclaimed.

"Who am I? Who are you to burst in here like this?" she demanded.

She looked to be about five or ten years older than me, with dark tan skin, black hair, and a black chromark.

"Where's Bice?" As long as I was here, I knew something I needed right away. I walked past her to a set of shelves on the wall and climbed onto a chair. Where was that box?

"You can't just barge in here like this! Mister Onyx won't like it. Who are you, anyway?" The woman got to her feet and edged around the opposite direction. Lainey casually stepped back a pace, blocking the door.

I found the box I wanted and opened it. Cybernetic eyes. I hadn't noticed when Caedan and I found them, but they were all my color. Loden meant these for me as backups. He could have mentioned that. I took one out and put the box back. I looked back at the stranger.

"I'm Beryl. This workshop belongs to me," I informed her. "I don't know who you are, but I intend to find out, once I talk with Bice and Rick."

"Is that a cybernetic eye?" she asked, staring at my hand. "Did the Architect make those too?" She looked up at my face and gasped. "Are they for you?"

"You tell me." I raised the eye up to my empty socket and slid it in place, resisting the urge to gag. I heard a click as it attached. The entire side of my face locked up for a moment, then a shiver ran through it. I clenched my jaw and shook my head at the bizarre feelings.

I blinked, and my vision cleared. I held my palm in front of my old eye, and I could still see with the new one! It worked! I had two eyes again. I breathed a sigh of relief.

"That's a big improvement," Lainey noted. "I can stand to look at you now."

"Well, thanks." I tried to roll my eyes at her, but it felt too weird. I needed to get used to… my new eye. What a bizarre thought.

The other woman studied me. "Fascinating. Just plug and play. Similar to so much of the rest of the Architect's work."

I looked her over. "The Architect? Are you talking about Loden?"

"I only know him as the Architect. That's what Mister Onyx called him. Said he built everything here."

"Mister Onyx?" I snorted. "Is Rick here somewhere? I need—"

"Incoming," Lainey warned, stepping away from the door.

Caedan burst into the room, baton at the ready. He spun toward

Lainey, raising the weapon, before a glance in my direction brought him to an abrupt halt.

"Beryl?"

"Mister Teal. Do you know this person?" the strange woman demanded.

Caedan whooped and dropped his baton. The next thing I knew, he had me wrapped up in a bear hug, lifting me off the ground. "They told me you were dead! That Incarnadine got you!"

"Not quite," I answered, hugging him back. "Not for lack of trying, though."

He let me back down and stepped back, an enormous grin on his face. "This is so streak!" He patted my shoulder again, as if to reassure himself that I was still here, still real.

"What is going on?" the woman asked, exasperation in her voice.

"Dusk, this is Beryl. He's the reason all of this happened."

"I thought Mister Onyx and the Architect—"

"It's Beryl," Caedan repeated. "It's all Beryl. He's our leader and he's back. Oh, right. Beryl, this is Dusk. She's our new tech girl. Rick brought her in."

"Where is Rick, anyway?" I asked. "And Bice? And Kelly?"

"Bice is outside with the priests," he said, thumbing over his shoulder. "Rick and Kelly are out on one of the four-wheelers. Don and Lovat should be on their way back from the weekly trip to Viridia. Man, they are going to be so pumped to see you!"

Lainey cleared her throat.

"Um, Caedan, this is Lainey. I probably would be dead if not for her."

"Good to meet you," he said, turning with a grin. "Any friend of Beryl's—" He broke off, staring at her face.

"Am I that fascinating?" she asked.

"No chromark. I told you, Lainey. To us, it's as unusual as someone walking around without a head." I headed for the exit. "There's a reason for it, Caedan, but I'd like to talk with everyone at once."

Lainey and Caedan followed me out of the cave. Caedan pushed past me and hurried to another area of our improvised headquarters. Things had changed in the weeks I'd been gone. More walls had been erected, creating rooms for individuals, I supposed. One of the four-wheelers waited alone. Lainey wandered over to look at it, while I waited for Caedan to return.

When he did, he wasn't alone. Bice rushed past him. When he saw me, he fell to his knees. "I tried to believe," he cried, real tears appearing in his eyes. "I tried. I prayed. And, and here you are!"

I hurried to his side and pulled him back onto his feet. "It's real, Bice. I'm alive. I'm here," I assured him. "I'm all right."

He reached out a trembling hand and touched my face. "You can't know what this means to me, Beryl," he whispered. "I'm, I'm speechless."

"That's a first." I chuckled and embraced him. "I came back as soon as I could," I explained. "It's a long story."

"It may have to wait," Bice said, pulling back. "We've got trouble here. Lots of it."

9

"What kind of trouble?" I tensed, taking a quick look around, but seeing nothing demanding attention.

"Rick has… assumed the leadership while you were gone," Bice explained. He took a deep breath and closed his eyes, gathering control over his emotions. "His methods have been a bit more aggressive than yours." He glanced at Caedan.

"Aggressive how?"

"We've been doing raids against the green and black troops every time we find them," Caedan answered.

"No wonder we kept seeing patrols," I said. "They're all over the place. They're looking for you!"

"We've attracted way too much attention," Bice said. "They're coming for us."

"This is bad." I shifted and paced a few feet. "Did everyone go along with this?"

"I argued against it." Bice gave a pointed look at Caedan. "Others didn't."

"I'm here for action," Caedan argued. "You know that."

"Action is one thing. Risking everything is another. Argh." I ran a hand through my hair. "I'm guessing Kelly went along with it too. And the others? Who's this new girl?"

"Rick has Mazarine on his side as well. He brought the girl back from a trip to Atramentous." Bice glanced at the cave. "Since then, I haven't been allowed back in the workshop."

"Allowed?" I shook my head. "That's ridiculous. Where's Rick now?"

"He and Kelly went to scout toward the north," Caedan offered. "They should be back soon."

Peri came running up at that moment. "Beryl!" He looked like he wanted to hug me, but wasn't sure if he could. I reached out and slapped his shoulder. "Good to see you, man." His hair had really grown out. He didn't look like a priest at all.

"But Lovat and Don," Bice said. "I'm worried about them. They should have been back by now."

"They went to Viridia? With all these patrols out there searching?" I spun around. "Caedan, where's a sword?"

"Uh, Rick's is in the workshop, but—"

"Introduce Lainey to Bice and Peri," I told him and raced back to the cave.

Dusk looked up as I entered, but returned to her work as I sought out the weapon I wanted. Once I had it, I hurried back out.

"What are you going to do?" Lainey asked. I couldn't help but notice Bice now held the cub.

"Find my friends." I strapped the sword onto my back.

"Want me to drive the four-wheeler for you?" Caedan offered.

"I can move just as fast without it."

"Don't run off on your own again!" Bice exclaimed. "You can't do everything."

"Fine. Caedan, you and Lainey follow me on the four-wheeler. Bice, if Rick comes back, tell him… No, don't tell him anything. I'm on my way toward Viridia." With that, I sent boosts into both legs and took off running.

Fewmets. What had Rick been thinking? Our entire operation hinged on keeping attention away from us. We wanted the dragons to fight each other, not us!

I glanced over my shoulder as I raced out of the Asylum. Lainey had been right. We'd disguised our base from above, worried about the dragons flying over, but it could be seen easily from ground level if anyone got close enough. And Rick had been attracting them toward us. Idiot.

I knew the path to Viridia well, having walked it at least four or five times myself. Don wouldn't take any major deviations from that path unless he had to. And he might have to, if he or Lovat spotted the enemy patrols before being spotted themselves. They might be far out of the path. If he was smart, he would have pushed toward the east then, closer to the mountains and the Blasted Lands. But I couldn't take time to do any kind of lengthy search. I would have to take the regular path to Viridia, and if I didn't find them by then, try searching toward the east.

I wanted to smack myself for not bringing along one of Loden's talkers. I couldn't let Caedan know my intentions. Hopefully, he'd figure the same thing out himself.

When I crested the top of a larger hill, I stopped to scan the horizon. Zooming my vision, I looked in each direction, watching for any kind of movement. Nothing to the east or south. To the west, I caught a flash of black. I tried to focus, but the distance was still too great. Returning my eyes to normal, I boosted my legs again and headed in that direction.

I crossed the railroad tracks and sought out another hill from which to search. I found a place among a few birch trees. Zooming my eyes in the direction I'd first noticed movement, I saw a group of black-clad men moving together toward the northwest. Sable Legion, then, from Atramentous. I didn't see a draconic, so it wasn't the same bunch Lainey and I'd encountered. But of course it couldn't be. We were miles and miles from that group. At any rate, this one didn't have any prisoners, and they weren't headed toward the Asylum.

Abandoning the west side of the tracks, I raced back to my original course, heading toward Viridia. Ordinarily, this trip would take at least a day. Even at my full speed, it would take many hours. Maybe I should have waited on the four-wheeler after all. It wasn't too late. I could stop, rest, and wait for Caedan to catch up. But if he'd brought Lainey, it would make the ride a bit crowded. And I didn't want to wait.

Out of all the friends I left behind when I crashed into the mountain, Lovat was the one I worried most about. He looked up to me, thought me to be some kind of hero or something. If he thought I was dead, he'd be devastated. I knew what that felt like. In the moments before the crash, thoughts of him helped me do everything I could to survive. And now he might be in trouble. I couldn't rest.

I kept running. An hour or more went by, and I could feel the burn.

My leg muscles had been unused for a couple of weeks, but I had just finished three days of walking, not to mention climbing. I thought I was stronger. My legs argued differently. I couldn't even describe the pain my blistered little toes were feeling.

I paused for a few moments to catch my breath and scan the distance again. Nothing. Now that I thought about it, this was a very bad sign. Bice said Don and Lovat should have been back already. If I hadn't found them yet, it meant they'd definitely run into trouble. I channeled another boost into my legs and kept going.

My haste almost took me right into them. I came down one hill and up another. Just before I reached the crest, I spotted figures going down the other side. I stumbled, fell, and rolled several feet before vaulting back up, only a few feet behind the people I'd seen.

Viridian Guard. Five of them, fully armored and carrying shockspears. Don and Lovat walked between them, not restrained, but clearly prisoners. And why would they bother to restrain them, anyway? A draconic walked beside them. No chance of escape with that thing around.

Until now. I had hoped to catch them unawares, but my fall drew their attention at once. The Guardsmen all came to a stop, readied their weapons, and faced me. These were trained experts, not new conscripts. The draconic turned at a more leisurely rate. It laughed when it saw me.

"Another fugitive!" it cried. "Were you coming to rescue your friends alone?"

"Beryl!" Lovat screamed.

I drew my sword. "That was the idea, yeah." Five Viridian Guard and one draconic. Not the best odds.

"Take him," the draconic ordered, waving in my direction. Four of the Guard rushed me, while the fifth hung back, hovering next to the prisoners.

One touch from a shockspear, and I would be down. Speed was my only ally here. I didn't like the idea of using lethal force against other humans, corrupted though they might be. But I had brought the sword, so…

I readied boosts for both legs and arms, building them up while I waited. The first Guard reached me and swung his shockspear. I ducked under it, releasing the boosts. From my point of view, he now looked as if he moved in slow motion. As I lunged past him, I sliced the back of his calf. Not only would it take him down without killing, it was probably one of the least-armored spots in his uniform.

Still ducking, I barreled into the next Guard, throwing my blade up to knock his shockspear out of the way. The impact of my boosted body striking his knocked him off his feet, but also gave me a severe jolt. I tripped over him as he fell and almost hit the ground myself. My legs screamed in protest as I boosted them yet again to keep my footing. I spun back to face the others.

And an enormous fist slammed into my stomach. Boosts or no boosts, it knocked all the air out of me and threw me back several feet. I rolled, trying to pull myself up, gasping desperately for breath. A green foot kicked my sword out of my hand and settled on my chest. I looked up into the face of the draconic.

It chuckled and leaned in closer to speak to me. "We've been looking for you."

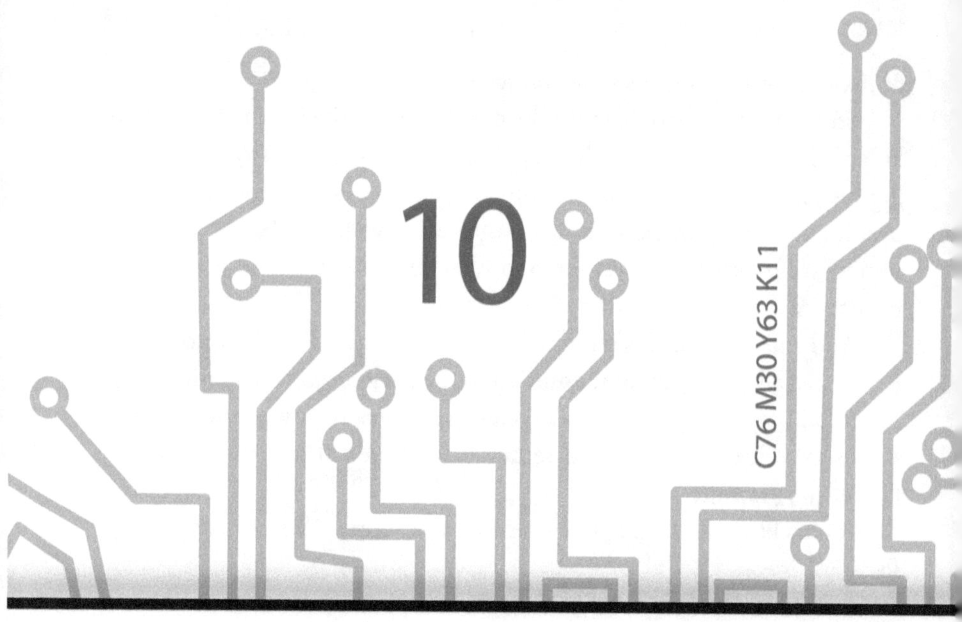

10

The draconic lifted its head. "We've been informed of a cybernetically enhanced rogue operating out here. Your attacks on our troops have made you the most wanted man in all of The Circle."

Thanks, Rick. Thanks a lot.

"Beryl! Beryl!" Lovat yelled at me. I caught a glimpse of Don holding him back.

I couldn't speak yet. I tried to channel a boost to my stomach area to help me recover. Whether it worked or not, I managed to gasp in a huge breath. "Which one are you?" I forced out the question, stalling for time. I needed to recover before trying anything.

The draconic cocked its head at me. "I am Calchas Green. You would do well to remember it, in the short amount of life you have left."

"Oh, Calchas. That's all?" I continued to suck in as much air as I could. I was almost stable. I trickled small boosts into my limbs. "I thought maybe I'd gotten captured by someone important, like Scamandian."

"Scamandrius," it corrected me. "Your attempt to antagonize me is amusing. But I have seen your future. A future where I disassemble you in front of my master."

"You talk pretty big for a third-rate draconic." I had no idea whether my insults made any sense at all, and didn't care. As long as I kept the conversation going, I could build up my strength.

"Of course, before that disassembly, you will tell me absolutely every-thing I wish to know about you and whatever group you work with out here," it went on, ignoring my taunt.

"I'm not telling you anything, Calchas." Calchas. Calchas. My mind tried to think of a clever insult or pun to make with the name. Nothing. I'd probably think of one an hour later.

"Oh, but you will." It gestured back toward the prisoners. "We have two of your companions here. More specifically, we have… a child." In a swift motion, the draconic lifted its foot from my chest, spun around and snatched Lovat away from Don's grasp.

"You monster!" Don snarled, lunging after it. One of the guards tapped him with a shockspear. He went down, shaking.

Calchas Green held Lovat with one clawed hand wrapped completely around his neck. "Over the centuries, I've found that threatening a child makes you humans so… pliable."

"Beryl," Lovat whispered. His eyes locked on to mine.

I pushed myself up on my elbows. "Leave him out of this! You, you're pathetic. Big giant lizard proving his power with a kid?"

Calchas Green ran one of its clawed fingers through Lovat's long hair. "So fragile. So easily damaged."

"If you harm him, I will kill you."

"Will you?" The draconic ran its claw along Lovat's cheek, cutting a narrow scratch. Lovat cried out. "There. I have harmed him. Now what?"

Now… I didn't know. My body was ready to attack, everything boost-ed, but… I couldn't. Not while that thing held Lovat. One twist of its hand, and it could snap his neck.

"I…"

Calchas Green bent closer. "Yes?"

I was about to say, "I surrender." But at that moment, two things hap-pened at once.

One, Calchas Green pitched forward, dragging Lovat down with him. Two, a loud explosion echoed through the hills. Lainey's rifle!

I rolled and snatched up the sword. I leaped to my feet and rushed to the draconic. Lovat broke free, crawling toward me. I grabbed him by the arm and yanked him up. "Get behind me, kid."

Calchas Green rose up from the ground. I caught only a glimpse of a huge wound on its back. A shot that could kill a giant cat only wounded a draconic. Nothing is ever as easy as I hoped it would be.

"What magic is this?" it roared. The four remaining Viridian Guard gripped their shockspears, looking wildly in every direction, trying to figure out what happened.

A second shot rang out. Calchas Green screamed as the left side of its face exploded. It collapsed onto its hands and knees. I didn't wait any longer. I shot forward and stabbed my sword through its damaged head, penetrating the brain. It slumped to the ground with a satisfying thump.

I whirled toward the Guards and aimed my bloody sword at them. "The power that took down the draconic is coming for you next, if you don't run," I declared in as menacing a voice as I could muster.

One of them hefted his spear as if to throw it at me, but hesitated. Two of the others ran at once, taking off toward the south. "Don't leave me!" screamed the one whose leg I'd cut. The last two looked at each other, then raced after the others, leaving only the injured one.

Don got up and walked over to him. "Give me your shockspear," he ordered. The Guard complied, terror in his eyes.

Lovat threw his arms around me from behind, almost tackling me. I dropped the sword and turned back to embrace him. "Hey, buddy. It's all right. We're all right."

"I knew you weren't dead! I knew it!" His words came out muffled from his face buried against my stomach. Had he gotten taller since I left? His hair certainly had gotten a lot longer.

Caedan ran into view and stopped to catch his breath. "You didn't leave anything for me to do!" he griped. Peri, only a few steps behind him, stopped in the same way. They almost looked like twins.

"You got Lainey here in time," I said. "That's what mattered."

Caedan glanced back in the way he'd come. I could now see Lainey standing up on a nearby hill. "I have got to get me one of those rifles!" Caedan declared. "Don. You all right, man?"

"I'm good." The gruff man stood holding the shockspear aimed at the Guard on the ground. He turned to look at me. "Glad to see you're not dead."

"Yeah, it's a long story." I pried Lovat loose and knelt down to look at his face. "Let me see that." I turned his face to look at the scratch. It didn't look deep. "You should be okay. We'll clean it up when we get back, and Bice can look it over."

"It don't hurt," he said, trying to look brave despite the tears that still ran down his cheeks.

"Lovat, I—"

He grabbed hold of me again, holding me like he never wanted to let me go. I submitted to his grip and watched the others. Lainey approached, carrying her rifle in both arms. Caedan introduced her to Don, who couldn't help staring at her unmarked face.

"Thanks!" I called. "You saved us."

She shrugged. "I figured you could use a little help." She walked over to look at the body of the draconic. "My aim wasn't very good. I meant to take off his head with the first shot."

"That was so streak," Caedan said, shaking his head and grinning.

In the aftermath, as my boosts faded, fatigue swept over me. I'd been boosting my legs for over an hour, and then did more in this fight. I sat down, pulling Lovat down with me.

"You all right?" Lainey asked, her forehead creased.

"I'll be fine. Just tired."

Caedan looked around. "Well, there's no way we'll all fit on the four-wheeler," he observed. "What do you want to do, Beryl?"

"You go on back. Let them know what happened. We'll follow once I get some strength back." I looked at the boy holding me. "But maybe Lovat should ride with you."

"No! I'm staying with you!"

"Sure, man. Sure." I patted him on the back, and fought a lump in my throat. I'd known he would miss me the most, but the strength of his emotions still caught me by surprise.

"We've got one problem," Don pointed out. "What do we do with him?"

I turned to look at the last Viridian Guard. He'd pulled his helmet off sometime after I cut his leg. He glared at me through his green chromark. "Traitors!" he snarled.

"We're not the ones working for lizards," I said. "We're about helping humans be free. Sound interesting?"

"The wrath of Viridia will consume you!"

I sighed. Of course the Guard would be the most indoctrinated of all Viridia's inhabitants. I didn't think we'd be able to get through to him.

"We could… take him with us," Caedan said. I looked up at him and knew what he was thinking. In Caesious, I'd been faced with a similar situation. I chose to bring Caedan back with me. That worked out pretty well.

Looking at this guy, I didn't think it would turn out the same way. But I thought about Rick and his more aggressive attitude. I had no doubt what he would do in this situation.

But I was not Rick. The image of the guard I'd once killed haunted me. Truth be told, it never stopped haunting me. No matter what, I couldn't kill this man now.

So what choice did that leave?

11

I knelt beside the prisoner and asked him: "What do you think we should do with you?"

The arrogance dropped off his face. "I, uh… let me go?"

I glanced down at his leg. "Your buddies bandaged you all right, but I don't think you can get very far by yourself."

"It's more than that," Peri said. "You cut his tendon. He'll need surgery to repair it."

I saw a sudden widening of the Guard's eyes. He knew what that meant as well as the rest of us. "So you have to ask yourself," I told him, "Are you valuable enough to the dragon to have surgery? Or will he just toss you aside, because he can always find more humans eager to join the Viridian Guard?"

"I'm…" He swallowed and didn't answer.

Caedan stepped up beside us. "I was part of the Cerulean Corps, until I met this guy." He gestured at me. "If you come with us, we'll treat you fair. And you might get an opportunity to do some really streak stuff."

"We don't have a surgeon," I said. "So I can't promise you we can get your leg fully taken care of. But you'll be alive. It's your choice. I'll give you a minute to think it over, but after that, we're gone."

I motioned to the others and we walked a few yards away. Lovat stayed close to me the whole time. "What do you think?" I asked them.

"You gave him the chance," Peri said. "Let's see if he takes it."

"And if he doesn't?" Don asked. "He's Guard. He saw what we can do. He'll tell them all about us."

"What will he tell them? That we've got some kind of magic and we killed a draconic? Will they even listen? For that matter, does he know anything more than the others who already got away?"

"Do you really think you can help with his leg?" Lainey asked.

"I don't know. Peri?"

"Maybe? I don't know as much medicine as Bice, but it doesn't look promising. Could we help him with, you know"—he gestured at me—"something cybernetic?"

"We can look around Loden's lab, but I don't remember anything having to do with legs. And like I told him: the dragon, or his boss, may decide he's not worth the resources and time needed to heal that kind of injury. He'd be taking his chances."

"So either way, he may never walk again."

"No. With us, he may never walk again. With the dragon, he may die."

Lainey pulled her hair to the back of her neck. "Is that true? They would kill him rather than let him recover from an injury?"

Caedan, Peri and Don all raised their eyebrows in near-unison. "Where have you been all of your life that you don't know this?" Caedan asked.

"We'll discuss that later," I said. "Let's see if our friend has made his decision."

We walked back to the fallen Guard. "Did you make up your mind?"

He'd pulled himself into a seated position, holding his injured leg. "What are you people doing out here, anyway? What's your goal?"

"Uh-uh." I shook my head. "I'm not telling you anything else, unless you come with us. You have to decide. And now. Or I make the decision for you."

"How far are we from Viridia?" he asked.

"Miles and miles," Don answered. "And the trains aren't running, so crawling to the tracks won't do you any good."

"You'd have to crawl all the way to the city," I agreed. "Or get lucky and run into another patrol. Your friends abandoned you, after all."

"I suppose… I suppose I'll have to come with you." His face fell as he said it. I guess this wasn't how he expected his career in the Viridian Guard to end.

"Good choice."

"I don't have much of a choice," he complained. "Try to get back and risk death, or come with you and… whatever you do with me."

"We'll treat you like a human being," I said. "What's your name?"

"Uh, Jaden."

"Jaden, I'm Beryl." I held out my hand. He reached up hesitantly and took it. I pulled him up onto his good foot. "Caedan, fetch the four-wheeler. Looks like you'll have a passenger after all."

Lovat picked up Jaden's helmet and put it on his own head. With the comically oversized helmet resting on his shoulders, he looked from side to side. "How do you see in these things?" he asked, pulling it back off.

Once Caedan returned, we helped Jaden mount the vehicle behind him. "Don't try anything funny," Caedan warned. "I can wreck this thing with a twist of my wrist."

"And we're all going to be close," I added. "Drive slow along with us, Caedan. I'd prefer we all got back at the same time." I didn't want Rick to see Jaden before he saw me.

"That's no fun," Caedan complained.

I almost told him to let me drive, then. But I needed to reestablish myself as leader here. Riding while others walked wouldn't do it, even if I was already exhausted.

Lovat finally noticed Lainey. He stared up at her face. She smiled back. "You." Lovat pointed at her. "You're like me."

"I guess I am," Lainey said. She touched her own face.

"Never heard of an orphan living that long, unmarked," Don observed.

"She's not an orphan," I said. "Let's get back to the Asylum and we'll talk over everything."

"Looking forward to it," Caedan said, gunning the four-wheeler's engine.

Driving the four-wheeler at a walking speed wasn't easy. Caedan would spurt ahead, then slow to almost a crawl while we caught up to him, then try to stay with us. But he never could. I gave him permission to drive up ahead, then make a wide circle around us, to scout for other enemies.

"But keep close," I warned, glancing at Jaden behind him. Caedan nodded and took off.

"Here we are, walking again," Lainey said. "Thought we were done with that for a while."

"Sorry." I triggered a boost into my legs to keep going, but the boosts themselves were getting weaker and weaker. I was hitting my limits. "This is what our life is like now. Walking from one crisis to another."

"Where you been, Beryl?" Lovat asked. "Rick said you were dead. But I knew you couldn't."

"Lovat, I can die like anyone else." I didn't want him thinking I was immortal. Bad enough he wanted to be like me. "So, you remember Incarnadine, right?"

He nodded.

"The dragon chased me, but I got away. Then I sort of crashed into the mountain. Lainey found me and helped me get better. Then I came back."

"Oh. Okay. Hue."

Heh. If only explaining to the others would be that simple.

We took a slight detour on the way back, so we could cross our favorite stream and get some clean water to drink. While there, I washed off Lovat's face and took a closer look at his scratch. It didn't look too bad, but I supposed it might scar. I didn't know how to determine that.

By the time we got back to the Asylum, the afternoon sun was on its way toward the mountains. Bice came out to meet us. Lainey's cat bounded along beside him, but got distracted by something until Lainey chased it down and scooped it up. Lovat wanted to see it, naturally. While they bonded over the kitten, we told Bice what had happened.

"I need you to check on Lovat's face, and then this guy," I said, pointing at Jaden. "We'll need to find a place for him, but not in the cave, obviously."

He shook his head. "You love to take in strays, don't you? I'll take care of it. But, uh, you have someone waiting to see you."

"He's back?"

Bice nodded. "Kelly too, but she's taking a nap."

"Did you tell him I was back?"

"Mazarine did. He saw you this morning."

Great. Several different scenarios ran through my head, none of them good. Bice went to see to Lovat and Jaden. I squared my shoulders and took a deep breath. No sense putting this off.

Caedan, Don, and Lainey joined me. "You good?" Don asked.

I nodded, seeing the figure emerge from the Asylum and trot toward us. I might be upset about what he'd done, but he was still my best friend.

Wasn't he? I stepped away from the others.
    "Hello, Rick."

He stopped and stared at me. For a few moments, no one spoke. He took another step forward.

"Maz told me you were back," he said at last. "I didn't… I…"

I didn't know what to say either. I didn't think I could say anything. Something in my chest rose up into my throat and cut off my vocal ability. It also made my eyes grow a little moister than usual, I think.

And then Rick charged me and grabbed me in a hug. I hesitated only an instant before throwing my arms around him as well. This was different from Caedan's hug. That one came from sudden joy and excitement. This hug came from deeper emotions. I don't know how to explain it, but when two guys form a bond, when they fight through stuff together, when they're on the same mission… I don't know. It's deep. I guess it's a kind of love or something. I am not saying this right at all.

Rick pulled away, clapped me on the shoulder and cleared his throat. "So, uh, where's the flyer? You didn't bring it back?"

"Sorry. I had to sell it for food."

Rick snorted, then glanced around at everyone else. "I see we have a lot to talk about here. The workshop?"

"Yeah. I want to talk with everyone at once. Well, all of our original team, that is."

"Right, right. Let's get to it." He paused and stared at my face. "Wait…

weren't you missing an eye the last time I saw you?"

"Like you said: a lot to talk about."

He nodded and hurried back inside. I explained to Lainey that I'd call her in when it was appropriate.

"No problem. I'll be out here with Glacier."

"All right. There are a few people still out here, but try not to talk to them too much until I can explain," I said. "Oh, and don't say anything at all to the blue draconic. Yet."

"The what?"

"I didn't tell you about the blue draconic?" I looked around. "I'll introduce you after our meeting. Gotta go right now."

Peri looked a little hurt to be left behind. "Sorry, man. I need to talk to the first team." That didn't sound right. "But, uh, keep it up, and you'll be right there with us very soon." That was a little better.

Lovat hadn't left my side. I gathered up Don, Caedan, and Bice, and we made our way into the cave and to the workshop. Dusk passed by on the way out, giving us all a funny look. I had to stop as we passed a side nook where Kelly lay asleep on a cot. I watched her for a moment, feeling that lump in my throat again. I swallowed and hurried on.

"I guess we're the all-boys club for the moment," Rick said. "I didn't want to wake Kelly. She's been really tired."

"It's all right. Let her rest," I said. I took a deep breath and looked around the room. I was back. I was here, with my friends, the ones that mattered, the ones that cared about me. We might have our differences, but we were united in our purpose and our devotion to each other. At least I believed we were.

"Where do we start?" Rick asked. "With what just happened, or backing up three weeks? Has it been three weeks? Maybe four?"

"I don't know. I was unconscious for most of it."

"Well, now you've got to tell us."

I found a seat and sank into it. I don't know if my legs could've handled anything else. "I might sleep for another week after today," I confessed. Then I started my story from the moment I blasted out of the Flame in Incarnadine, and described what happened next. Naturally, the biggest consternation came when I revealed where Carl Roberts and Lainey said they came from.

"But there's nothing outside The Circle!" Caedan protested.

"That's what we've been taught," Bice said. "Does it surprise you that the dragons were lying?"

"How do we know these two are telling the truth?" Rick asked.

"We don't," I said. "But you saw Lainey outside. No chromark. She's never had one. If they're not from outside The Circle, how is that possible?"

"Could some orphans have fled to the mountains and—I don't know—formed some kind of secret society of their own?" Caedan suggested.

"Would they have the kind of technology they have?" I asked. "You saw her rifle and what it can do."

"What can it do?" Rick wondered.

"It's a projectile weapon. A very powerful one. That's not something someone whipped up in the mountains."

Bice rubbed his chin. "I'm really puzzling over this one. If there are people outside The Circle, why keep it such a secret from us?"

"To keep us subservient," I said. "To keep us from knowing about life without dragon rule."

"But if it's a whole civilization, with their own technology and everything, wouldn't it behoove the dragons to at least trade with these people? To make deals with them? They wouldn't have to involve anyone but their trusted servants. It's just strange."

"Like everything else here. You know, the more Lainey learns about life in The Circle, the more she keeps saying how weird it all is. Everything is different for her."

"What did she tell you about life outside?" Rick asked.

"Not enough. She's keeping things to herself. I think her dad warned her not to tell us too much."

"Why? Why not tell us?"

I shrugged. "Secrets. I don't know."

"Can we trust them?" Don wanted to know.

"I think so." I shook my head. "They had no reason to help me, but they did. And I'd be dead if not for them, no question."

"If we can learn the tech secrets of that rifle, it could make a huge difference," Rick suggested. "Do you think she'll let Dusk look at it?"

"I don't know." I hesitated, looking at the table surface in front of me. "Who is she, Rick? Bice says you brought her from Atramentous?"

"Sure. I know her from way back. I took a scouting mission there a couple weeks ago, thought I'd look her up, and found her. She's totally on board with our mission."

"You've never mentioned her before. Was she a member of your rebel group?"

"Not exactly. She was more like Stacy is for us now: on our side, but not really part of the group."

"So why'd she agree to come join you now?"

He gestured at the workshop. "I told her about this. She's a tech person. We needed one. Worked out great."

"Loden left this place to me, Rick. I'm not all that comfortable with someone else scrounging through it."

"You were dead, Beryl." He leveled his gaze at me. "I had to move on, take what actions I thought were necessary to continue the mission."

"That's what we need to talk about next: your actions."

Rick shot a look at Bice. "What have people been telling you?"

"You've been doing raids?"

"Yes. Like you did when you went after the red draconic. We've taken down some troops from both sides."

"Going after the red draconic was a mistake, not to mention it didn't work. And now they're all looking for us!"

"They're looking for enemies," Rick argued. "Not us in particular."

"Sure looked like it. We just rescued Don and Lovat here from one of their patrols!"

"And you brought back a prisoner, I saw. Good job."

"And killed a draconic," Caedan added.

"You killed another green draconic? That's fantastic!"

"We're getting off the point," I said, slapping the table. "You've brought trouble down on us. It's only a matter of time before they find this place now. And then what happens to all of Loden's work?"

"They're not looking for me, Beryl. They're looking for you."

Rick's statement hung in the air, and a chill trickled down my back. "We've been informed of a cybernetically enhanced rogue operating out here," Calchas Green had said. Maybe it was true.

"Do you know why Kelly and I were gone when you got here?" Rick went on. "We were scouting north, because there are gold patrols that way." He stood and pointed. "Gold troops, Beryl. I haven't done anything to the golds. Not a thing. But you antagonized them at the Hub, and they're looking for you. What's more, they're not just randomly patrolling like the green and black. They are systematically searching everything between the Hub and the Blasted Lands. You say it's only a matter of time? You're right. But the threat is from the north, not the south."

I didn't know what to say. Rick sat down again. "I haven't done anything without asking myself whether you would do it," he said. "Not one thing."

"I wouldn't ban Bice from the workshop," I shot back. It felt lame to say it, but I was scared and annoyed.

"I wanted Dusk to have the place to herself while she catalogued and studied," Rick said. "I banned everyone."

"That ends now."

He shrugged. "You're the boss. I'm happy to let you take over again." He looked up at me. "But let's not try to go back to the way things were. We can't. We have at least three of the dragons looking for us. What are we going to do about it?"

13

We sat in silence for a few more moments. Finally, I stirred. "There's a lot I haven't heard about," I said. "I'd like to know everything else that's happened since I've been gone. Then maybe we can make some decisions."

"Well, um." Rick looked at the others. "We escaped from Incarnadine, obviously. We hid out in Marcus and Cerise's place for a couple of days until the furor died down, and then we slipped out."

"With the books?" I couldn't believe I hadn't asked about the very purpose of our entire mission yet.

"Yes," Bice answered. "They're very, uh… fascinating."

"I want to hear everything you've learned," I said. "As soon as we can."

"Of course. But you may not like some of it, especially since… we're missing the first book."

I looked at Rick. "The one that got left behind?"

He nodded.

"It just happened to be the first book, the one that reveals the beginning of The Circle and how the dragons got here? All the stuff we really want to learn?"

"Looks that way."

"Ugh." I slumped back. "I hope there's some good stuff in the other books."

"We'll talk later," Bice promised.

"What about Olive?" I asked. "Did she get back to Viridia all right?"

"She's there," Don spoke up. "Saw her this morning."

"And she still thinks she was working for the Viridian Guard?"

"That was absolutely crazy, but it worked," Rick said, shaking his head. "I still don't know how you convinced her. She was quite distraught that you gave your life for Viridia, by the way."

"Oh, yeah?"

"Lots of tears. Some wailing. I don't know if I've ever heard you described in such glowing terms. It was embarrassing, really."

I couldn't argue with that. I wondered if I would ever see her again. I wondered if I wanted to. "And, uh, how did everyone else handle it?"

"We didn't believe you were dead, at first." Rick flexed his hands together. "We've seen you survive all kinds of things, so we... held out hope. For a while."

"I didn't give up!" Lovat chimed in. I smiled at him, seated on top of another table. He never did like chairs.

"I know you didn't."

"The rest of us... we waited there for two days. When you didn't turn back up, and we heard what happened in Caesious, we came back here."

"Oh, right! I heard the dragons fought!"

"And brought down the entire tower," Caedan said. "It's hard to imagine."

Of course. Caedan grew up in Caesious. It would be like me hearing the Emerald Ascendancy had been destroyed.

"Wait. Wasn't Stacy there? Did she get out okay?"

"She had already left," Don said. "Scared her, though."

"I'll bet." I looked back to Rick. "Do we have any word on how bad the dragons hurt each other?"

"No, nothing definite. But neither of them have been seen since then."

"So, even if the books don't end up being that big of a deal, we still took down the whole peace summit," I concluded. "In some ways, that was more important."

"But we thought we lost you doing it," Bice said. "That wasn't worth it."

"I'm not—" I winced. "I'm not that important, Bice. The cause is what matters."

"Not to me. Every life is sacred."

"And that brings up the guy we just brought in." I looked to Rick. "You probably would have killed him. I couldn't. He was a helpless prisoner."

"So you brought him back here?" Rick wrinkled his brow.

"We gave him a choice." I explained the injury and what we'd told him.

"I don't like it," Rick said when I was done. "But you knew that. I can't ever agree with bringing an enemy into our camp."

"Like Caedan? Or Mazarine? Or Protogonus Blue, for that matter?"

"Just because it sometimes works out doesn't mean it always will."

"Everyone is our enemy, until we show them the truth," Bice spoke up. "I'll talk with him, and then bring him to meet Protogonus. I think that will shake up his worldview."

I bet it would. If a child of the "gods" told you they weren't really gods, it would shake anyone up.

"Speaking of the others, maybe it's time to consider bringing our blue friends in all the way?" Rick suggested.

"We should definitely consider it, but not right now. There's too much other stuff going on."

"Next meeting," Bice suggested. I nodded, feeling the weariness push at me.

"You never explained the eye," Rick remembered.

"Oh." I got up and found the box with the eyes. "Remember when we found these, Caedan?" I flipped it open and showed the others.

"Too hue," Lovat said.

"I put one of these in place when I got back this morning." I closed the box. "Turns out my eye wasn't real either."

"How much of you is?" Caedan wondered.

I shrugged. Good question. I didn't know the answer. Time and time again, I survived things I shouldn't. I had no idea how much Loden had done to my body.

"So... what are our next moves?" Bice asked. "We have new people to integrate here. I'll work on that and get Peri to help me. I'm assuming neither of them should come in here."

I almost said I trusted Lainey enough, and that I'd already brought her in once, but decided against it. "Yeah, yeah. That's good. Don, I forgot in all the craziness, but any news from Stacy?"

"Nothing much. She did say a messenger from Auric visited the

Emerald Ascendancy. She wasn't able to hear anything about the visit; only that it happened."

"All right. Nothing much we can do about that just yet. I want you to get to work on disguising our base some more. Lainey pointed out that it could be seen from the ground just fine. Not sure what we can do about that, and it might be too late, but it's worth a try. Recruit whoever you need to do the labor, including me."

He nodded.

"Rick, you said the gold teams were doing a systematic search. How much time do you think we have until they get too close?"

"Three or four days."

That soon? Ouch. "All right. Start with the north side, Don. And we need to make some contingency plans for if we're discovered. Where do we run? How much do we take? Do we seal off the cave somehow? Rick, Caedan, figure out the answers to those questions."

"You got it."

I paused. "You know, once you get to know her, ask Lainey if there's a place in the mountains we can go, anywhere near here. She might know."

"I'm sure she knows a lot. It's just whether she tells us."

"You're right. I'll keep trying to learn what I can from her myself."

"What are you going to do next?" Caedan asked.

"Sleep. I've been channeling so much boost energy that my body is about to shut down." And I felt it too. I might collapse at any moment.

"Take the cot by the wall there," Rick suggested. "We'll make sure no one disturbs you."

"Thanks." I looked around. "I don't... I can't tell you all how I feel, seeing you all here, being here again. When I was flying into the mountain, I thought about you and what you'd think, and..."

"It's all right, Beryl." Bice gave me one of his biggest smiles. "You don't have to say anything else. We know."

I nodded and swallowed. One by one, they passed by me and left the room. Don patted my back. Bice hugged me again. Caedan punched my shoulder. Lovat gave me a big squeeze, then ran off. Rick nodded, started to leave, then paused.

"I think you'll have to have one more conversation before you sleep." He stepped aside and someone else entered the workshop.

Kelly.

Rick tapped his own forehead and saluted me, before leaving the two of us alone. Kelly entered slowly. Her eyes still held a tiredness to them, as if she hadn't gotten enough sleep.

"Beryl, I..." She sniffed and looked away. "When they told us you were back, I told myself I wouldn't cry when I saw you... but I can't help it." She looked back and I could see her eyes filling up. "I'm so happy you're alive. I just—"

I stepped forward and she fell into my arms, sobbing. I held her as gently as I could. I didn't know for certain what to think here. We were still friends, even though she and Rick were together, right? Were these tears just for a friend? Or something more? Yes, I know it's stupid, but I couldn't help thinking about it.

At last, she pulled away and wiped her eyes. "I hear you brought another girlfriend with you."

"What? No. She's not my—"

She shoved me. "I'm teasing, you idiot."

Oh. Right. I snorted, then frowned again. "Kelly, are you all right? You don't look so good."

She glanced back at the door, then took a few steps to look out, making sure no one else was around. She came back, and stood there, wringing her hands together, as if she didn't know what to say next. I waited, wondering why this was such a big deal.

"Beryl, I'm... I..."

A thousand possible endings to that statement raced through my head, although at least half of them included her professing her love for me. But none of them prepared me for what she actually did say:

"I'm pregnant."

My mind blanked out. I couldn't understand for a moment or two. "You're what?"

"I'm pregnant. It's not that strange a concept, Beryl." She scowled at me.

"Right, right. Sorry. I'm just… are you sure?"

She took the chair I'd been sitting in. She leaned against the table and buried her face in her arms. "Yes, I'm sure. You remember I was getting sick to my stomach back at Incarnadine."

"I thought Marcus got sick too."

She sighed. "I don't know. Maybe it was sympathy, or maybe he was faking it to make me feel better, or maybe he really did get sick from something else. But it wasn't the same. And since then I've been constantly tired."

"Well, maybe—"

She lifted her head. "So I had Stacy send me a test. I took it a few minutes ago. I'm sure now."

"Oh."

My thoughts shifted through multiple emotions: anger at Rick for letting this happen to her, concern for Kelly's long-term future, but most of all, worry about the immediate future. If we had to abandon the Asylum and run for our lives, would she be able to do it? She'd have to have one of the seats on a four-wheeler, if we were still able to use those. I needed to co-ordinate with Rick and… then I realized. "A few minutes ago," she'd said.

"Rick doesn't know yet?"

"No." She groaned and let her head fall again. "I don't know how to tell him. I don't know how he'll react. He's not… he's not the most responsible person. You know."

I did know. And yet… "He's my best friend," I said. "I have to believe he'll handle this okay. I can be there when you tell him, if you want."

"No, I don't want him to know I told you first. Ugh." She looked up again. This time I noticed the dark circles under her eyes. "I'm so glad you're here. I needed someone to talk to, but I don't want him to know I needed someone to talk to. Isn't that crazy?"

"Not, not really. I think I get it." Thinking about it, I guess she didn't have any other real friends here. She'd never been close to Don or even Bice. Caedan wasn't exactly the listening type, and everyone else was… new and/or suspicious. She couldn't slip off to Viridia to talk with Stacy. "So hey, at least we've got more girls here now, huh?"

"I don't know them yet, Beryl. I need you."

I always wanted to hear those words from her, but not necessarily in this context. "I'm here, Kelly. Whatever you need from me."

"I just… I'm not ready to be a mother. And definitely not while we're at war. I can't believe I let this happen."

I put my hands on her shoulders. "It's going to be all right, Kelly. We'll take care of you, no matter what."

"You can't even take care of yourself, Beryl."

Ouch.

"Sorry, I didn't mean that. I know you'd sacrifice everything to protect me, or just about any of us. That's just who you are."

That was a little better.

"Do you… I mean, um, you want me to send Rick back in here while I go somewhere else?"

"No." She got back to her feet. "I'm not ready to tell him yet. I have to decide what I want to happen first."

"Oh. Okay."

She looked at me. "Thanks, Beryl. This helped a lot."

"You're welcome." I honestly don't know that I said anything worth-while in the entire conversation, but if it helped…

I waited until she left the room. Then I staggered over to the cot. I'd used the last of my boost energy to stay upright while talking to her. I desperately needed to sleep, and… I fell into the cot, asleep before my body stopped falling.

"Beryl? Beryl!"

I struggled to open my eyes. Bice's dark face looked down at mine. I lifted a hand and rubbed at my eyes. "What's going on?" I blinked a few more times. "I just fell asleep."

"You've been out almost an entire day," he said. "I'd have let you keep sleeping, but we have a situation."

I groaned and swung my legs off the cot. Bice took a step back as I sat up. Had I really slept an entire day in these clothes? I didn't feel like I'd gotten that much rest. Aches erupted everywhere on my body as I stood up. I guess I really abused it in the search and rescue.

Rick burst into the workshop. "Did you get him? Oh, good. He's finally awake."

"What's happening?" I asked. I licked the roof of my mouth a couple of times, trying to generate some saliva. I hated dry mouth.

"Remember those gold patrols? They've gotten a whole lot closer in the past twenty-four hours," he told me. "If we don't stop them soon, they'll find us."

"And by stop them, you mean…"

"What do you think I mean? This is no time for playing it safe, Beryl. Everything's in danger here."

"Sorry. Still waking up." I shook my head. Bleaking sleepiness. I needed… huh. Why not? I tried channeling a burst of boost energy throughout my head. The effect was instantaneous. "Wow." I jumped to my feet, my head clear and eyes wide.

"You all right?" Bice asked.

"Yeah, great. Now. So… what do you suggest, Rick?"

"We set up an ambush. You, me, Caedan, and your new friend with the rifle thing. You killed a green draconic yesterday. How about a gold one today?"

"There's a draconic?"

"Yeah, it's leading the main patrol. Seems pretty determined too."

"Taizong Gold," I muttered. "Gotta be."

"How many draconics are on a first-name basis with you by now?"

"Too many." I looked around for the sword. Where had I left it? "Get the others together. Let me go pee, get a drink and a snack, and then I'll be ready. I'll make one alteration to your plan, though."

"What's that?"

"We'll set up the ambush, but I want to do something before we attack." I found the sword and picked it up. "I want to talk to it."

Rick snorted, but headed out of the cave.

"Do you think you can talk this one into doing anything?" Bice asked.

"No, not really. But the gold dragon seems mighty busy for not being in this war. I want to figure out what he's up to, if I can."

"I'll pray for you, then."

I nodded. Bice still believed in some power, some god, above it all. I couldn't get there yet. The idea of gods still pointed me to the worship of the dragons, as corrupt and twisted as anyone could imagine. I wasn't eager to find out if anything else might want or need my worship.

I took care of the basics and then hurried to meet the others. Lainey met me halfway.

"Interesting place you have here," she said.

"Yeah? I'm sorry I wasn't able to show you around, introduce you to everyone. After all that, I kind of collapsed."

"Kelly told me. So your cybernetic thing takes a lot out of you, huh?"

"When I use it too much, sure. My body can only handle so much." And that, I realized, was crucial. It meant a lot of me must still be human. Otherwise, why would I get so tired? Suddenly, my exhaustion seemed like a blessing.

"Some of your friends are a little pushy," Lainey added.

"What do you mean?"

"They really want to know more about… where I come from."

I stopped. "Can you blame them? I told you it was a big deal."

"But I can't tell them. My father told me not to."

"I understand." Except I didn't. Not really. "But it's not going to stop the questions." I started walking again.

Lainey followed. "All right. Guess I'll have to use threats."

"If that works." I chuckled.

At the four-wheelers, Lovat complained about being left behind again.

"You said things would change after Incarnadine!" he accused me.

"I did. You're right. And things are changing." I gave him a quick hug. "Ask Bice about the books he's reading. He's learning stuff about the dragons that we can use. And once we do, I'll need you. Right now, I'm trying to protect you, and everyone else here."

"I still want to go."

Rick climbed onto one of the four-wheelers behind Caedan and gave me an impatient look.

"You have to trust me, pal. Everyone has their own special abilities. I need these three right now. Other times, I'll need you. That's what a leader does: choose the right people. Can you trust me?"

Lovat's shoulders slumped and he backed off. I hoped this wouldn't happen every time. I couldn't justify taking him into danger.

I jumped onto the other four-wheeler, and Lainey climbed on behind me. "Ever ridden something like this before?" I asked.

"Not exactly, but… close enough."

"Good. Hang on to me. Here we go."

Caedan and I gunned the engines and raced out of the Asylum, heading north. I had an appointment with a gold draconic.

We rode for about ten minutes before Rick signaled a halt. We parked the four-wheelers behind a copse of trees and continued on foot. About five minutes later, we spotted our quarry. We hid in some tall grass, waiting and watching.

"Can you zoom in on them?" Rick asked.

I nodded and sent a boost into my eyes. I couldn't hear anything, but every time I did it now, my mind imagined the sound of parts moving in my bionic eyes. The concept still unnerved me, but I couldn't deny the advantages. At least I'd never have to wear glasses in my old age. If I got there.

I focused in on the figures moving along next to a set of railroad tracks. I think they were part of a spur which bypassed the Hub, connecting Viridia and Auric directly. The figures resolved into a gold draconic and four of the golden-armored soldiers. No one had ever mentioned a name for them, now that I thought about it. I tried to get a closer look at the draconic. Sure enough, its left hand and forearm had a different appearance, the cybernetic materials not quite matching the color of its scales.

"It's Taizong Gold all right," I said, letting my vision return to normal. "Third time I've seen it now."

"And you still want to talk to it?" Rick asked.

"Yeah, I do. Last time, it told me Auric wanted to speak with me." I paused. "And before that, it wanted to take me back and rip out my cyb implant."

"To be fair, they all want to do that."

I laughed. "True. The point is: I'm curious. I want to know why the gold dragon is so interested in me."

"Caesious said his name as he died," Caedan recalled. "That has to mean something."

I nodded. Another mystery I'd like solved. But all of them were secondary to our main goal: continuing the war and killing the dragons. "If I can get any good info from it, this will be worth it. If not, be prepared to shoot it."

Rick pulled out his little hand crossbow. Lainey unslung her rifle. Caedan looked at them both and chuckled. "She might have you beat, Rick."

"You think?"

"Move into position," I told them. "I'll walk out in the open and get their attention."

Rick pointed to two different spots. "I can hide there by that tree, and Lainey there at that rock. You all right with that?"

"Sure," Lainey said. As before, nothing seemed to faze her. She'd gone from hiding in the mountains to hunting draconics without even asking many questions.

I waited for them to move out, then I stood and strode out into the open. I was curious to see how long it would take the golden gang to notice me.

The answer: not long at all. One of the soldiers, who wore an odd attachment on his helmet, pointed me out to the others. As one, they all turned and came in my direction. Taizong Gold took the lead. Keeping in mind the ambush points, I came to a stop and waited for them to come to me. As they drew near, I noticed little details. The odd attachment looked like some kind of visor, binoculars of some sort, I guessed. The draconic wore loose-fitting gray-green pants again. It carried no weapon, but the soldiers all bore their long swords. None of them carried the larger pole weapons I'd seen at the Hub.

"That's far enough," I called when they were about forty yards away. "I hear you're looking for me."

The draconic took three or four more steps beyond the soldiers and stopped. "Beryl. I suspected you survived the disaster at Caesious."

I spread my arms. "Here I am, same as always. And there you are, ugly as always. I see they patched up your hand."

Taizong Gold flexed its cybernetic left hand. "Indeed. Made some improvements as well. But it's still not as impressive as your own tech, I believe."

"Is that why you're searching for me so much?"

The draconic gave a signal to the soldiers and they backed even further away, leaving it out in the open. Curious behavior. It wasn't going to challenge me to single combat again, was it?

"I told you before that Auric wishes to speak with you," it declared. "After I described your… performance at Caesious, he was even more intrigued. I have sought you out to extend his invitation."

"Invitation to what?"

"To come to his city and speak."

I blinked. "You can't be serious." A dragon inviting me to come visit for a chat?

"I am completely serious, as is my master. He is most earnest to meet you."

"This is nuts," I muttered to myself.

"You will, of course, wish to discuss this with your allies," Taizong Gold went on, "the ones who are no doubt waiting in ambush." It pointed at the rock where Lainey hid. "That seems a likely place."

"Send your soldiers away and then we can talk," I said.

"Of course." The draconic turned and gave an order. The soldiers, as one, spun on their heels and marched away. I waited until they'd gone almost out of sight before I gave my own signal, beckoning the others to come join me.

Rick approached with a dark look. "Why are we revealing ourselves to it?" he demanded. "We should just kill it!"

"Did you hear what it said?" I asked as Caedan and Lainey joined us. "It wants me to come to talk to the dragon!"

"Of course it does! You said it yourself: they want the secrets of your implant. If you walk into that city, you're never coming back."

"Yeah, Beryl," Caedan agreed. "This is nuts."

"I agree it's crazy," I said. "But why? That's what I don't get. If it just wanted to capture me, why not send a bigger force? Why extend an invitation?"

"Who knows why the dragons do anything?" Rick waved his crossbow in the direction of the draconic. "They're crazy!"

"No, they're not. That's why we're so crazy to fight them. They've ruled for a thousand years. They're smarter than we are."

"Then no matter what you do, the dragons win," Lainey spoke up.

I stared at her. "What?"

"If they're that far ahead of you in intelligence, then how can you win?"

"Because we can take advantage of their weaknesses, like their arrogance, to do things they don't expect."

She gestured with her head toward Taizong Gold. "So how does this one's arrogance factor in?"

"That's what I'm trying to figure out. Is the dragon so arrogant that he believes I'll accept this invitation?"

"There's more to my offer!" the draconic shouted to us.

I stepped apart from the others and looked back at it. "I'm listening."

"I'm perfectly aware that you do not trust this invitation. Your experiences growing up under Viridia would have naturally predisposed you to mistrust against all dragons."

"Go on."

"So I am empowered to make an offer." Taizong Gold spread its arms wide, mocking my earlier pose. "I am ready and willing to be a hostage with your people while you visit almighty Auric."

"You're what?"

"I will submit to being a prisoner with your"—it waved at our group—"whatever this is, until you return safely from your visit with my master."

"Uh, let me talk this over." I huddled with the others again. "Now what?"

"There's no way we take him back to the Asylum," Rick said.

"Agreed. Is there somewhere else we can hold him?"

Caedan and Rick looked at each other. "We've been scouting new locations…" Caedan said slowly.

"In case we had to run," Rick put in. "But they're just empty places we considered."

"This is an opportunity I'm reluctant to pass up," I said. "The dragon is serious about this. And considering how valuable and limited the draconics are, I can't imagine he'd give up one of his children just to get a look at my brain."

"I wouldn't put anything past them," Rick argued. "But... you may be right. Auric is different from the others. I don't know what that means, but he might be sincere in the offer."

"Suggest a delay," Lainey said. "Tell him you're in the middle of something, but you will make the visit later. That gives you time to set up this other place."

"Might work," I said.

"Let's be clear," Rick emphasized. "What are we getting out of this? What do we stand to gain?"

"Information. Both from visiting the dragon, and from whatever you can get from the draconic."

"You think we can turn it?"

"I think we should try. Let Protogonus Blue talk to it. See what happens. What's the worst possibility?"

"It's all a trap. You get killed. The draconic escapes, murdering some of us in the process." Rick shrugged at my look. "You asked."

"Caedan? You're being quiet. What do you think?" I asked.

Caedan tore his gaze away from the draconic. "Sorry. I still think it's nuts."

I nodded. I didn't expect him to trust this draconic, since it almost killed him. But that experience taught me something: Taizong Gold kept its agreements, but only to the exact letter. We would have to be careful.

I turned back to the draconic. "I'm willing to accept your offer, under certain conditions."

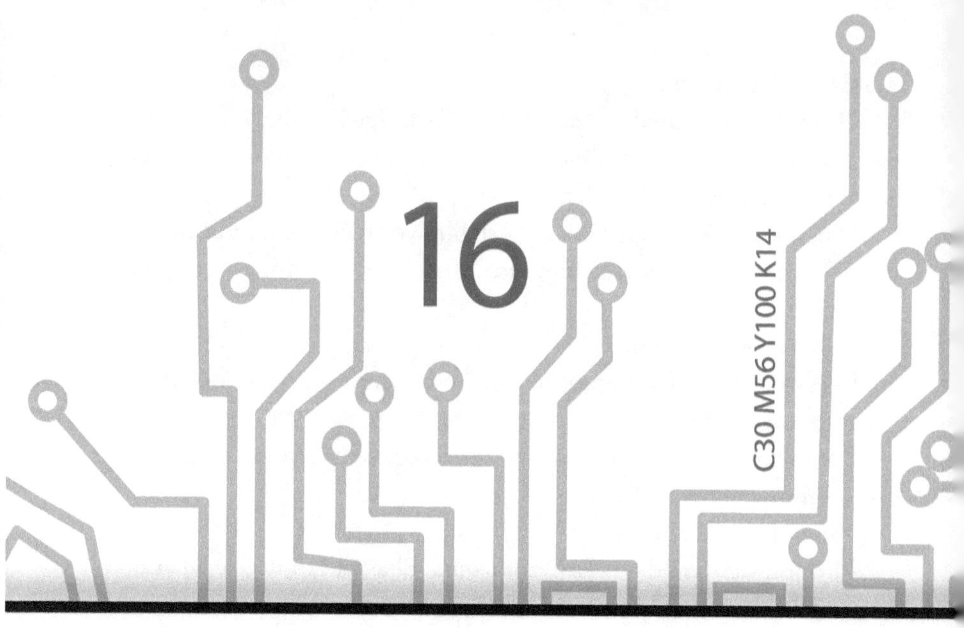

16

"What are your conditions?"

"I need a little time. We're in the middle of something here, and I need time to wrap it up before I can come to Auric."

Taizong lowered its head. "How much time?"

"A week?" I whispered to Rick.

"Make it two weeks. We have to deal with the green patrols too, remember?"

"Two weeks!" I called.

"Far too long," the draconic answered. "Auric has plans in motion that will not be delayed. The entire makeup of The Circle may change by then."

I looked back at the others with wide eyes. "Well, that's an audacious claim," Rick noted.

"I have my own plans in motion," I answered Taizong. "And they don't include bowing to a dragon's whims."

"Ten days, then," the draconic suggested. "That is the most I can offer, and I am certain Auric will be disturbed by it."

"All the more reason." I glanced at Rick, who gave a slight nod. "Ten days it is, then. We will meet here and make the trade-off."

Taizong Gold nodded, turned, and walked away.

"That's it?" Caedan asked. "Really?"

"Sorry you didn't get to fight today," I said. "But maybe something good will come out of this."

"I want to go with you," Lainey spoke up.

"I don't think that will work. Auric only wanted to see me."

"Why not? You made him change it once. Change it again when he comes back."

"Why would you want to put yourself in that kind of danger?" Just when I thought I was starting to understand this girl…

"I'm here to learn about this place. Visiting the gold city seems an ideal opportunity."

I looked back at Taizong Gold still walking away. "We'll talk more later. We've got ten days. Let's figure out how we're going to use them."

Back at the Asylum, we gathered everyone except for Jaden. I greeted Mazarine, and Protogonus Blue for the first time since my return. All together, I explained the gold dragon's offer. "Any thoughts? Suggestions?"

"Did you make another decision all by yourself?" Kelly asked. She looked a little more rested, at least.

"No, I had these guys with me," I answered, a bit irritated. "And we have ten days. I can change my mind."

"But if you refuse the offer, they're likely to return with a large army to flush us out," Mazarine observed. "I think it's the right decision."

Bice shook his head. "You just got back, Beryl. Are you that eager to place yourself in danger again?"

"No, I'm not. But it's an opportunity, maybe. Unless you can find us something in those books to act on, this is the next step we can find."

"So you want us to create a fake headquarters?" Don asked.

"Yeah, but finishing the camouflage on this one takes precedence. Let's get that done first."

Fatigue pulled at me. I wanted to take action myself, but apparently my body still needed more rest. I needed to talk with a couple of people before that, though.

Don took over, explaining his plans for hiding the Asylum better. He was clearly out of his element speaking in front of a group, but he did well enough. By the time he was done, he'd given a job to almost everyone. I applauded, then snagged the first person I needed.

"Dusk, can I have a word?"

She eyed me through her glasses. The thick lenses made her chromark appear distorted. "Certainly, Mister… what should I call you?"

"Beryl is fine. Tell me. How much progress have you made with Loden's notes?"

"Quite frankly, they're a mess," she answered. She pushed her glasses up her nose. "The man was an incredible genius, but not the least bit organized."

I nodded. "That's about what we determined too." I glanced around. "Here's the thing. We want to find tech that's useful against the dragons, but… somewhere in there, I hope to find something about me."

"About your cybernetic parts?"

"Yes." I hesitated, but if she was going to be around, I would have to trust her. "I don't actually know how much I'm capable of. If we can find Loden's notes, if they exist, it would be a huge help."

"I'll look, but it seems unlikely. I've gone through the workshop and pulled all of his writings together in one place. I've sorted through most of them. While I haven't read very much in detail, I can usually tell what a particular notebook or stack of papers is about. I haven't seen anything on human enhancement yet."

"But some of the stuff in there is human enhancement," I protested. "The eyes. Some hands. Maybe more." We walked into the cave entrance.

"Yes, I've seen the hands. But as yet, I've found no notes on them. Very frustrating. At the same time, there are boxes of things that have no notes." She made a helpless gesture. "I found a whole box full of batons that seemed to channel some kind of electrical charge like the shockspears used by your Viridian Guard. But the charge isn't enough to harm anyone. It seems completely pointless. Much of the lab seems that way."

"All right. Well… let me know if you find anything."

"Of course, Mister… Beryl. May I ask for something?"

"Sure."

"Mister Onyx is very insistent that I examine your new friend's projectile weapon. Can you send her to the workshop?"

Lainey was outside somewhere, probably playing with her cub. "I'll ask her, but she may not be ready for that."

"You can't order her to do it?"

I frowned. "Maybe I need to explain something to you." I gestured at the others setting off to start on the work. "Everyone here is here by their own choice. I'm in charge, but I'm not like the dragons. I don't get to force everyone to do what I want them to do."

"A central authority guarantees efficiency."

"That may be so, but I'd rather be inefficient and free, than efficient and become like the dragons." I repeated that to myself in my head. Did it make sense? I thought so. We entered the workshop

She shrugged. "Very well. Ask her, then. I'll be in here."

"Have you found anything at all interesting, something that could help us with our mission?"

"Not specifically. I did figure this one out." She picked up an odd-looking metal device from the table. "I've already shown it to Mister Onyx."

"What is it?"

She put her hand inside an opening and held it up. It looked like… a drill? She activated it and watched it turn. "It's a drill."

Dusk nodded and turned it off. "I have no idea what purpose it would serve, except to dig a straight hole for planting a fencepost or something."

"How strong is it? Could it be used in mining, maybe?" I tried to think of a reason Loden would build such a thing.

She shrugged again. "I haven't tested it that much yet. Maybe. Many of the devices in there are like this: they have a purpose, but they don't seem overly practical."

"All right. Well, let me know if you find anything else interesting."

"Yes, sir."

I watched her leave, and shook my head. Strange woman. I needed to find time to talk with Rick about her some more. Her arrival still seemed odd.

As I stepped outside, Lainey approached, holding the cub. "You have a very eclectic group here. So many personalities and motivations."

"Motivations?" I scratched an itch on the back of my head.

She nodded. "They're not all here for the same reason."

I jerked my head up. "They're not? You think someone is working against us?"

"No, I just meant…" She frowned. "You have a singular focus. Kill the dragons. The girl in the cave is only interested in technology. Your friend Rick… I'm not sure what he wants."

"He wants the dragons dead. We started all this together."

"Maybe he does. But he wants something else too. I'm not sure what it is."

Rick's actions while I was gone gave me pause to consider her words. But I knew Rick. I didn't know Lainey that well yet. Could she really be so insightful as to figure something out about him that I hadn't picked up on yet? After one day?

"And then there's that blue thing."

"The draconic? Did you talk with it?"

She nodded. "A little. Like everyone else, he tried asking me about the world outside your valley."

"And?"

"I told him as much as I've told anyone else."

"Which is hardly anything," I pointed out.

She shrugged. "I'm here to learn, not to educate."

"You can't blame us for wanting to know more. I mean, our purpose is to set humans free, and you come from a place where they already are. I'd like to know how that works out."

She gave me an odd look, one I'd seen her do before, but I still couldn't translate it. Not quite raising the eyebrows, but maybe lifting them ever so slightly, while also cocking the head. "I never said we were free."

"You're not?"

"I'm not saying we're not. I just never said we were."

Glacier yowled. Lainey scratched the cub's head.

"I guess I assumed it," I said. "You're here, just the two of you, investigating. The dragons would never let two humans cross the mountains to spy things out."

Lainey bent over and nuzzled Glacier. When she looked up, she had a smile on her face again. "Once I learn everything I can about this place, I'll tell you what you want to know. Or as much as I can, anyway."

"All right. Looking forward to it."

"Which is why you need to take me along to the gold city."

"Ha! I'll think about it. We've got ten days."

She nodded. I saw Bice approaching and waved him over. "It's time," I told him.

"Time for what?"

"Tell me our big mission wasn't for nothing. Tell me everything you've learned from the Cerulean Books of Lore."

Bice led me to one of the halfway-enclosed "rooms" of the Asylum. Mazarine sat there, paging through one of the enormous Cerulean Books of Lore. He looked up when we appeared.

"Ah. I wondered how long it would take before this conversation."

I took a seat on one of Don's crude benches. "Tell me everything."

"That could take a while," Bice warned, sitting down beside me.

"I've got ten days." I yawned. "Well, minus sleeping."

"As I'm sure Bice informed you, we're missing the most crucial of the books, the first one," Mazarine started. Even though he was ostensibly on our side now, I wanted to slap him almost every time he talked at length. He spoke as if everyone else in earshot was far beneath him, either in intelligence or social standing, I suppose. "However, we do gain hints of the early days from the second book." He pulled it over to him and opened it.

"When does that book start?" I asked.

"They aren't necessarily straight-up histories," Bice explained. "Each book contains some history, and it's somewhat sequential, but there's a lot of other stuff too. Discussions of technological advancements, theorizing about draconic reproduction, and so many, many other interesting topics."

"The history parts of this one involve the building of the cities," Mazarine took over. "There are references to sources of power. I believe you already know a little bit about that particular topic."

I knew what Bice had told me: that the seven cities of The Circle had been built atop some kind of sources of power, the "magic" wielded by some of the priests and draconics. Bice himself could do some pretty impressive stuff with it.

"It's curious, isn't it?" Bice asked. "It's written here in these books, but Caesious never shared that information with his priests or draconics, like Viridia did."

"The red draconics use it," I said. "I ran into it with at least two of them."

"And so do the gold, a point to keep in mind with this 'hostage' you plan for us to watch."

I nodded. I would need to remind Rick about that aspect as he prepared Taizong Gold's prison. Would it be a prison, exactly? I didn't know what else to call it.

"But the dragons themselves don't use this power, right?" I seem to remember Bice mentioning that.

"Not as far as we can tell," Mazarine answered. "There's no reference to them using it. But…" He hesitated. "I believe the power sustains the dragons."

"What do you mean?"

"It's like food to them. It keeps them alive."

I wrinkled my brow. "But I thought that's why we have such large herds of cattle and sheep out here. Don't they eat those?"

"You've seen the size of the dragons. How many animals would they have to eat to maintain that?" Mazarine shook his head. "No, the herds are for us. The dragons live on the power."

"So if we could separate them from it, would they die?"

"I think it would have to be a very long separation," Bice said. "They leave the cities often enough without difficulty."

"But maybe we could destroy one of these sources of power," I mused. "I wonder if that would have any other effects."

"To continue…" Mazarine cleared his throat. "As you know, each of the dragons is different from the others in power."

"In what they breathe out, right?"

"That's primarily how it manifests itself, yes. Viridia uses poison. The red dragons fire. My former lord Caesious had a form of lightning."

"Black is acid," I concluded. "But what about gold? I don't think I've ever heard that."

"That's because Auric is the most mysterious of all the dragons," Bice said. "We know less about him and his city than anything else in The Circle. And he managed to keep that mystery in these books."

"Who wrote the books, anyway?"

"My predecessors," Mazarine said, his face beaming. "The first high priests of Caesious."

"But you weren't even allowed to read them," I pointed out.

His face fell. "No. Somewhere along the way, Caesious decided it was too much knowledge for humans to possess."

"Getting back to the cities," Bice said, "there are a lot of references to something called 'opposition.'"

"Someone opposing the dragons?"

"No, no. Not a person or group. The references are very vague, implying that it was more thoroughly discussed in the first book. The nearest I can theorize is that it has something to do with the dragons' powers and the sources under each city."

Something tickled at the back of my mind about that. But before I could consider it further, Mazarine's next words blasted all other thoughts away.

"There's a big discussion early here," he said, flipping a few pages forward, "about a proposed expedition outside The Circle."

"An expedition?" I leaned forward. "For the dragons themselves, or sending their servants?"

"That was part of the discussion. Auric argued strongly against the idea, though Amaranth seemed just as passionate about doing it. She wanted to send a draconic from each city, and—"

"Wait, wait, wait, wait." I slapped my hand down on the book. "You said 'she.' Amaranth is a female dragon?"

Mazarine and Bice looked at each other. The bald high priest shrugged. "So it appears. I'd never heard such a thing myself, but she is constantly referred to as female in these books."

"But, but…" All of my understanding of the dragons and draconics fell apart. "What does that mean? Can she have baby dragons with the others? Are she and Incarnadine a couple? If the draconics are children of the dragons already, how does that work with her? Does she even have her own draconics, or are they all Incarnadine's?"

Mazarine spread his hands helplessly. "We don't know any of that."

"You know as well as I do that the draconics are a mystery," Bice said. "They believe themselves to be children of the dragons. The stories claim that the dragons transform themselves into human guise and mate with women, who then give birth to the draconics. Things don't turn out so well for the women."

"And they're limited in number, and are re-born if they die," I added, "or so Protogonus Blue says. I never bought into that 'children of the dragons' stuff before now. I just thought they were their own race."

"If so, shouldn't they grow in number?" Bice asked.

I didn't have an answer to that. "So does Amaranth turn into a woman? Because that would be…" I stopped. I didn't even want to think about that.

"If I may continue," Mazarine said, "the dragons as a group ultimately decided against this expedition. It was deemed too dangerous."

"Too dangerous? What is out there?" I turned and looked outside the enclosure. Lainey sat on the ground, playing with Lovat and the cub.

"That is the only reference we have found," Bice said. "You'll have to get your new friend to answer the rest of it."

"Amaranth and Onyx were the only dragons to support it. The others all disagreed," Mazarine went on.

"How much do the books talk about Onyx, anyway?" I asked. "Was he just like the others?"

"I'm trying to do this in order," Mazarine complained.

"It's all right," Bice said. "Of course Beryl has questions. We all do." He faced me again. "Onyx is a bit of a mystery from what we've read so far. He comes across just as evil and tyrannical as the other dragons, but… he seems to have had trouble getting along with them. I think they might have actually been relieved when he died."

"The destruction of the seventh city may not have been solely a punishment," Mazarine added.

"What do you mean?" I wrinkled my brow. What else could it be?

"The other dragons may have been making sure that none of Onyx's followers survived to spread his particular… heresies."

"Heresies?"

"The black dragon's priests taught that rather than all being equal, there was a hierarchy among the dragons," Bice explained.

"Let me guess: he was at the top?"

"Of course."

"Don't all the dragons teach that, sort of? I mean, the Viridian priests proclaim him to be our god, right? And I assume each city does the same."

"Yes, to a certain degree." Bice glanced at Mazarine. "Priests proclaim the godhood of their own dragon, and to a lesser extent, the other dragons. But they only encourage worship of that city's god. The problem with Onyx is his priests openly proclaimed him to be greater than the others, and started trying to spread that to the other cities."

"In effect, they would travel to each city, and proclaim 'yes, your dragon is a god, but ours is a greater god,'" Mazarine explained, sniffing.

"Wouldn't his death sort of end all that?"

"Yes and no," Bice answered. "The other dragons feared his followers might promise a resurrection or something, and continue to undermine the other dragons. Besides, none of them wanted to rule over another city full of humans."

I looked to Mazarine. "That doesn't sound good for Caesious."

He shook his head. "I can only hope they learned something from the earlier disaster."

I wouldn't count on that. And yet the people of Caesious hadn't done anything against their dragon; we had. And they weren't spreading "heresies," so maybe they would be all right... for now.

"How did they kill him?" I asked. "The black dragon, I mean."

Mazarine gave an exaggerated sigh before pushing his current book away and pulling another one to him. "This is the one with missing pages," he grumbled.

"Missing pages?"

"There are pages torn out of the middle," Bice said. "Recently torn out, in fact."

"And they're about the fall of Onyx?" How frustrating can you get? It must have been Incarnadine's people. Maybe I should go back to the Flame and find the missing book and pages.

Mazarine pointed at the spot where I could see the remains of torn pages. "At least a dozen pages missing here, right in the middle of the story of the fallen dragon."

"Do the rest of the pages tell how they killed him?"

"There is some... debate about that topic," he admitted, turning a page.

"The information comes from Viridia," Bice told me. "His agents captured some of the leaders of the uprising."

"Here it is," Mazarine announced. "Under severe torture, the ringleaders finally described their plan. They waited until a day that the dragon was gone, then rose up against his draconics and soldiers. With the numbers on their side, they obtained a swift, but costly victory. And then they laid a trap for Onyx within his own lair."

"What kind of trap?"

Mazarine shrugged. "It doesn't say."

I stared. "The most… spectacular event in the history of The Circle, and they don't even know how it happened?"

"To be fair, they don't know how the blue dragon died either." Bice laughed at that. "The dragons are not all-knowing."

I slapped the table. "I wanted to learn from them, how they killed one, so maybe we could do the same."

"Maybe that's why they didn't include the details," Mazarine suggested. "These books are written with a certain… arrogance."

I'm sure he knew nothing about that. "Let me see that passage," I said. I pulled the book across the table and looked where he pointed. Two words popped out at me immediately: the name of the draconic who interrogated the rebels.

Troilus Green.

"You have got to be kidding me!"

"What is it?" Bice asked.

I pointed it out. "Troilus Green! It was around back then!" Even as I said it, I felt stupid. Of course the draconic had been around, assuming Protogonus Blue told the truth about their lifespans and reincarnation. Why wouldn't it? Still, the fact that my first nemesis had been involved in the information leading to the Blasted Lands gave me mixed feelings.

I shoved the book away. "None of this is doing us any good!"

"We're learning all kinds of things we didn't know before," Bice pointed out.

"But none of them are things we can use! Nothing that will help us defeat the dragons."

"Maybe. Maybe not. The books are thick and hard to read. We still have a lot to get through."

I gave him a skeptical look. "You're telling me that in two weeks' time, you two haven't read all of them yet?"

"I have," Mazarine offered.

"He's read them, yes," Bice said, "but only once, straight through. Now he's going through them slowly, taking notes. I'm doing the same, but I'm two books ahead of him. We're getting there. Give us more time."

"All right." I sighed. "I want you to pause that plan, and go through looking for everything you can find on Auric."

"There's not a lot," Mazarine said.

"Then it shouldn't take long. But I want every detail, no matter how small. If I'm going to be talking to this thing in ten days, I want to know all I can beforehand."

I got to my feet. "Anything else?"

"You should talk to the new guy," Bice suggested.

I struggled to remember who he meant. "Oh. The Guard. Jaden."

"Yes. I've had a couple of talks with him, but haven't given much away yet. I figured that was your department."

"Right." I should have asked Dusk if she'd seen any tech related to legs. So many things happening all at once. Kelly's situation, above all others, kept shoving itself back to the forefront of my thoughts. And yet it was the one thing that I couldn't do anything about. "Where is he?"

Bice led me to another "room." Don (and whoever helped him) came up with some ingenious ways of segregating the space out here. Walls were built out of whatever they could scavenge: fallen trees, dirt, discarded railroad ties. And I think maybe he dismantled part of an old loading bay next to the main railroad line. In some places, the haphazard barriers almost made me feel claustrophobic.

Jaden sat on a bed that looked made out of wooden loading pallets. His injured leg sported fresh bandages. He'd stripped off the Viridian Guard uniform and wore only shorts and a tank top. He looked up as I entered.

"Finally! You didn't tell me how boring this would be. Maybe I should have gone back to Viridia!" His tone didn't sound like he meant any of it, like he was trying to force humor, but it didn't work. Nervous, perhaps?

"I'm sorry, man. We don't have much in the way of entertainment out here." Rather than intimidate him further, I sat down on the ground and crossed my legs. "How's the leg?"

"It hurts. A lot. Can't you do anything else about that?"

"I'll be completely honest with you. I don't know. Bice over there knows a lot about medicine. He's kept me alive several times. But like I told you before: we don't have a surgeon. We do have a stash of fortek. I'll have our expert look through and see if anything can help you."

Jaden stared at me with blue eyes surrounded by skin a couple shades lighter than Bice, but far darker than mine. His black hair was cut in a short, precision style, probably a requirement with the Guard. "What is all this?" he asked. "You have forbidden technology and weapons. Renegade priests. Chromatic hells, you killed a draconic!"

"Yeah, pretty crazy, huh?"

He pointed in a vague direction. "And that one girl. She didn't even have a chromark! That's not possible for someone that old! I used to work in that department. No one can live like that!"

"You gave out chromarks?"

"Before the Guard, yeah." He shrugged. "I got bored with it, and enlisted. But you're avoiding my questions and asking about me. Don't think I don't notice."

"You're smart." I shifted my legs. This wasn't the most comfortable position. "Smart enough to know you had to come with us, or risk the dragon's wrath. Now you're probably wondering if you can gather enough info on us and escape with it, so he'll welcome you back."

"Of course I've thought about it," he said. "Along with around a dozen other ideas. But I need to know more to make a solid decision."

"I want you to stay. And join us."

"You've got to tell me who you are first."

"Right. How do I explain this? We're a group of people from a bunch of places, all teamed up together for one purpose: to end the reign of the dragons." I watched his face for reactions. "Preferably by killing them."

He snorted. "The gods don't die."

"Tell that to Caesious," I said, keeping my eyes on his.

"That was… you aren't…" He frowned. "You can't be serious."

"I'm completely serious." I held out my hand, palm up. "You've seen what we can do. You know I have cybernetic enhancements. You know we have forbidden weapons. Our goal is for all humans to be free."

He studied my face, then shook his head. "You almost convinced me. But this is ridiculous. You got lucky with the draconic, but you're nothing more than a little band of rebels taking advantage of the war's chaos. The girl has makeup on, right? Covering the chromark?"

I kept watching him. "Bice," I called. "I think it's time he met Blue."

"I'll fetch him," Bice answered.

"Blue? What's that supposed to mean?" Jaden asked.

"Give it a few minutes. It's not as young as it used to be."

I smelled it before the arrival. I doubted I would ever get used to that. A moment later, Protogonus Blue stepped into sight. "Greetings, Beryl

Godslayer. You wished to see me?"

Jaden scrambled back on his bed, looking around for any kind of weapon. "Holy Viridia preserve me!"

"Well, that's not gonna happen." I laughed. "Jaden, meet Protogonus Blue, child of the late Caesious, and a part of our rebellion. Ask it if the dragons are gods."

"They are not," the draconic said calmly.

Jaden composed himself and stared at Protogonus Blue for a few moments. "It's a trick," he said at last. "A costume or something."

"You mean you can't smell it?" I asked.

The draconic gave me an odd look. Had I insulted it? Oh well. It stepped up beside Jaden's bed and leaned forward. "Feel here my scales and claws, servant of Viridia. Or is that not strong enough proof for you?" It took one of the claws on its right hand and pressed against its left forearm until it punctured the thick skin. Very dark red liquid oozed out. "Behold the blood of a draconic. Is this a trick?"

Jaden did not know how to react. He stared at the draconic, then back at me. Finally, he closed his mouth and swallowed. "I… perhaps I spoke in haste."

"Perhaps," I repeated. "Ready to listen now?"

He nodded.

"It is well to listen to those who have information challenging your beliefs," the draconic said. "Thus we learn, and thus we grow. I myself had to confront such information a few months ago, at the death of he whom I considered both father and god." Protogonus Blue gestured at me. "This man was responsible for that death. Consider. If humans can kill dragons, then are dragons truly gods?"

Jaden didn't answer. I didn't blame him. How do you answer when someone is tearing apart your fundamental beliefs?

"Talk with each other," I told them. "Figure out the truth." I looked at Jaden. "And when you're ready, there's a place for you here."

"I'm not… I don't think I could fight against my own people."

"I get it. I'd rather not fight against any other humans. But there are some who will never see the light. If I have to fight them, I will. But our main target is the dragons themselves." I thought for a moment. "But even then, you don't necessarily have to fight to be a part of this. We have several here who aren't involved in the fighting. Whatever it may be, we have a place for you."

"Even with a bad leg?" He pointed at it.

"Since that's my fault, I can hardly blame you, can I?"

I left the two of them together. Once I was out of their sight, I bent over and took several deep breaths. Despite my cockiness there, I had been super nervous. At least it seemed to be working out. One by one, our group grew. Only about a million more to convince.

The ten days passed faster than I expected. Don put everyone to work, starting with the further camouflage of the Achromatic Asylum. We blocked off most of the path with mounds of dirt and plant life. We left three exits toward both the north and south. We then camouflaged each of those exits with a flap that folded down when needed, blending in with the surrounding landscape.

We went on scouting expeditions each day to keep track of enemy patrol movements from Viridia and Atramentous. After they discovered the body of Calchas Green, the patrols became larger and better equipped. I suppose we should have felt flattered they were taking us seriously now. Rick suggested engaging them from time to time and leading them away. It was a good plan. After a couple of brief skirmishes, we always retreated in the direction of the Hub, and the patrols began shifting in that direction. They never came close enough to appreciate our new camouflage, such as it was.

Lainey pointed out that the new landscape still didn't quite match everything around it. Don countered that he couldn't make grass and trees grow on command. So Lainey took it on herself to transplant a number of trees and bushes into positions that would further add to the disguise. Some of them were quite heavy, so of course, I had to do the carrying.

After a few days, Lainey herself fit right in with the rest of the team, for the most part. People—including me—still caught themselves staring at her unmarked face, and she remained tight-lipped on details of life outside The Circle, no matter how much others pestered her. On a couple of occasions, I know Rick stepped over the line in demanding answers. Still, I saw her talking and laughing with the others quite often. Caedan in particular seemed quite taken with her… or at least her rifle. Lovat, on the other hand, enjoyed the company of Glacier. The white cub grew with each passing day. Lainey went hunting to obtain fresh meat for her on a regular basis.

The only person she didn't seem to get along with was the other new girl, Dusk. On the rare occasions that Dusk left the workshop, she didn't associate with anyone much, except Rick. I checked on her progress from time to time, but she hadn't found anything about my implant… yet. I just knew it had to be in Loden's notes somewhere.

I anxiously watched Kelly every day. She still hadn't told Rick about the pregnancy, but she seemed to recover her health well enough to participate in the work around the Asylum. Aside from occasional fatigue, she seemed fine. It didn't stop me from worrying, though. She would have to tell him soon. And what would we do when her time drew near? Bice had some medical knowledge, but delivering a baby? I couldn't ask him about it, of course, but I did try casually inquiring about the extent of his medical knowledge. The conversation didn't go as far as I'd hoped.

Jaden recovered enough to limp around. Bice wasn't sure about the significance of the injury to his tendon. It might heal enough to let him walk normally, or it might not. Jaden kept quite and observed everything, lending a hand when it was possible. I did have an idea of something I wanted him to do, but no time to set it up.

My relationship with Rick returned to our close friendship… but I could feel an undercurrent of tension. We'd always had somewhat different ideas about the future. Rick had trouble trusting new people, and seemed to resent my bringing in Jaden, and even Lainey. Yet he brought in his own friend, Dusk. I couldn't figure him out sometimes. But while we worked together on common goals, we got along and enjoyed each other's company.

Once the camouflage was completed to Don's satisfaction, we moved on to our new "fake headquarters." We had a lot of discussion about how extensive to build it. We wanted it to be convincing enough that Taizong

Gold wouldn't doubt it to be our primary base, but building an entire headquarters for no other reason than misdirection seemed excessive… not to mention a lot of work.

Rick and Caedan chose a spot northeast of the Asylum, and very close to the Blasted Lands. They found a large gorge with steep walls stretching at least a dozen feet tall. The space between the walls, while nowhere near the size of the Asylum, looked sufficient enough for half a dozen people to live. Don set about building a roof and an entrance, the two most critical parts of the design. Caedan suggested we make it look like we had a cave exit in the back, even though we didn't. Together, we dug out the beginnings of a cave, but only a few feet inward. Then we used a pallet of tree branches to "conceal" it. Anyone could tell what was being hid. As long as no one opened it up and stepped inside, it would look like some kind of tunnel.

The third most important thing to construct was a place for keeping the draconic. No one thought we could seriously keep it contained if Tai-zong Gold decided to break the agreement. But we could definitely make things difficult for it to get out. We discussed various traps and such, until Lainey pointed out that the most effective deterrent was her rifle. "And since I'm going with Beryl, I'll teach Caedan how to use it," she announced.

"I haven't said you were coming," I said.

"Yet. You haven't said it yet. But I'm coming."

In the end, I did cave on Lainey's request. I'm not sure how much of the decision came from her insistence, and how much came from worrying about going on my own. I had a long conversation with Bice about it, and he agreed, though he warned about the danger to Lainey (and myself).

"We can give her a fake chromark, but if anyone discovers she's un-marked, I don't think any agreements will hold," he said. "That's too much of a… shock, I suppose."

"And that's why I don't want to take her."

"But at the same time, it's not good for you to be alone, Beryl. I would have suggested taking someone else along, in any event, and since she's offering, I think you should take her." He laughed a bit. "I would almost volunteer to go myself."

"Do you want to? I'd be glad to take you instead!"

"No, no. Someone needs to be here to keep an eye on things with Rick back in charge."

I nodded. I needed to be sure to leave some strict instructions for Rick. And what if I didn't return? What then? I didn't want to think about that. I couldn't think of everything, could I?

Lainey wanted to go, so Lainey got to go. I considered having Jaden make her fake chromark, with his experience, but I had Kelly do it instead. I figured Lainey would be more comfortable with her, and besides, I wanted them to be friends. When Kelly suggested it might be a struggle to create without painting over an existing mark, I did have her bring Jaden in for advice. In the end, Lainey's new chromark looked absolutely real to my eyes. The only trouble might be in maintaining it. We had no idea how long the trip to Auric would take. I made sure to pack the special makeup, and practiced using it, with both Jaden and Kelly supervising.

As promised, Lainey taught Caedan how to use the rifle, but warned him about the limited ammunition. He was absolutely thrilled. She left Glacier in the care of Lovat and Bice. I think the cub would have come with us, if she'd let her. It followed her around with unusual devotion for a cat.

It took a lot of careful thought to decide how best to position everyone for the exchange. We decided Rick and Peri would be the ones to escort Taizong Gold to the fake headquarters, while Caedan followed them nearby with the rifle at ready. Once there, they would be welcomed by Bice and Protogonus Blue. I hoped that combination would be enough to shake the gold draconic's own beliefs.

Kelly would be in charge back at the Achromatic Asylum, keeping an eye on things with Don, Lovat, Mazarine, and Jaden. Dusk, of course, would keep at her job in the workshop.

On the morning of the trade-off, we dressed and prepared. I wanted to bring a sword along, but gave it up. It wouldn't look right, carrying a weapon to an invitation to talk. And despite what silly stories Loden had once told me, no one ever killed a dragon with a sword. It would be like trying to kill a grown man with a toothpick.

I met Lainey, once again wearing the clothes she'd arrived in: tan shirt and shorts. Her green chromark looked completely wrong on her, and yet made her appear more… normal. I rebelled against the feeling. Shouldn't her mark-less face be our natural state, the most normal of all? Yet we'd been raised to see our marks of slavery as normal and right. Ugh.

"Are you ready for this?"

She nodded. "Looking forward to it."

"You know there's a strong chance we never come back, right?" I'd told her many times, but had to do it once more.

"Yep."

I swear. Nothing fazed her.

Once at the meeting spot, Caedan hid with the rifle while the rest of us walked out to the open area where we'd met Taizong Gold ten days earlier. We didn't have long to wait. About ten minutes later, the draconic approached with one human.

"You sure this is the right play?" Rick whispered. "We could take it out now. Add to our draconic kill count."

"And bring down the dragon's wrath on us. No, I need to find out what he wants," I answered. "Something strange is happening here."

"That's for sure," Peri muttered.

I stepped out and called to the approaching draconic. "That's far enough! Let's talk terms."

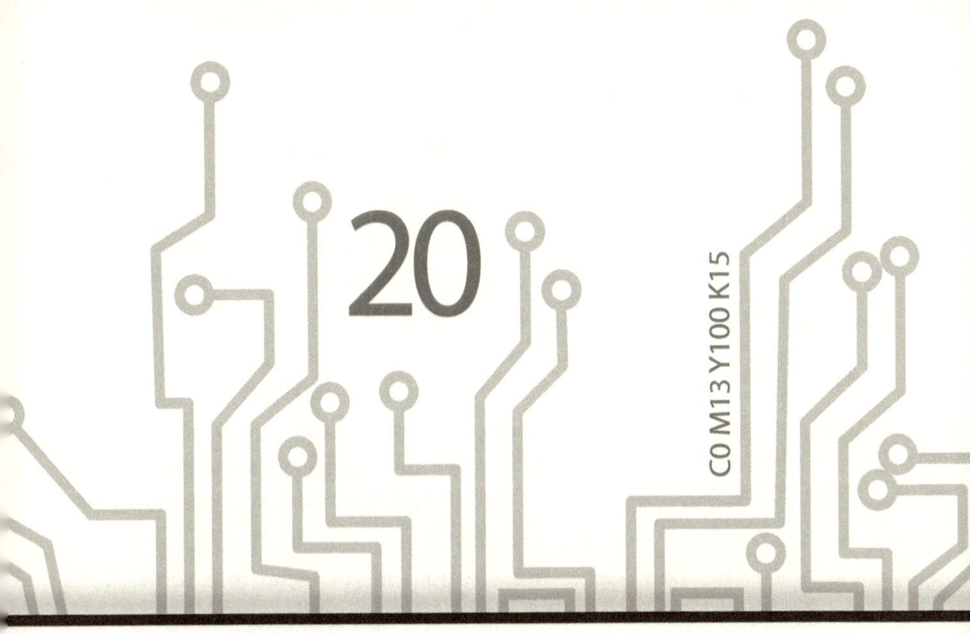

20

Taizong Gold stopped and held out a palm. "Haven't we already made our agreement?"

"I know how agreements with you work," I answered. "I want to nail down specifics."

"Very well. Proceed."

I pointed at Lainey. "I'm bringing a friend with me. For the duration of our trip to Auric, the visit there, and our return trip, do you guarantee that no harm will come to us?"

It cocked its head. "The agreement was for you, not you and your woman."

"She's a friend," I repeated, "and I'm not coming alone. Take it or leave it."

"As you wish. On behalf of the almighty Auric, I pledge safety for the two of you."

"For the entire trip and visit and trip back?"

"Yes. You have my word."

"In return, you've offered to be a hostage with my people," I went on. "Do I have your guarantee that you will not harm any of them for the duration of your time with us?"

"Unless harm is attempted against me, I will harm no one."

I looked at the other three. "Am I missing anything? Any way this could be twisted against us?"

"I don't see anything," Peri said. The others agreed.

I turned back to Taizong Gold. "Very well. We have an agreement. These two will escort you to where we're staying."

The draconic nodded, then gestured to the man beside him. "And allow me to present Captain Tawn of the Aurelian Sentinels. He will be your escort and protector throughout the journey."

Captain Tawn snapped his heels together and gave a short bow. "It is my honor to serve almighty Auric in this fashion," he declared.

The captain wore a stripped-down version of the golden armor I'd seen on the other soldiers. He wore no helmet, revealing a stern and weathered face which reminded me of Don in some ways. For the first time, I noticed a distinction in the golden chromarks: a very thin black edge outlined them against the skin. Otherwise, the gold might blend into some skin tones, I suppose. Tawn's skin had an almost yellowish hue to it, now that I considered it. His short hair was jet black with no facial growth.

Lainey and I stepped forward and began walking. Captain Tawn fell into step beside us. I looked back to watch Taizong Gold walking away with Rick and Peri. They looked comically small next to the monstrous draconic. I immediately doubted the whole arrangement. Even with using a fake headquarters, even with Caedan watching with the rifle, I couldn't help fearing we were inviting our own destruction into the camp. Without my advantages, could the others really take on a draconic if it became necessary?

It was too late now. We couldn't make such an agreement and then back out at the last second because of cold feet. I took a breath and faced front.

"How will we be traveling to Auric?" I asked.

"It is a short walk to a branch line of the railroad," Captain Tawn said. Was everything he said going to sound so crisp and focused? "We have a private car waiting there to take us to the city."

"Lead on, then."

As he said, we took a short walk before emerging from a fold in the earth and discovering the branch line. I had to admit to surprise. We'd traveled through this area multiple times and never seen this. We could learn from their camouflage tricks.

A train engine sat at the ready, a single passenger car hooked to it.

Captain Tawn escorted us to the car's entrance. We entered, finding ourselves alone, and took seats at a table next to a window. The captain went forward to notify the engineer.

"First time on a train?" I asked Lainey in a low voice.

"We have trains," she answered.

"But have you ridden one?"

"No," she admitted.

The captain returned and sat at a separate table across from us. Almost as soon as he took his seat, the train gave a jerk and started forward. In only a few minutes, we reached a high speed and turned onto the main line leading toward Auric. So far, I saw no differences between this train and the one I'd ridden between Viridia to Caesious. Of course, the last time I'd been on a train was Loden's special edition, our weapon against the blue dragon.

"So you've never been to this city, correct?" Lainey asked.

"No. Until we started all this, I'd never been outside Viridia." I glanced at the captain, then whispered, "Try not to ask questions like that out loud. It will make them suspicious of you."

She pulled her hair back and considered. "How was that suspicious?" she whispered.

I leaned in close. "Almost no one ever leaves their home city here. We're not allowed to. That's part of how the dragons control us."

"But what if you have relatives in another city?"

"That doesn't happen." I thought about it for a moment. "I don't even know how that could happen."

Lainey looked like she wanted to ask more, but instead, she leaned back and watched out the window. I looked out as well, seeing hills and trees rolling past us. After about an hour, we crossed a bridge over an enormous river, the largest amount of water I'd ever seen. Seeing the water moving so fast below us amazed me, but Lainey took it in without any change in her expression. It made me wonder what natural wonders she'd seen outside The Circle.

At some point in the past few days, Lainey mentioned living in a city, at least for part of her life. Another city. One of many, based on what she'd just said. And people could travel between them. She wouldn't say things were great outside, but the hints she dropped sure made it sound that way to me.

When the view turned monotonous again, I settled back to think. In many ways, I envied the rest of the team. I really wanted to see and hear the conversation when Protogonus Blue met Taizong Gold. I couldn't guess how the gold draconic would react. Could we win another one over? It seemed unlikely, but I never would have imagined we'd have even one on our side.

Of course, it could all backfire. This might all be an elaborate trap. Had we prepared enough for that eventuality? The more I thought about it, the more I worried. The draconic kept his bargain with me back at the Hub, but… it was a draconic. How could I possibly trust it?

Lainey's hand touched mine, startling me out of my worry. "Hey," she said. "Are you okay?"

"Yeah. Sorry. I'm just thinking about the others."

"They'll be all right." She couldn't know that, of course, but her reassurance helped somehow. I smiled and looked back out the window.

"We approach the city," Captain Tawn said a few minutes later. It was the first time we'd heard his voice since boarding the train.

"Will the best view be on the right or left?" Lainey asked. The captain pointed to the right, where we already sat.

I leaned close to the window to catch my first view of Auric, my fourth city to visit in the past few months. If this kept up, I might get to see all of them. I suppose it only made sense. I wanted to free all of the humans, not just those in Viridia.

"There it is," Lainey said.

I saw several tall buildings come into view. Then the train swerved a bit to the left and the full city lay out before us. I expected to see buildings of gold and yellow everywhere. But to my surprise, gold wasn't even the predominant color. I saw a good deal of it, but also red, white, brown, black… The sheer number of colors in use was stunning. The architecture appeared different from the other cities as well. I saw a lot of pointed roofs with rounded corners leading to unusual tips. Many buildings sported wraparound roofed decks, or balconies at higher levels.

"It's beautiful," Lainey observed.

"Yeah," I agreed. "Until you get down to the street level and see the ugliness of our daily lives."

"You will find no ugliness here," Captain Tawn declared.

"I would expect a servant of the dragons to make that claim," I said.

"But I've never been one of the elite. I know the truth of how common people live."

"You know how it is in Viridia," he argued. "This is Auric. Our people live their lives to the fullest."

"Sure they do."

"While you are here, you are welcome to tour any parts of the city you wish, speak to anyone you wish. You will find no complaints."

"Of course I won't." I knew arguing him was pointless, but I couldn't help it. "Because you or someone like you will be standing over my shoulder. No one would dare complain in front of you."

"Auric is different."

"It's ruled by a dragon, isn't it? They're all the same. They're evil incarnate."

"But what if one of them isn't?" Lainey whispered.

The train passed into an enclosure, slowing to a crawl. A few moments later, it came to a complete stop.

"We've arrived," Captain Tawn said. "If you'll follow me…?"

He led the way back out of the passenger car. We exited into a train station. I'd seen the train stations of Viridia and Caesious, of course, and this one didn't appear much different. I did see occasional architectural distinctions, such as more window panes, larger hallways, etc., but a train station is a train station.

I kept an eye out for the strange devices I'd seen the golden soldiers erecting on the tracks back at the Hub. But I didn't even see any soldiers other than our escort. Captain Tawn spoke with an official-looking woman in a gray uniform. When they finished, she hurried away down a hallway while the captain returned to us.

"Are we going straight to the dragon, or…" It struck me that I hadn't seen any type of massive construct in the city that would mark the dragon's dwelling. Maybe I just hadn't been looking in the right direction.

"The almighty Auric will see you this evening," the captain explained. "In the meantime, we have arranged lodgings for you, a place where you can relax after your travels."

"Cool. Sounds good," Lainey said. "Let's go."

I couldn't help feeling wary about anywhere we might be taken. Taizong

Gold's first words to me back at the Hub weeks ago still came to mind. Auric's servants had standing orders to bring any cybernetic technology back for examination. This entire journey might be nothing more than an attempt to follow those orders.

Captain Tawn led us down a brightly-lit hallway sloping down for a while. When it leveled out, he introduced us to a tech I'd never seen before: a moving sidewalk. Judging from Lainey's expression of delight, she'd never seen one either. Following our guide, we stepped onto what looked like an endless series of slats rolling out of the ground. Once on the slats, we were carried along at a reasonable pace. We could probably walk faster than this device, but I could see how it was helpful, especially in such a long passageway.

In fact, we traded one such moving sidewalk for another three times. I couldn't tell how far we might have come, but these passages must stretch for miles beneath the city itself. Fascinating.

We came to another stop, and Captain Tawn led us to a stairway. We ascended three flights and found ourselves within the first floor of a large building. This floor was mostly open with many seats and small tables scattered around. Large desks with workers manning them stood at either side of the building, near the entrances. An enormous double staircase led up to the next floor before splitting off into balconies encircling the whole place.

We climbed these stairs as well. I wondered at the use of the moving sidewalks, but not elevators. I think I preferred avoiding stairs than long walks. But just as I was thinking it, we approaching elevator doors at the top of the stairs. They couldn't put them on the first floor?

The captain took us in the elevator up to the sixth floor, where we emerged into a hallway lined with flat carpet and dim lighting. We passed multiple unmarked doors, until Captain Tawn opened one and gestured for us to enter. "These will be your rooms until Auric is ready for you," he explained. "If you require anything else, press this button beside the door and a servant will come to take your request." He gave us another short bow, and turned to leave.

"Wait!" Lainey exclaimed. "You said we were welcome to tour part of the city. How can we do that?"

Tawn paused. "I will have a guide sent to escort you." He gave yet another short bow and left, closing the door behind him.

Lainey and I looked around. We stood in a type of living room, I suppose, with a number of nice chairs, a couch, some end tables, and a kind of countertop with a small refrigerator attached. A sliding door to the right led into a sumptuous bedroom with an enormous bed.

But my attention was drawn to the outer wall of the room: a massive single window pane looking out over the city below. Lainey and I both walked up to it and stared down. From here, we could see many of the unusual roofs I'd noticed on the way in.

"It's even more beautiful from this view," Lainey said.

I didn't answer. I didn't want to compliment anything related to the dragons.

"Do you really think the people here hate their lives?" she asked.

"I don't know how many of them would admit it, but I know what life is like under the dragons' rule. We are nothing to them. We have no freedom, no true joy in our lives."

Lainey gestured at the people we could see walking along the street below. "These people don't look like slaves."

"Slavery comes in many forms," I argued. "Many slaves don't want to admit their own slavery."

"What?"

"Sorry. I'm not saying this right." I thought a moment. "You can be enslaved to something, trapped. But if it's all you've known your entire life, maybe you've just accepted it as the way things are. Maybe you don't think it through to the logical end."

"So explain the logic to me."

I pointed to the people again. "They live here. They work here. They raise their children here. But can they travel to other cities, like we talked about on the train? No. Can they choose to have as many kids as they want? Can they study the science and technology they want to study? Can they worship something other than the dragon?" I shook my head. "They're slaves, even if they don't admit it."

"And you want to set them free."

"Yes. It's as simple as that."

A soft knock at the door heralded the arrival of our guide: a young woman who looked remarkably similar to Captain Tawn in the face. She wore loose clothing of dark colors trimmed in gold. Her shirt hung low over her pants and had wide sleeves, a tall collar, and a row of gold buttons down the middle. She introduced herself as Kiro, and suggested we start as soon as possible, since our appointment with the dragon held an uncertain time.

Lainey and I followed her back to the elevator. As we descended, Kiro asked if we were interested in any specific part of the city.

"We don't know anything about your city," Lainey said. "I suppose any area is fine."

"I want to see the poorest sector," I said. "Show me the slums."

Lainey frowned at me, but Kiro merely nodded. "I am instructed to take you wherever you like," she answered. "We can start just outside, and make our way toward the lower regions."

Lower? Interesting terminology. I filed it away in my mind.

At the second floor, we descended the stairs and made our way to the front doors of this building. We stepped out into a fairly busy street. We watched people walking, biking, and riding in unusual two-wheeled vehicles pulled by runners. Most of them wore clothing similar to our guide's, though I noticed a few wearing long robes with very wide belts. Kiro suggested we follow the sidewalk to the left. With no other obvious options, I agreed.

Lainey stopped another young woman passing us. "Excuse me," she began, "we're visitors—"

"Ah, Viridia!" the woman exclaimed, pointing at Lainey's chromark. "Welcome! How can I help you?"

"How is your life in this city?" Lainey asked. "Do you enjoy it?"

The woman pulled her hair back. "Do I enjoy it? I have a good job, a good family. What more can I ask for?"

"Do you worship the dragon?" I asked, in spite of myself.

She blinked at me. "What an unusual question. Of course I worship the almighty Auric. He gives us life!"

"He doesn't give you life!" How could she think such a thing?

"Perhaps…" She paused. "Perhaps your dragon does not. But ours does." She hugged herself and looked up into the sky. "And it is glorious when he does."

As I suspected, this woman had been planted here to speak to us. Everyone around probably had. I had no doubts Kiro worked for the dragon or his soldiers. She might even be a soldier.

"Let's keep going," I said. "I want to see more."

We walked along the sidewalk. Kiro occasionally pointed out some of the buildings, talking about when they'd been built or their purpose. Every description ended with some variation of "for the glory of Auric." I didn't ask whether she meant the city or the dragon. I already knew.

I could think of only one way to get an honest opinion. When Kiro stopped to greet someone else, I whispered to Lainey, "I'll be back in a few minutes."

"What?"

I ran.

I raced down an alley, followed by a shout from Kiro. "Please wait, sir!" I ignored her and kept going. I turned right at the next street. This wasn't Viridia, so I needed to keep careful track of my movements, unless I wanted to get completely lost. Though the architecture was different, streets were still streets. At least I could count on that.

Another left, another right, and then straight for three blocks. Running the streets seemed no different than Viridia, at least. People got in my way. People got out of my way. People did their own things. Most just stared in confusion at the crazy man running down the street. No one else was running, after all.

As the buildings grew less impressive, I slowed to a walk. The foot traffic decreased as well. Soon, I began to recognize the stooped walk and downcast eyes I'd been looking for. These were people from whom I might hear the truth. Then I could tell Lainey…

But what good would that do? It would just be my word then. I reproached myself for not thinking this through. I should have brought her along, somehow.

At any rate, I shouldn't waste the opportunity. I stepped in front of an older man. Like most, he wore the loose-fitting shirt over pants made of a soft material, though I noticed patches in the elbows and one of the knees. "Excuse me."

He looked up and did something of a double-take on seeing me. "Oh, ah, hello."

"I know, I know. You don't see many visitors from other cities. Neither do I in my city, to be honest." I tried to smile reassuringly. "Can I ask you something?"

"What is it?" His eyes darted about, looking for anyone watching us.

"Do you have a good life here? Or are you a slave?"

"A slave? No, I—" He looked around more pointedly. "Is this a trick of some kind? Are the Aurelian Sentinels watching?"

"No trick. I ran away from them. Just tell me the truth."

His eyes widened. "You ran away from them?" He took a step back. "No, no. I can't help you. I love my life. Everything is wonderful." He turned and hurried away.

I didn't need any further confirmation. His actions said enough. Fear still ruled here, at least for the common people. But something made me hesitate. It seemed almost too easy. If the earlier people had been planted by the Sentinels or whatever, then surely they would have anticipated me running away. I'd implied as much, after all. Wouldn't they have planted people in the surrounding areas as well?

But if the old man was a plant, why had he confirmed my belief? Was it all part of some elaborate scheme by the dragon, to show me exactly what I expected to see? I shook my head. "Stop it," I told myself out loud. I was getting way too paranoid. These conversations probably meant exactly what I thought they meant. No need to see a conspiracy in it.

I retraced my steps and met Kiro and Lainey looking for me. "We should go back," I said.

"I agree," Kiro answered, frowning at me with her whole face. "We don't know when Auric will call for you." She turned to lead the way.

I gave Lainey a shake of my head in answer to her raised eyebrows. We could talk alone.

Kiro took us back to the large building, up the stairs and elevator, and back to our room. She bid us farewell and shut the door behind her.

"What happened?" Lainey almost exploded. "Did you find the poor people?"

"I did." I looked out the window at the street below. "They're no different from the people in Viridia, where I grew up. They live in fear of Auric and his Sentinels."

Lainey's shoulders slumped. "Are you sure?"

"Pretty sure." I moved away from the window and checked out the refrigerator. I found milk, various juice combinations, and water. I took a bottle of a juice I didn't recognize and tried it. Tangy, but smooth. Not bad. I looked back to see Lainey watching me.

"I'll give the gold dragon credit for a nice facade," I said at last, gesturing toward the window. "This city is definitely... nicer looking than Viridia. Much nicer. That place is ugly."

"Why do you suppose that is?"

I shrugged. "If I had to guess, I'm thinking it's just the different personalities of the dragons. Sure, they're evil tyrants, but they're not all exactly the same."

"So maybe this gold dragon actually cares about humans. Maybe only a few don't like him. Maybe the ones scared of him are scared because they're doing wrong."

"No. No way. The dragons are all evil. To them, humans are... nothing. They don't care about us any more than they care about those herds of cattle and sheep we saw out in the fields. We're nothing to them."

The vehemence in my voice must have gotten through to her. She took a step back and regarded me with an unusual sadness in her face. "I knew you wanted them dead, but it's more than that to you, isn't it?"

I sat down on one of the chairs and looked away.

Lainey's hand touched mine. I looked up as she knelt beside me. She took my hand in both of hers. "Tell me." Her eyes, so big and green, stared into mine.

"I don't like telling that story." The blood dripping from golden curls filled my head. I hadn't thought about that image in months. Why? Why had I let it go?

"If you want me to understand..." She hesitated, then went on: "If you want me to understand why you do this, you need to tell me. I want to know."

"Only my friends back at the Asylum know this." I took another drink of the juice. "I don't... I don't know how to tell you. You don't know what it's like."

"Then tell me." She squeezed my hand.

I looked at the carpet. It looked made of tight curls of yarn, or something like that. "I had a baby sister." With those words, my voice broke. A tightness filled my chest and made speaking difficult. It took a few minutes to compose myself.

Over the next half hour, I managed to get the story out, piece by piece, torn from my soul. It was even more difficult than when I'd told Rick and Kelly and the others. They understood the basics, and I had Bice to help explain the dragon religion. This time, I had to explain those details myself. I hated every moment of it. At one point, I threw the juice bottle across the room. A few moments later, I slid from the chair onto the carpet, on my knees.

Lainey, like any compassionate human being, was horrified. She moved closer to me on the floor, moving one of her arms around my shoulders. She patted my back, a little awkwardly. "I'm so sorry, Beryl," she said. "I didn't know."

"How could you?" I turned and looked into her face, a few inches from my own. "You haven't lived it." My voice wavered with each word. It was all I could do not to burst into sobs. "You haven't lived every day with the anger, the hate, and, and the fear."

"The fear? That you would die too?"

"No." I looked into her eyes, willing her to understand my anguish. "Until Rick came along, I couldn't get close to anyone. I didn't dare get close to anyone. I was afraid of what would happen to them. I worked with Kelly, and I really liked her, but I couldn't, couldn't get close to her. I never tried to ask her out, because I was afraid. I'm still afraid." I lowered my gaze again. "I don't care what happens to me. But when I think of what the dragons will do to my friends, it destroys me. That's all I care about now. It's why I had to get back as quick as I could, from the mountains." I repeated the words again, realizing the truth of them more than ever before: "I'm afraid."

23

Lainey squeezed my shoulder. "You can't protect everyone all of the time, Beryl. Bad things are going to happen. That's life."

"But bad things don't have to happen from the dragons!" I shook my head and wiped my eyes. "If I can protect them from that, if I can keep the dragons from hurting the people I, I care about, then… then maybe my life will be worthwhile."

Lainey took my face in her hands and turned it to look at her again. "Listen to me. You say you want freedom, right?"

"Yes…"

"Your friends are free. They're the freest people I've ever met. But you can't protect them all of the time."

I stared into her green eyes, so close to mine now.

"If you knew that one or more of them were going to die… if you knew that for a fact… would you want them back under the slavery of the dragon instead? Or let them live this freedom that they have now, even if it's only for a little while?"

I struggled with an answer. I put a name to the question: Kelly. Would I want Kelly living the freedom we had now for the past few months, knowing she would die sometime in the near future, or would I want her safe, but living in Viridia again?

"I can't. I can't answer that," I finally admitted. In a few words, Lainey had pierced through to my fears and shaken my beliefs. How did she do that?

Lainey lowered her gaze. "I have one more question, Beryl. I hope you can answer this one." She looked back into my eyes. "You've talked a lot about the value of human life. One of your big arguments against the dragons is how little they think of our lives. You even struggle to fight against other humans, because you value their lives."

I would have nodded if she hadn't still had her hands on my face. "Yes. All human life is valuable."

"Then why do you think your life is not?"

My eyes widened. "What?"

"A moment ago, you said maybe your life would be 'worthwhile' if you kept your friends safe. Isn't your life already worthwhile? Aren't you already valuable?"

"I…" I didn't know what to say again.

"You can't have it both ways. Either all life is valuable, including yours, or no one's is."

"You've trapped me. Of course I have to say my life is valuable. It's just—"

"No," she interrupted. "It's not 'just' anything. It's valuable. Period. No qualifiers."

I managed a little smile. "All right."

She smiled back. "You've been through some horrible stuff, Beryl. But you're still fighting. That says a lot."

I swallowed. "Thanks. You…" I didn't know how to word it. I wanted to tell her no one had ever been able to pull those kind of emotions out of me before, except maybe Bice. I wanted to tell her how amazing I thought she was. Instead, I just stared at the face so close to mine: the green eyes, the pink lips parting ever-so-slightly. I leaned in a tiny bit more. So did she. But only for a moment.

Lainey dropped her hands from my face, and leaned back on her heels. "Wow. I think I need one of those drinks now." She got to her feet and headed for the fridge.

What was I thinking? Lainey had shown no romantic interest in me from the moment we met, even though there had been plenty of opportunities to do so. We'd been alone together a lot. In fact, I may have spent more time alone with her than I ever did with Kelly. Or Olive, if I'm thinking of all the girls that I'd... been interested in. Fewmets. I couldn't even think about these things in the right words!

Lainey took her drink bottle and walked over to a large mirror on the opposite wall. She tilted her head back and forth. "This mark should be good for a day or maybe two, if I'm careful," she said. "You don't think they'll try to keep us that long, do you?"

I got back to my feet, feeling unusually drained. Heavy emotions tended to take as much out of me as physical exertion. I felt like I'd just run a mile. "The dragon wanted to talk with me. That's all the draconic said. And the captain said it would be this evening. I hope we can leave right afterwards."

Lainey turned away from the mirror and plopped down in one of the chairs. She swung her legs up over the arm and sat sideways. "You haven't said much about what he's going to talk about."

I took a seat near her. "That's because I don't know what he wants."

"You must have some idea."

"No, I don't." I paused. "Well, that's not entirely true. I know that he knows some things about me."

"What does he know?"

I ticked off my fingers. "He knows I have cybernetic implants that he wants. He knows I defeated one of his draconics in combat. He knows I know, sort of, what he's up to at the Hub. And he knows I led the red dragon into the peace summit."

"And these are not the actions of a normal human being," she observed. "Or even one of Viridia's servants, right?"

"Yeah, I guess I sound like I'm all over the place." I considered it for a moment. "But Taizong Gold told me the dragon wanted to talk to me before he would have known about the peace summit. Hmm."

"Do you think the dragon knows what you're up to?"

"I don't see how." Fatigue pulled on my eyelids, but the sight of Lainey's legs hanging over the arm of the chair kept distracting me. "One of the advantages we have is that the dragons are so arrogant, they can't conceive of a ridiculous plot like ours."

"You mean they can't imagine humans wanting to overthrow them?"

"They can't imagine humans thinking they had a chance at overthrowing them!" I pointed out the window. "They made an example of an entire city once, and they constantly remind us of that. It's one of the ways they rule: taking away hope."

"Not from you."

I shrugged. "Maybe." Did I still have hope? I guess it came and went. Sometimes I thought we would win, eventually, but most of the time I guess I thought we'd all end up dead. Huh. Maybe that answered her earlier question.

Our talk turned to more mundane things after that. After about an hour, I grew sleepy enough to take a nap on the couch. When I woke, the setting sunlight through the window cast a dark red glow across the room. Lainey sat beside one of the short tables, eating something.

"What's that?" I asked, stretching.

"Oh, you're awake. They brought some food in a few minutes ago." She gestured at a tray in front of her. "I decided not to wait for you."

"I don't blame you. Not sure why I got so sleepy. I don't usually take naps." I sat down to look at the food with her.

"I think it's this place." Lainey gestured in a circle. "I've felt kind of a drain on me since we got here. I napped a little while you out. I just woke up first."

"Huh." I picked up a piece of what I assumed was chicken and took a bite. A little sweet. Curious. "I've never heard of a place that would make you tired."

"Maybe it's an effect from the dragon."

She might not be wrong. Bice and Mazarine had not uncovered as much information as I'd like about the gold dragon, but there were hints about his powers. Apparently, he did breathe fire like the red dragons, but one of the books did speak of him weakening his opponents. Maybe the book meant that literally.

"This food is different," I observed, using another bite of the chicken to scoop up some rice. "Ever had anything like this before?"

"Not exactly like this, no. But I've had similar."

We ate almost everything on the tray. By the fading light, I knew it had to be early evening at least. The sun was about to disappear over the mountains. They would come for us soon.

The thoughts had only just crossed my mind when a knock came at the door. It slid open and two men entered. Captain Tawn stepped past the other one and bowed to us.

"The dragon will see you now."

24

Captain Tawn led the way, and the other man followed behind us. He had an odd look to him, with his neck craned forward and a stoop to his stride. He couldn't possibly be a soldier, could he? I kept glancing back at him as we rode the elevator. He had black hair, like the captain, but longer, tied back in a ponytail that reached the middle of his back. He also sported a ridiculously long mustache. I wondered if it tickled his neck when he turned his head. His clothing looked no different from the richer people we'd seen in the streets, except for one distinction: he wore a pair of black gloves. In his hands, he carried a strange-looking orb about eight or nine inches in diameter. It appeared to be formed of a series of interlocking glass panels. A faint glow from within made them appear cloudy.

"What's that?" I asked.

"It belongs to Auric," the man said in a deeper voice than I'd expected.

"Is it far to the dragon's lair?" Lainey asked.

"Not far," Captain Tawn answered. Only then did I notice we were descending further than the six floors we'd ascended. The elevator continued on down for some time before coming to a stop. The doors opened to another immense tunnel stretching away into the distance, lit by sconces every ten feet or so. I could see another of the moving sidewalks just ahead.

Captain Tawn stepped out and gestured forward. "Ciaru will take you the rest of the way," he declared.

The other man nodded and led the way to the moving sidewalk without another look at us. Lainey and I glanced at each other and followed.

We reached the end of one sidewalk and proceeded to the second before our guide spoke. "You have been afforded a great honor," he said. "Auric rarely speaks to anyone, let alone"—he glanced at our faces—"Viridians."

"Yeah, I'm not big on the idea of honor here," I said. "I'm not a fan of any of the dragons." The moment it came out of my mouth, I realized I might have said too much. I still didn't know what Auric knew about me, nor why he wanted to talk.

"Not even Viridia?"

"Especially not Viridia." That one I couldn't resist, especially not after telling Lainey my story.

"Interesting." Ciaru led us onto a third moving sidewalk. "Almost there now."

I appreciated the moving sidewalks now. For some reason, fatigue continued to drag at my muscles. I would hate to walk all this way. Up ahead, I could see a change in the lighting. It looked like quite a few more lights, but I couldn't tell much about them yet. We would be there in a few seconds.

"I'm already frightened," Lainey whispered to me.

"You should be," I said. "The dragons are terrifying in person."

Ciaru apparently overheard me. "Have you met one in person before tonight?"

I didn't answer. At first, it was because I didn't want to give anything else away, but then the sidewalk came to an end, and we stepped into the gold dragon's chamber. I stared, awed in spite of myself.

A cavern stretched out before us. I would call it enormous, but the word didn't seem… big enough. Viridia's cave was enormous. This one… Three of Viridia's cave would fit within this one. Hundreds of floating lanterns filled the entire place with light, casting myriads of shadows in every direction. Awed as I was by the overall view, it took a few minutes before I examined the nearest lantern. It looked like a miniature replica of one of the houses in the city, with a peaked roof and curved corners. What held them in the air? They moved slowly, drifting as though suspended in some form of liquid. The entire place was beautiful beyond all my expectations.

It was also conspicuously lacking a dragon.

"So lovely," Lainey murmured.

"Thank you," Ciaru answered, walking forward with the orb tucked under one arm. He gestured with the other to encompass the entire cavern. "We've worked hard to make it what it is today."

"And yet all of this is just for the dragon," I pointed out. "You already said he rarely speaks to anyone else."

Ciaru turned with an amused smile. "If you were a thousand years old, you might want a pleasant place to live as well."

"Not at the expense of others," I countered. Sure, I could see the beauty. But I could also see the exploitation of humans that had created it.

"If your cybernetic abilities are as impressive as advertised, you may have a chance to test that yourself."

"What do you mean?"

"Your power may make you effectively immortal, Beryl. As the humans around you die of old age, and you live on, perhaps your view of them will change."

Lainey turned to look at me, and her expression almost crushed me. "I'm human!" I snarled. "Surgical procedures don't change that!"

Ciaru raised his eyebrows. "Is that what it is?" He turned and walked further into the cave.

"So where's the dragon, anyway?" I demanded. My mood was shifting from bad to worse.

"He's always with us. But while we wait for his manifestation, perhaps we should dispense with some preliminaries." Ciaru turned back to face us, holding the orb with both hands now. "For example, the original invitation was for you alone. Who is your companion, and why is she here?"

"This is Lainey," I answered. "She's here because I want her here. And I revised the agreement with Taizong Gold."

"We are aware of Taizong's negotiations with you. We will honor his agreement, but it was curious." He studied Lainey. "Why?"

"I wanted to come," Lainey said. "I wanted to see the city. And the dragon."

"To witness the full glory of a dragon is a privilege given to only a select few. Perhaps you will be one of them tonight."

"Perhaps? Are you saying he may not even show up?" I clenched my fist. "He invited me here. I want to know why."

Ciaru rotated the orb in his hands. "You are a conundrum, Beryl.

From what I can tell, you do not seem to be acting in the interests of Viridia, yet you bear his mark. You possess impressive cybernetic enhancements,
designed and implanted by an absolute genius. You first encountered us
in the presence of a soldier from Caesious. Then you led Incarnadine into
attacking the peace summit. You seem to keep… interesting company." He
stared at Lainey again. I could almost feel his eyes peeling away her fake
chromark.

"And that's enough for the dragon to want to talk to me?"

"It is your actions that bring curiosity. Why are you doing these things?
Your agenda is a mystery."

"I'm not here to explain myself. My agenda is my own."

"We can guess part of it. You seem bent on keeping this war going." He
finally stopped staring at Lainey and turned back to me. "And Auric will be
ending it. He is curious as to why you oppose peace."

"I'm not opposed to peace." I made a point of looking around the
cavern. "If the dragon isn't going to show up, then we'll be going. I didn't
come all this way for a light show."

"What were Caesious's last words?"

I blinked. "What?"

"You told Taizong that Auric's name was one of the last words of Caesious. What did he say, exactly?"

"Maybe I'll tell that to the dragon, if he shows up."

"I told you: he is always with us." Ciaru's deep voice trembled as he
said it, and I had a sudden horrifying suspicion.

Ciaru bent his head. Golden tongues of fire erupted around him. Once
they reached a dozen feet or so from his body, they swirled in around each
other, forming a semi-transparent orb of golden flames around the man.
And then he began to change.

Lainey and I both took several steps backward. Ciaru grew, his body
growing longer and longer, even as it swelled out. The orb of flame grew
with him, obscuring the finer details, but allowing us to see just enough
to fully understand. His face elongated as well. His mouth split open into
jaws lined with gigantic teeth. Horns grew and spiked out in every direction. Even his mustache transformed into some kind of bizarre growth
that stretched long and thin back from his nostrils. Golden scales appeared
across every inch. His feet transformed into clawed monstrosities. His
hands, however, burst out of their gloves as they grew, revealing them to be

almost entirely cybernetic. I noticed a few other spots along the serpentine body where scales had been replaced. A pair of strangely long and thin wings erupted out from his back, flaring into the air, then folding down across his body as it continued to grow longer and larger.

The orb he'd been holding grew with him. My entire apartment back in Viridia would fit inside it. Multicolored lights flashed around the panels. Brief images exploded into view on each of them. I was almost certain I saw a view of the city from above before the entire orb dissolved back into cloudiness.

The circle of flames exploded out from him. Lainey and I both threw our arms up instinctively, but the fire dissipated before it struck us. I felt a sudden burst of heat, as well as an abrupt weakening of every muscle in my body. Beside me, Lainey staggered and almost collapsed. I caught her, sending boosts into my limbs to keep me from doing the same.

Before us, the dragon stretched himself out to his full length, rising up on his hind legs for a moment, then crashing down to face us. His mouth opened and I stared into the enormous maw, remembering the mouth of the red dragon almost closing on me.

"I am Auric, first child of Chroma, creator of The Circle, and the immortal god of this city. From this moment forward, your lives continue only by my grace."

Two thoughts fought for dominance in my head. One, dragons could take on human form. I'd heard that before, but dismissed it as a legend. It didn't make sense. But I couldn't deny what we'd just witnessed. Suddenly, the stories about how draconics came into being didn't seem so fanciful.

But the second thought infuriated me. If I had known, if I had guessed we were already talking with the dragon… could I have attacked him in his human form and killed him here and now? How vulnerable were they in human form? Could they be killed with a quick stab of a sword after all?

"You… you were human!" Lainey exclaimed.

"It pleases me to take that form and walk among my people from time to time," the dragon rumbled. His voice echoed through the chamber. "It also provides me with… other opportunities that I do not possess in this form." I could see its eyes ogling Lainey's body. Yes, a dragon can ogle a human. Disgusting. My fury grew at the insult.

"You can make yourself look human, but you still don't understand us!" I snarled. "You'd think after a thousand years, you might have learned something about humanity. Maybe gained a little empathy for those you've enslaved!"

"You operate under so many misconceptions." The dragon shifted its weight, curling like a tremendous snake. His shape was certainly different from the other dragons: long and serpentine, with much smaller legs. The air grew warmer, and an unusual smell struck my nostrils. It wasn't the same as the poison and waste I'd smelled in the green dragon's lair. This smelled more like smoldering charcoal. The giant orb sat to one side, apparently forgotten or unneeded for now.

"I don't think so."

"You call my people slaves, but I do not. They serve me, but it is necessary. All of it is necessary."

"I'm sure you've found ways to justify it in your twisted mind." As I said it, Lainey pulled on my arm. Everything I said sounded antagonistic. I wasn't sure whether I cared or not.

"Without me, and the other dragons, you would all be in far greater trouble," the dragon declared. "I am your salvation."

"Salvation?" I exploded. "You're insane! You've actually bought into the worship stuff? You're no god. You're a monster."

I glanced at Lainey for the first time since the dragon's transformation. Her eyes were the widest I'd ever seen them. Her lower lip trembled. I reached out and grabbed her hand. She tore her gaze from the dragon and looked at me. "It's all right," I said. "We'll be all right."

"It's not what—" she began.

"I invited you here," the dragon boomed. Smoke curled from its nostrils.

"Yeah, why is that?" I glared back up at him. Concern for Lainey diverted my anger, but only for a few seconds.

"I wanted to see if you are what Taizong believed you to be. Alas, from your actions, you seem to be working from a flawed premise." The dragon's head rose and turned with each sentence, as if he couldn't keep it still. "You achieved surprising results in each case. I wanted to see you myself, and evaluate you."

I'd had it with this thing. With all of them. I wished I had something witty to say, something to tear into its smug superiority. But I couldn't think of anything at this point.

The dragon's head stopped moving. It stared down at us. Only then did I notice the floating lights. They had all moved to encircle the dragon at equal distances. The light of the cavern now centered completely around him. The warmth of the cavern also grew, becoming almost oppressive. "You are an angry child. You are unworthy of knowing the facts. I am unsure how you have succeeded—or even survived!—so far, but I am inclined now to think that luck played a tremendous factor."

"I'll take luck," I said. "I'll take skill. I'll take whatever I need to bring you down."

"Fascinating. You genuinely believe you have a chance at such an undertaking. Perhaps you did witness the last words of Caesious, after all."

I'd really said too much. Now he knew my intentions. But what would he do about it? Hunt us all down? Destroy our base? An icicle of fear pierced through my anger. What was I thinking? Yelling at an ancient dragon as if he were an equal?

"I know more than you suspect," I said at last. "I've looked at the Cerulean Books of Lore."

For the first time, I think I surprised him. The dragon's head curled backward, like a serpent readying to strike. But he recovered fast enough; I'll give him that. "And what did you learn from these books?"

I didn't want to give away everything I knew, of course. But I figured I could let a few things slip. "I know about your sources of power." I pointed at the ground. "Is yours right below this cave? Is this where you feed?"

The dragon's forearm reached up and scratched a spot on his neck. "Of course not. The opposition would be too strong." He eyed me at an angle, as if daring me to show I knew what he meant.

Opposition. Bice and Mazarine talked about that word. They thought it had something to do with the dragons' power. But I had no idea what it meant yet. "Of course," I answered. "I should have remembered that part."

The dragon snorted, sucking smoke into its nostrils, then spewing it back out in a twin burst. "You know enough to be dangerous, but not enough to have understanding. I would enlighten you, but as I said: you are an angry child. I will not waste my time on such as you, at least not at this point. This audience is ending." He started to turn away.

"And what would it take for someone to be worthy in your eyes?" I demanded. "Does any human being rise to that lofty standard?"

Auric turned back and considered me. "A human would have to prove himself on the same level as a dragon. In a thousand years, I have only met one who met such a standard."

"You mean able to outsmart a dragon? I've already done that." I couldn't help wondering who that one might be. Whoever it was might have lived hundreds of years ago. It couldn't be relevant to right now.

"So you say. Very well. I will pose you a challenge, then. Succeed, and perhaps I will tell you more of the truth that will put things into perspective for you. Fail… well, if you fail, the war ends anyway, and everything goes back to normal."

"What kind of challenge?"

He stretched out one of his feet, claws scraping across the ground. "I am going to stop the war. Your challenge is simple: try to stop me."

"Oh, I'll stop you."

"Not unless you put together the obvious clues you already have." The gold dragon's wings split off from his body and spread out around him, reaching from wall to wall. The lights spread to match his movements.

"Clues?"

Auric looked down at me from his full and impressive height. "You've seen my servants at work. You've heard a word you know nothing about. If you can put all that together, then you'll be able to stop me. Otherwise, the war ends, and The Circle returns to its ways… with a smaller population."

A chill ran down my back. Smaller population? What did he mean?

"But that is only the first part of the challenge: defeating me. The second part is harder. You must defeat yourself."

"Myself?"

"You hate us. That is clear. And you hate Viridia most of all. That also is clear. You know we draw our sustenance from the sources. I will tell you where Viridia's source is."

My mouth fell open. If we knew that, it might change everything! Destroy the source and we destroy the green dragon, or at least the bulk of his power.

"Finding it is simple. Look for a place of true green."

I instantly knew what he meant. But how did this translate to defeating myself?

"But, of course," Auric went on, leaning in a bit, "if you go after Viridia, you will not be able to stop me. So you must choose. Your revenge, or saving human lives. Choose wisely."

"Wait." I raised my hand to implore him. "We can talk more about this. Tell me—"

"This audience is over." The dragon sucked in his breath and all of the lanterns went out. Neat trick. The only light remaining came from the sconces in the tunnel behind us.

"Let's go," Lainey whispered, pulling at me.

"No, wait." I peered into the darkness. Was the dragon still there? Had he reverted to human form again? The heat and smell persisted, but I couldn't see anything else, not even that weird orb. "Dragon! We're not done! I want to know what you did to Onyx!" Bice and Mazarine hadn't found much more in the books about Auric, but they gave me a few hints to work with. This was my favorite one.

A hiss came from far above. "Why do you mention that name?"

"It wasn't just a human rebellion against him, was it?" I called into the darkness. "You never got along with him. You or Viridia. You were glad when he died, weren't you? Did you help the humans overthrow him?"

"Again you speak of things you do not understand." This time, when he spoke, I caught a glimpse of sparks high above my head. Not in human form then.

"Maybe so. But I'm learning. I'll figure it out eventually."

"Perhaps. But you'll have to learn humility before that ever happens."

"Like you?"

Again with the hissing. This time, the sparks turned into what looked like liquid fire dripping. Lainey and I dodged backward as it struck the ground in front of us. Even in the warm air, I felt the heat radiating from the liquid.

"If you persist in this discussion after I have ended it, I will consider our agreement at an end as well."

"Kill me and my friends kill your draconic!"

"He will be born again. Will you?"

More of the liquid fire spilled out, falling and splattering closer to us. I turned with Lainey and sprinted back up the tunnel. The moving sidewalk would be too slow.

"You're crazy!" Lainey exclaimed when we stopped to catch our breath. "How could you talk to him that way?"

"I'm sorry. I just… I got too angry."

"He called you an angry child. Maybe he was right!" She was trembling. Her fear made her say things she didn't mean. Or at least I hoped so. Come to think of it, I'd never seen her angry before. Her little nose flare might be one of the cutest things I'd ever seen.

"Let's keep moving," I suggested, pointing to the next moving sidewalk. I let her step on it first before following. She moved a couple of steps ahead of me.

"Were you trying to get us killed?" she demanded.

"No! I… I'm sorry. I hate them so much. I didn't… I didn't think about what I was doing."

"No, you didn't."

We rode the sidewalk in silence until it reached the third one. "What do you think he meant about stopping the war?" I asked. "It must have something to do with the Hub."

Lainey didn't answer for a moment. "What's the Hub?" she asked at last.

I explained the importance of the location where the train tracks intersected, and then what Caedan and I had seen Auric's soldiers doing. As

I did, I tried to think through how he could possibly stop the war. "He dared me to stop him," I concluded. "I think I can, if I can figure out what it is he's doing."

"So now you want to impress the dragon? Show it how smart humans can be?"

"No, I don't care about that." Maybe. I guess I did care about it a little bit. "But he all but said he would be killing a lot of people. I can't let that happen."

"Of course you can't." Her tone was odd, but I couldn't tell if she was still angry, or… something else.

I knew already I would work to stop the gold dragon, and ignore the taunts about Viridia. We could go after that target afterwards. And yet… we had a good size team now. Maybe we could do both. Maybe I could find a way to destroy the green dragon's source while Rick stopped the gold dragon…

We reached the elevator for our return upward. I stopped and looked around. Lainey paused in front of the elevator doors. "What is it?"

"No one's come to meet us," I said. "Do we go back to the room? Or…" I looked down the tunnel in the other direction. "We could go anywhere."

"How far do you think your agreement will keep us safe?"

I sighed. "You're probably right. Let's just head up." Besides, I still couldn't shake the fatigue.

Captain Tawn stood waiting for us when we exited the elevator. "Considering the hour, it has been decided that you should sleep here, and I will escort you back tomorrow morning," he announced.

Neither of us argued with him. As we walked back to our room, a thought occurred to me: "Does everyone struggle with this… fatigue… around the dragon? How do your people get any work done?"

He glanced at me and didn't answer at first. "It is no secret that Auric's presence drains those around him at times," he said at last. "But it is a localized effect. Everyone has plenty of energy elsewhere."

I suspected as much, but wanted confirmation. As we entered our rooms again, Tawn told us he'd come for us an hour after dawn. He bowed again and left us alone.

"You can have the bed," I told Lainey. "I'll just take a pillow and sleep on the couch."

She nodded. After we both got some water from the fridge, we prepared to sleep. I tossed the pillow onto the couch and considered which direction to lie. Feeling warm, I pulled off my shirt. I hadn't slept in a building since... well, I guess I did sleep on the floor of the Vermeils' apartment in Incarnadine several weeks—or was it months now?—ago. And I've slept in a cave a lot since then, but that doesn't count. Anyway, it felt weird.

Lainey emerged from the bedroom door, holding her own pillow in front of her. "Beryl?"

"Huh? Oh, sorry." I tried to pull my shirt back on, but got it caught on my elbow. I struggle for a few seconds until I got it straightened out.

Lainey giggled. "It's not like I haven't seen you without a shirt before."

Oh, right. Still, it felt like the thing to do for some reason. Stacy would have laughed at me. "Did you need something?" I asked.

"No." Lainey walked a few steps closer and took a deep breath. "I apologize for yelling at you down below. You know much more about these dragons and the situation than I do."

"Hey, it's all right. You were scared. I don't blame you." Just standing felt awkward, so I crossed my arms. No, that was worse. I uncrossed them. "I was pretty stupid in the way I handled it, anyway."

"All right." She turned to go back into the bedroom.

"Lainey..."

She turned back. "Yes, Beryl?"

"I just... Part of what got me so angry was the way he looked at you. Like he wanted you. I couldn't take that."

She clutched the pillow a little tighter.

"I mean, you're my friend. If something that horrible happened to you, I don't know what I would do."

She nodded, then looked down at the pillow. "I miss Glacier."

I smiled. "I'm sure Lovat's having a great time with her."

"Yeah."

"We'll be back tomorrow."

"Yeah." She shuffled back into the bedroom.

I stared after her for a few moments, then dove onto the couch. I punched the pillow. "Idiot," I muttered. "Calling her a 'friend.' Are you trying to kill every possible relationship with a girl?"

I ran the conversation through my head a dozen or more times, changing what I said and imagining what else could have changed. Then I called myself more names for letting my imagination go too far. Finally, I forced myself to think about the dragon's challenge again.

Or not the challenge itself, but the reasons behind it. If the gold dragon understood I was fighting to end the rule of the dragons, why tell me anything? Why not just eliminate me and everyone with me? It wouldn't take him much effort, after all. What could he possibly gain by feeding me information and then daring me to stop him? Throughout the war so far, he had remained apart. His troops had not fought against any of the others. They took the Hub and that's all. Every indication pointed to the gold dragon wanting to end the war. So why dare me to stop him? Why ask me to prove myself to him? Was this some convoluted plot to blame humans for whatever actions he did take?

The Hub. It all came down to what they were doing at the Hub. His soldiers had set up devices on each of the tracks leading to the other five cities. Or four of them. I couldn't remember. Were those devices intended to threaten the cities somehow? We'd used a train to kill a dragon. Could this dragon use a train to kill a city? The thought chilled me.

I never did tell him what the blue dragon said at the end. "The Circle will fall. Auric." I'd puzzled over those words many times since then. By "The Circle," I had always assumed he meant the dragons' rule. And he knew his death would lead to the others falling as well. But I never could figure out why he named Auric at the end.

With such perplexing thoughts in my head, I finally fell into a troubled sleep. In one of my dreams, Lainey's cat grew to gigantic size and ate a dragon. Then it turned to look at me, and I woke up.

I almost leaped out of the couch. Every part of my body suddenly felt invigorated and full of energy. I looked around the room, illuminated only by dim light coming from the streets below. I saw nothing unusual. Worried, I walked to the bedroom door, which Lainey had left open a couple of inches. I peered through the gap. I could just make out her form, so small in the huge bed. She shifted and mumbled something, but appeared to be sound asleep.

I turned away and walked to the giant window. From here, I could see down across much of the city. It surprised me a bit to see so many lights on at this time of night. Maybe I wasn't the only one waking up energized all of a sudden. And then I saw it. A brighter light outshone everything else. I raised my hand to shield my eyes, but they adjusted faster than I expected.

Another advantage to cybernetics?

The glow came from my left and illuminated mountains, so I assumed north. I craned my neck to see, nervous about leaning against the window itself. The gold dragon. Of course. It looked spectacular, a shining gold silhouette against the darkness of the mountains beyond.

Distantly, I heard a sound. I looked down into the street and saw dozens of people who'd emerged from the buildings and homes since I first looked out.

They were cheering.

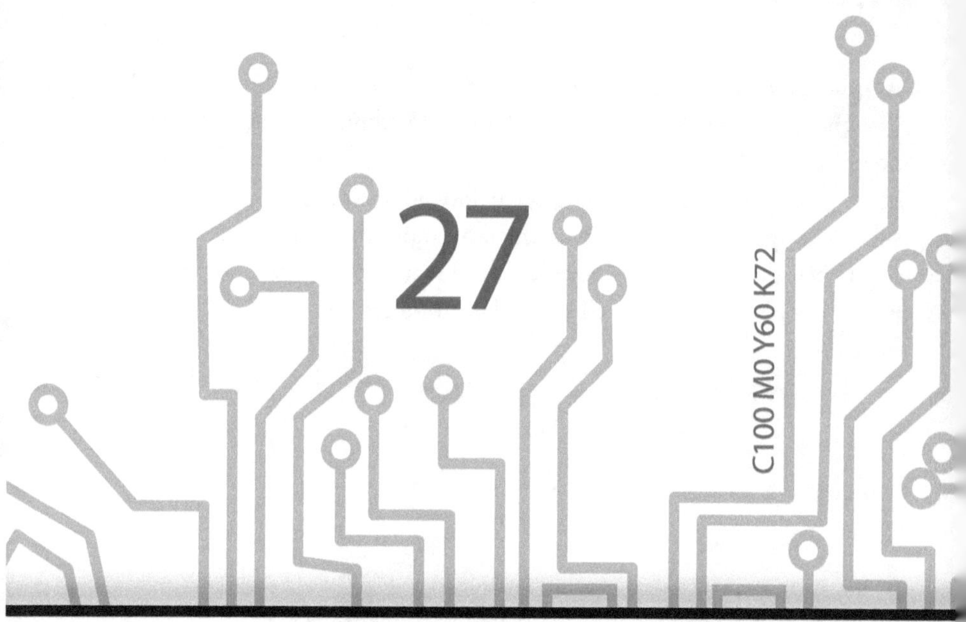

27

Our journey back to the meeting place was uneventful. During the walk and ride to the train station, and on the train itself, I pondered what I had seen and felt in the night. The gold dragon's power involved weakening those around it, yet by all appearances, it had energized an entire city instead... the exact opposite of its power. Was this the meaning of "opposition"?

The people in the street cheered. Perhaps the dragon did this on a regular basis, and they enjoyed the feelings. "Auric gives us life!" I had to admit I had never felt better. It took me the better part of an hour to relax again. Even though the people recognized the event, I couldn't help but wonder how much of the display had been for my benefit. If so, the dragon's motives continued to baffle me. I couldn't figure him out.

Escorted by the ever rigid and mostly silent Captain Tawn, we left the train and walked out to the meeting spot. Apparently, Lovat was on duty to keep an eye out for us. He waved to us from a nearby incline and then took off running.

"He'll fetch the others," I said to the captain, who only nodded. "You don't talk a lot, do you?"

"I have nothing to say to you, except what my god commands."

"Right. Your god. I don't suppose he told you to tell me more about the project at the Hub?"

"I know nothing of such matters."

"Of course you don't."

"Your city is very beautiful. You should be proud," Lainey spoke up. She'd also been quiet throughout most of the morning.

Tawn gave us another of those short bows. "Thank you. We are quite proud of our architectural accomplishments."

"How much of the design is inspired by the dragon and how much of it comes from your people?"

The captain blinked, the closest I'd seen to him expressing emotion of any kind. "We, uh, we like to think that Auric and his people are one; the inspiration comes from both."

"I see," Lainey said. "And do you personally worship Auric as your god?"

"I do."

"You believe there is none higher?"

I wondered where Lainey was going with this line of questioning, but we had nothing better to do while we waited.

"Of course. The other dragons are also gods, but they pale before the brightness of the almighty Auric."

"Then I must ask you another question."

Tawn nodded.

"If Auric is the highest god, why did he refer to himself as the child of Chroma?"

"Ah, I see the confusion." Tawn did not look fazed at all. "Chroma is not a person. It is a reference to the celestial home of the dragons, the place from which they descended when they came to enlighten us."

Huh. I'd never heard that before. I always thought "Chroma" was short for "Chromatic hells!" It's the way we used it in Viridia, anyway.

"Thank you." Lainey made a clumsy attempt at duplicating one of Tawn's bows. "You've been very informative, Captain."

Was I imagining it or did he actually smile?

"Beryl!" The shout came from behind us. I turned to see Rick, Lovat, Taizong Gold, and Protogonus Blue. The group moved slowly to accommodate the aging blue draconic. But Lovat didn't do slow. He burst apart from the others and ran to meet us, Glacier in his arms.

The cub, much larger now than when I'd first seen it, complained mightily at the treatment. If Lovat hadn't dropped it right when he reached us, I'm pretty sure the cat would have given him some severe scratches. Lainey fell to her knees and pulled Glacier toward her, cooing. Lovat gave me a quick hug, then tried to look tall and fierce. At least, that's why I guessed he thought of himself, staring with narrowed eyes at the gold captain.

"A blue draconic," Tawn observed.

"Fascinating, isn't it?" I asked, then walked to meet the others. The captain trailed behind.

"…given me much to think about," Taizong Gold was saying to Protogonus Blue as I approached. The two draconics put their palms together in an odd arrangement. I suppose it was like shaking hands for us.

The relief at seeing the others all right almost erased all of my earlier thoughts, but as I passed near Taizong Gold, I remembered. I put out my hand. "A word, if you will?" Wow. When did I become so formal? Captain Tawn must be rubbing off on me.

The draconic nodded, and we took a few steps away from the others. "You possess an intriguing collection of allies, Beryl," it said before I could speak. "Though their attempts to portray that hovel as your headquarters were laughable."

"Whatever you say." I glanced at Captain Tawn. "Listen, I don't know how much Protogonus Blue there persuaded you about anything, but I have a request."

The draconic lowered its head a fraction. "I will not betray my sire."

"Your what?" I shook my head. "Never mind. I won't ask you directly. I'll just make a guess about what's happening at the Hub, and you tell me if I'm right or wrong."

"I do not think—"

"Auric is going to threaten the other dragons to stop the war, and if they don't, he'll use those devices you've built to destroy their cities," I said in a rush.

Taizong Gold looked at me for a moment. "I will not say whether your guess is accurate." He glanced at the blue draconic. "But, if such a thing were true, it seems that an example would have to be made to prove such a capability." With that, he left me and joined Captain Tawn. The two walked away together without another word.

Rick walked up and slapped me on the back. "So what have we learned? Anything good?"

"It's all bad," I said, watching the gold ones leave. "We need to get back to the Asylum and speak together. I think the gold dragon is about to kill thousands of people all at once."

With some help from Caedan and the four-wheelers, we made it back to the Asylum in a very short time. As I hopped off, I told Rick, "Get everyone together. I want them all to hear this."

"Even that Viridian Guard guy?"

"Yes. If he's sticking around, he needs to know what he's getting into."

Kelly hurried to greet us, giving Rick a hug, and then doing the same to me. I couldn't help glancing at her belly to see if she were showing the pregnancy yet. I didn't think so, but her shirt was hanging loose. Maybe she did that on purpose.

"I'm glad to see you both still alive," she observed. "Everything went well, then?"

"Sort of. I'll explain everything once we're all gathered together. Everything okay here?"

"No troubles."

I nodded and started toward the water barrels. Kelly exchanged some words with Rick, then caught up to me as I got a drink. "You still haven't told him?" I asked.

"No, I… I'll tell him tonight." She patted her stomach. "I won't be able to keep it secret much longer, anyway."

I hesitated. "Kelly, we haven't talked about… I mean… do you want this?"

"Rick and I will discuss that."

"Of course. I just… I don't know." I stopped talking before it got more awkward. Instead, Kelly took it to a different awkward subject:

"So how are things going with Miss Outside-The-Circle?"

"Going?" I took a sip of water. "Oh. No. I told you. We're friends."

"Right. Friends. Like Olive?"

"What? No. Olive was…" I sighed. "I couldn't be honest with her. I mean, it was fun, having a girl, you know, like me, but… I can't talk to her about what matters."

"And you can with Lainey."

"I don't know. This time it's more like she's the one who can't be honest. She's hiding a lot." I looked across the Asylum and spotted Lainey playing with Lovat and Glacier. "I don't understand why she won't tell us about life outside."

Kelly leaned against one of our barrels and laughed. "Listen to us, talking about romance and stuff while the world falls apart around us."

I shrugged. "It's a part of life, right? And isn't that what we're fighting for? Life?"

Her hand drifted to her stomach again. "Yeah…"

Bice and Peri came around one of the dirt walls and approached us. "Hey guys," I called. "Rick tell you we're about to have a meeting?"

"We got the word," Bice said. "Good to see you still alive, Beryl." He moved in close and gave me a side-hug. "I need to speak with you about Mazarine," he whispered. "It's disturbing."

"Sure, Bice. Once we talk about all we learned in the past two days." I pointed to the others approaching. "Looks like we'll meet right here."

Protogonus Blue and Mazarine joined us, followed by Jaden on a crutch, Don, Caedan, Lovat, and Lainey. Finally, Rick and Dusk emerged from the cave and took seats near the rest of us. Kelly moved next to Rick with an odd look at Dusk. Wow, our group had really grown. Loden would be proud.

The group looked to me with expectation. They were all curious about my visit with the gold dragon. I may as well lay it on the line to start out. I pointed to the east.

"We live not far from the Blasted Lands. You all know what happened there." I looked from one face to another. "The thirteen of us may be all that stands in the way of it happening again."

28

"How so?" Peri asked. "Does Auric know what we're doing here?"

"I don't know," I said. "He's a mystery, even after talking with him. One minute, he acts like he knows everything we're doing, the next he seems perplexed by it, and the next he acts as if he doesn't really care what we do. But…" I raised a finger to make sure everyone paid attention to my next words. "He basically told me what he was going to do next, and dared me to stop it."

"Why would he do that?" Mazarine wanted to know.

"I don't know. Sometimes it seemed like he wanted me to impress him, to prove myself to him for some weird reason." I explained the threat, and reminded them of what Caedan and I had seen at the Hub. "I'm guessing the devices on the tracks can destroy a city, or at least do massive damage, and I'm also guessing they have something to do with the 'opposition' powers."

"That's a lot of guessing," Kelly pointed out.

"I know. The dragon also mentioned decreasing the population of The Circle, and then Taizong Gold pointed out that a threat is no good unless you first prove that it can work."

I let that statement sit with them for a moment.

"You think they'll launch one of the devices first," Rick said, "and then use the results to enforce peace on the other dragons."

"Right. And what would be the obvious target?"

"Caesious," Peri said immediately. "The city without a dragon."

"We cannot allow this to happen," Protogonus Blue rumbled.

"I don't intend to," I said. "I believe we can stop it, now that we know."

"All we'd have to do is destroy the tracks," Caedan pointed out. "Shouldn't be too difficult, right?"

"We'll probably have to deal with the Aurelian Sentinels, but they can't guard the entire line."

"If this is an explosive device powerful enough to destroy a city," Rick said slowly, "then you want to stop it as far away from the city as possible. Even if it explodes somewhat near to the city, it could still kill hundreds. We just don't know."

I still wasn't entirely clear on the whole concept of "explosions," but Rick had experience there. "The dragon hinted that it had something to do with this concept of 'opposition,'" I said. "Bice, you remember that term from the books?"

"Yes, of course. Something to do with the powers of the dragons," he replied. "But we weren't able to figure out what it meant, exactly."

"I think it's what the name says. It's the opposite of the dragon's power."

"That's why it's so cold at Incarnadine!" Caedan exclaimed. "Cold instead of hot!"

I hadn't even thought of that yet. But of course it made sense.

"So the city's are full of this… opposition power to the dragons?" Kelly asked. "Why would they even stay there?"

"Not the whole city," I explained, "only a specific spot in the city. It's the spot from where the dragon draws its power. The primary spot for the, uh, magic that his servants use."

"Magic?" Lainey asked.

"I'll explain later."

"The opposition power apparently spreads throughout the city, at least to some degree," Rick mused. "Maybe that's why the cold is felt all through the city."

"And maybe it's stronger since there are two red dragons," Bice suggested.

"I still don't understand how targeting these spots would destroy a city," Kelly complained.

"We don't know," I said. "Maybe it would unleash that power in a huge burst? Maybe it would do the opposite? Maybe just the act of destroying the power source would destroy the city?"

"The point is: it's a threat to our city, and we have to stop it," Peri said. "We'll find a way."

"Did you learn anything else from Auric?" Rick asked.

I hesitated. I almost didn't want to tell them the other thing, because it showed how perceptive the dragon had been toward me. But Kelly and I had just talked about keeping secrets. "He told me where the green dragon's power source is," I said. "He was taunting me, wanting to see if my hate for the dragon would make me ignore the threat to humans."

Rick almost jumped to his feet. "He told you Viridia's power source? Where is it?"

"It doesn't matter right now. We'll deal with that after we stop the gold dragon and save Caesious." I looked around at everyone again. "We started this war. It doesn't stop until the dragons are dead. We can't let the gold dragon stop it on his own. At the same time, we're all about preserving human life. If he's threatening to destroy a city full of people, that takes precedence over everything else." I swallowed. "Even killing another dragon."

"Why not both?" Rick asked.

"I thought of that," I admitted. "But it can wait, Rick. The green dragon's not going anywhere."

"But if he finds out we know, it'll make things harder," he argued.

"How would he find out? Is the gold dragon going to tell him that he gave away his secret?" Even as I said it, I wondered about Auric's motivations again. Did he want Viridia dead? And then it hit me: he believed Viridia killed Caesious and started the war! Exactly as we planned it…

Rick scowled but didn't answer.

"All right, people. Any thoughts, ideas, questions?"

"How much time do we have?" Caedan asked.

"I don't know. That's one of our problems. We also don't know if the gold dragon will send his demand first, or the demonstration first."

"So we need to keep an eye on both," Bice said. "Watch the Hub, and watch for messengers to the other cities."

"Right. Lovat?"

The boy jumped to his feet and saluted me.

"You're our best scout, man. I need you keeping an eye on the Hub.

But I want you to work with Caedan and Peri. Caedan's in charge." I turned to him. "Just watching for now, but set it up so you can get word back to us as fast as possible."

"The talkers have a maximum range of about three miles," Dusk spoke up. "You could set up a relay system with them to get a message from the Hub to here in a very short time, depending on how many you use."

"Great idea! Caedan, if you need more people to set that up, do it."

"Stacy wants one of the talkers," Don said, startling me with his voice as usual.

"Why haven't we given her one before?" I shook my head. "Sometimes we miss the most obvious things. Dusk, how many do we have now?"

"There were six in the original set. I think you lost one when you wrecked the wings, so that leaves five."

"One for Stacy, one at the Hub, one somewhere in the middle, and one here, leaving one more as backup." I counted them off on my fingers.

"Viridia is more than three miles away," Dusk pointed out. Did she have to sound so smug?

"Yes, we'll have to set up a weekly time to check in with her. That will take the place of our visits, since it's getting so dangerous out there. Don, I'll leave that up to you."

He nodded.

"After last time, we'd better send an escort with him for the last trip," Rick pointed out. "It should probably be you, Beryl."

"I can do it," Kelly said.

"I meant someone who can fight," Rick told her.

"You don't think I can fight?"

"No, I mean… against the Viridian Guard. Beryl's the most equipped to handle them."

"He's right, Kelly," I said. "But… if you want to talk to Stacy, we can set you up at the three-mile point to test the talkers."

"Three miles is the maximum," Dusk said. "You should try to keep it lower than that."

"Got it. Kelly?"

"Sure. That'll work."

I looked around again. "Anything else? Anyone?"

Rick looked like he wanted to say something, but shook his head instead.

"All right. I don't know about the rest of you, but I think I missed lunch somewhere along the way. Let's break up and get busy. Caedan, I want the Hub being watched by tonight. Don, Kelly, we'll wait until the morning to visit Viridia. Everyone else… be ready, and be thinking. If you have any more ideas, tell me, or talk to Bice if I'm not available. He's always good at telling me when my ideas are stupid. Oh, and Protogonus Blue… I need to talk with you."

Everyone split off to go about their tasks, leaving me with the aged draconic. Bice stayed near, reminding me he still needed to talk as well.

"You are becoming a fine leader," Protogonus Blue rumbled. "That was well done."

"Thanks, I guess." I looked at the others going in different directions. "I'm just making it up as I go."

"What can I do for you?"

"You seem to have made an impact on the gold draconic. Do you see potential there for the future?"

The draconic lowered its head and did not answer at first. I waited for what seemed like an entire minute, at least. "I do not know," it said at last. "Needless to say, he was quite shocked when I revealed myself to him. He refused to consider any questions about Auric's deity. But… I believe I shook him up."

Speaking with him reminded me of something Stacy told me weeks ago. I hadn't been able to mention it to anyone else yet. "I've got a question. Why would the green dragon want Troilus Green's body?"

Protogonus Blue lifted its head. The reptilian face held an expression I'd never seen on a draconic before. Eyes wide, nostrils flared. It looked a little like anger, but… I couldn't figure it out until he spoke.

"If Viridia has recovered his son's body, then you are in the gravest danger of all."

Oh. Now I understood the expression. It was fear.

"What are you talking about? You said he would be born again, but as a baby, without his previous knowledge at first." The whole reincarnation thing was crazy enough already.

"That is normally the way of things," the draconic acknowledged. "But it may be that Viridia is desperate enough to try something else."

"What else? It's a dead body!"

Bice, seeing my agitation, got up and came to join us. "What's going on?"

I pointed at Protogonus Blue. "He's saying they might bring Troilus Green back to life!"

The draconic shook its head. "No, that is not what I am saying. I will try to explain."

"Please do," Bice said.

"As we have discussed, when a draconic is reborn, he regains most of the memories of his past lives, but not until he is of age." The draconic tapped its own head with a claw. "This sudden rush of memories can be… quite traumatic. When it happens, a draconic seeks out its sire for comfort and aid in understanding. There is a… mystical bond between the two of them at the time."

"Great. More magic." I rolled my eyes. Why couldn't anything make sense any more?

"If you wish to call it that, I suppose. It is more of a sharing of minds." It stared off into the distance. "I well remember the last time it happened with me. I thought I had truly touched the divine. Caesious's thoughts were so far above my own…"

"And he's dead now," I snapped.

"Beryl," Bice said with a warning in his tone. I bit my lip.

"At any rate, Viridia may be seeking to perform a similar ritual, to connect with his fallen child."

"You're saying he's going to try to form one of these… 'bonds' with the dead body of Troilus Green?" Every time I thought I understand how twisted the dragons truly were, something like this came along, pushing my disgust even further.

"Something like that. Because of our nature, we have very persistent memory. There are many who believe the memory survives after the body itself is dead… at least for a while."

"I do not wish to be rude," Bice said, "but this sounds a lot like the superstitious beliefs you've told us about before, like some twisted form of necromancy. It can't possibly be a real thing, can it?"

The draconic shrugged. "I do not know the extent to which science—or magic as you called it—has advanced within Viridia. Every dragon keeps technological secrets from the others."

"Because they're all dying," I muttered, "and they want to outlive each other."

Protogonus Blue blinked. "That is a distinct possibility."

I got up and paced. "This changes things. We can assume it hasn't happened yet, because we don't have a green dragon tearing this place apart right now, but it could happen any day now."

"Remember what you told Rick," Bice said. "We have to save the city first."

"I know. But if the green dragon finds out about us, not only will it come after us, it may stop us from that mission too. Can we risk that?"

"I don't see that we have a choice." Bice put a hand on my shoulder. "When this all started, Beryl, you were letting your anger and hate drive you. You've moved on from that. Don't go back to it. We'll deal with Viridia, after we save the people of Caesious."

He was right. I knew it. It didn't mean I had to like it. "I'll check in with Stacy about this tomorrow," I said. "Maybe she's heard something."

Bice glanced at the draconic, then motioned me away. Oh, right. He still wanted to talk with me about something. I hoped it wouldn't be long; my stomach kept reminding me of the skipped lunch. "What is it?" I asked when we were alone.

"It's Mazarine." Bice lowered his head and shook it. "I thought we'd converted him, Beryl. I really did. With the books and everything, I thought he'd never turn back."

I tried to understand. "What are you saying?"

Bice looked at me. "He didn't mean to tell me, but his arrogance let it slip out. He says he's serving a new god now."

Maybe it was the stress of the last few days, or the hunger, but I didn't grasp the significance. "Bice, the religious side of things is your specialty."

"You're not understanding. Think about it. He's spent his entire life dedicated to the service of a dragon that he saw as his god. That dragon is now dead, but he says he's found another god?"

"But he—" I stopped. I think I did get it now. "You think he's chosen one of the other dragons as his new god? That he's going to betray us?"

"I can't be sure." Bice looked over his shoulder. "Like I said, he didn't mean to tell me."

"How could he even have contacted one of them? He hasn't left the Asylum since he got here! Has he?"

"No, and that's why it's confusing."

"All right, Bice." I sighed. As if we didn't have enough to worry about. "All we can do is keep an eye on him. I trust you. Do you think he's got Peri or the draconic on his side?"

"They don't talk with each other very much any more, so I don't think so." He straightened up. "I'll let you know if I hear or see anything else."

"Do that. And if you need help and I'm not here…" I looked around at the others moving about. "Well, you know who you can trust better than I do."

The trip to Viridia the next day passed without incident. Don, Kelly, and I took our usual path, and only had to divert from it once to avoid a Viridian Guard patrol. I wanted to talk with Kelly more about the pregnancy, but Don's presence made it impossible. I did manage to find out she had decided to wait to tell Rick until after she talked with Stacy.

We left Kelly at a location we guessed to be a little over two miles from the city. Don and I made our way to the Citrine, the theater where we met with Stacy. Only when we drew near the door did I suddenly remember something important.

"Uh, you'd better go in first without me," I told Don. "Find out if Olive is here. I don't think I'm ready to explain why I'm not dead."

He nodded and went to the door. I concealed myself in the shadows across the alley and waited. A few minutes later, Don re-emerged with Stacy. She was wearing jeans and a tank top this time, not one of her crazy stage outfits. I stepped out of the shadows, only to be caught up in another huge hug.

"You idiot!" Her voice was muffled against my shoulder. "Bringing a dragon to a peace summit!"

"Hey, he chased me there," I answered. "Good to see you too, Stacy." I had been a little worried she might have gotten caught up in the destruction.

As quick as I could, I explained my story, our current situation, and our plans. Then I told her about Troilus Green.

"I haven't heard anything since they brought the body back," she said. "But everything's been kind of crazy since you crashed that dragon."

Crashed the dragon. Ha.

"This I do know: something crazy is going on at the Emerald Ascendancy. They've stopped the tours, increased security, and I've heard some of the workers aren't even being allowed to go home at night." Stacy glanced around the alley.

"At first, I thought it might be in response to your raid on the Flame," she went on. "But how would they even know about that? No one's talking, but there's something brewing, for sure."

"Fewmets." Maybe Protogonus Blue was right. Argh. If only we could be sure about the timing of everything. Which would happen first? The attack on Caesious, or the attempt to find Troilus Green's memories?

"You can't break into the Emerald Ascendancy again," Stacy said, reading my thoughts. "Last time, you had inside help."

"That was before I knew all my capabilities," I argued.

"The place is full of soldiers and all the remaining draconics. Unless you're bringing another dragon again, you're not getting inside."

"Wouldn't that be something?" I laughed. If only I could pull off something like that.

"Beryl…" She hesitated and glanced around again. "A lot of people saw you. You know, when you were flying. Talk spread fast throughout the cities, maybe encouraged by a few actors who also saw it." Her eyes darted back and forth while she grinned. "And you've become quite the legend. The flying man chased by a dragon. Most think you died in the chaos, but… a few are still telling the story of how you escaped."

A legend. How about that?

I gave Stacy the talker and explained how it worked. "Kelly is waiting a couple miles away to hear from you," I said. "Try it."

She followed my instructions and held the device up to her ear. "Kelly?" A big smile split her face. "Hey, girl. What's happening?" She glanced at me. "Yeah, they're both still here. Why? Oh. All right." She lowered the talker. "She says for the two of you to head back while we have some girl talk."

"Sure. And when you're done, set up a regular time with her that we can check in with you. This will be our last one of these visits for a while."

She nodded. "The world's getting more and more dangerous."

No doubt about that. Everywhere we went brought us danger.

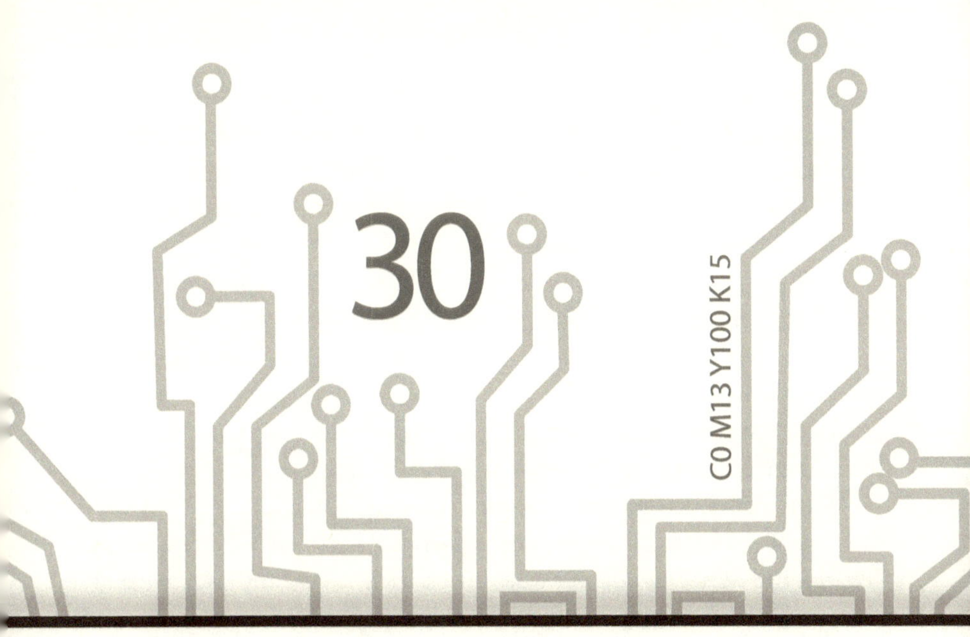

We left the city and met up with Kelly again. She seemed a little more cheerful after talking with Stacy, but didn't enlighten me about the conversation. As the sun vanished behind the mountains, we set out walking again. We could get a little closer to home before making camp for the night. These trips always ended up this way.

When we found a place to sleep in a grove, Don slipped off to relieve himself, and I got a brief chance to talk to Kelly alone. "Good talk with Stacy?"

"Yeah, it helped. She understood."

"So you'll be telling Rick tomorrow?"

Kelly spread out her bedroll. "I guess I have to."

I really didn't understand her reluctance. If it were me, I would certainly want to know. "I'm sure he'll be okay with it."

"Are you?" She looked at me with half a smile. "Are we talking about the same Rick?"

"If there's one thing I've learned about Rick, he's loyal to the people he cares about," I said. "How many times has he come after me now?"

"He's loyal to you, Beryl," she said, stretching out. "The rest of us? I'm not so sure any more."

"I don't understand."

"You were gone for two weeks. You didn't see."

At that moment, Don returned. Stacy rolled over and didn't speak any more. Reluctantly, I got ready for bed myself. No sooner had I gotten my own bedroll spread, then the talker crackled to life.

"Beryl? Beryl!"

It was Rick's voice. I snatched it up. "I'm here. What is it?"

"It's happening. It's happening now!" Static obliterated a few words. He must have been on the very edge of the talkers' range. "…messengers sent out. They're on their way to all the cities… except Caesious. Auric's about to strike!"

I ran out of the grove, hoping it might help the reception. "How are the messengers traveling?" I demanded.

Static continued to interrupt him. "…rails. Some kind of…" I kept moving. Rick's voice slowly became clearer, but I still missed a few words. "By the time Caedan got the word to us back… Asylum, they were already… way. I've been… four-wheeler to get… touch with you."

"All right. Listen to me, Rick. We'll stop the messenger to Viridia and see what the message holds. Tell Caedan and Lovat to watch the track to Caesious!"

"…ready doing that."

"Good. Once I know more, I'll get back to you. Have everyone ready to move fast!"

I ran back into the grove where Kelly and Don waited. "Change of plans! We have to stop the messenger from Auric!"

In short order, we gathered our things and made our way down to the railroad tracks. They hadn't been in use much since the war started.

"If we just follow this, we'll meet the messenger coming."

"And then what?" Kelly asked.

"I'll boost everything I've got and knock him down." I didn't know what means the messenger was using to ride the rails, but it couldn't be anything too big.

"Why don't we just block the tracks?" Don asked.

"With what?"

He shrugged. "Anything we can find. It doesn't take much to throw even a train off the rails."

"Really?" For some reason, I'd always seen the trains as the height of technology, able to withstand just about anything. At least until we crashed one into a dragon, anyway.

Don nodded. "With your strength, we can move some rocks and block it good."

He had a fair point, so I agreed. Don turned on his flashlight and sought out some good sized rocks. With the help of my implant, I managed to get a dozen or so in place on the rails. Kelly and Don dragged some large branches on top of it all for good measure.

Now came the waiting. I would much rather have kept moving along the tracks until we met the messenger, but Don's plan made more sense. Even if the enemy plowed right through our makeshift barricade, I would still be ready to charge in and take him down in the middle of it all. And we were still a good five miles or more from Viridia, so no one there would know.

Unless one of those patrols came along. That would be awkward.

We didn't have to conceal ourselves much while we waited. It was a cloudy night with only a sliver of a moon peeking through every once in a while.

"You all right?" I asked Kelly.

"I'm fine. You don't have to keep asking."

"Sorry."

We waited in silence for the next ten minutes, maybe a lot more. My eyes grew heavy, and I started to nod off a little. The bad guys needed better schedulers.

"Light," Don said.

My head jerked. I looked down the tracks and saw what Don saw: a small light coming toward us, growing larger by the second. "This is it." I got up into a crouch, readying myself for whatever it might be.

With the light coming almost right at us, I couldn't get a good look at the vehicle. "Come on, Loden. Why didn't you give me night vision or something?" I muttered.

"Are you seriously complaining about not having even more super powers?" Kelly whispered.

"Shhh."

The light struck our makeshift blockade. At once, it slowed. The driver no doubt realized he couldn't just plow through this obstacle. Unfortunately, it also looked quite obvious that someone planted the obstacle. He would be on his guard. It wouldn't do him any good against me, though.

As the vehicle came to a stop almost right in front of us, we finally got a look at it. Smaller than a typical train car or engine, it sported a sloped front end with a forward-facing window. The sides were open, revealing the driver, a member of the Aurelian Sentinals. The back end of the vehicle looked to have a small storage area, but not much else. In all, it had been clearly designed for a single person.

I launched forward, closing the gap between our hiding spot and the tracks in a couple of seconds. The driver managed to turn his head in my direction just before I leaped. Arms extended, I tackled him and yanked him completely out of the vehicle. We both landed in the dirt on the other side of the tracks, rolling over and over.

In the darkness, I couldn't be sure how much armor the Sentinel wore. At least he didn't have a helmet, so I gave my fist a small boost and punched him in the face. The boosts gave me speed and strength, but they did nothing to protect my knuckles. That hurt. But the Sentinel stopped moving. I got to my feet and called for Kelly and Don.

Don's flashlight blinded me for a moment, before aiming down at the unconscious Sentinel. Then it almost blinded me again, reflecting off the gold armor plates. "Fancy," Don observed.

"Should have worn his helmet." I shook my hand, wiggling my fingers. Ouch. Ouch. Ouch. As the effects of my boosts wore off, I could feel a handful of bruises on the rest of my body from that stunt. I was used to that by now.

Kelly climbed onto the vehicle. "This thing is interesting. Too bad we can't take it back with us."

I considered it for a moment. Together, Don and I might be able to turn it around. But then only one person could ride it, and it only worked on the rails. Not worth the trouble.

"Have you checked to see if he has the message on him?" Kelly asked.

Oh, right. With the help of Don's flashlight, I searched the Sentinel for pockets or anywhere else he might conceal a message. "Not finding it."

"There's a box up here, but it's locked," Kelly said. I climbed up beside her and checked it out, then hopped back down. From behind the vehicle, I stood on the tracks and grasped the lid of the box. With a boost to both arms, I yanked. The lid of the box ripped off and I stumbled back a few steps.

"You're so handy with the little jobs." Kelly reached into the box and lifted an official-looking envelope. Her flashlight reflected from gold trim around its edges. "This must be it."

Don and I both came beside her as she ripped open the envelope. She pulled out a large document and examined it.

"Yeah, here we go," she said. "Auric is informing Viridia that it's time for the animosity to be put aside. He's demanding an end to the hostilities and a return to normal business within The Circle."

"And if not?" I prompted.

"If not, he threatens to destroy the city of anyone who defies him. To prove his capability, he will…" She swallowed. "Sorry. I knew this was what you expected, but it's still insane." She took a breath. "He says he will destroy the city of Caesious in twenty-four hours."

"Twenty-four hours starting when?" I demanded.

"That's not clear…" Kelly read over the whole letter again. "I guess it means from the moment they get this letter?"

"But would all the dragons get the letter at the same time?"

Kelly shrugged. "It may not be precisely twenty-four hours, but he docs warn them to remove any of their people from the target city, if they want to save them."

"We're going to save all of them," I said, clenching my fists. "Twenty-four hours isn't much time, but…"

"It's hardly any time! Can we even get to the Hub that fast?"

I thought it over, recalling our previous trips. "Not on foot, not from here. Rick and the others should be able to reach it, though."

Kelly hopped off the vehicle. "You need to be there. You should take this thing."

"She's right," Don said. "You're the strong one. They'll need you."

"I don't want to leave you two…"

"Don't be ridiculous. We'll be fine." Kelly shoved the document into my hands. "We'll get back to the Asylum in our own time."

I wasn't going to say it, but it was exactly what popped into my mind when I heard the twenty-four hour time limit. I didn't know how fast this little device could cruise along the rails, but even with it, I would be hard pressed to get there in time to help the others.

Sleep? Who needs sleep?

31

As anticipated, Don and I (mostly me) managed to get the vehicle turned around on the tracks. I climbed into the driver's seat and studied the controls.

"What about him?" Don asked, pointing to the unconscious messenger.

"May as well just leave him there. He'll be in trouble for failing his mission."

"You don't want to try to recruit him too?" Kelly asked.

"I'd love to, but we don't have the time." The controls looked simple enough. It wasn't like it needed steering. I flipped a switch and the engine coughed into life. It sounded almost just like our four-wheelers. Another lever seemed to control the speed. All I needed to find was the brake. I guessed it must be another knob that had been pulled out.

"Here I go," I said. "You're still sure about this?"

"Go. Save the city." Kelly waved me on.

I pushed the knob in and gently moved the speed lever. The rail rider—as I began calling it in my head—jerked hard, almost throwing me off, and then started to move forward at a snail's pace. I moved the lever and the speed increased, bit by bit. In a few moments, I was speeding down the track, going at least as fast as our four-wheelers, and probably faster. I kept the light on to watch the track ahead. When I hit the first major turn in the rails, I discovered something important: slow down for turns. The rail rider almost flew off the tracks before I cut the speed. From then on, I paid attention to oncoming turns, and adjusted the speed accordingly.

Riding the rails was a much smoother way to travel than our four-wheelers. The light shining on the endless pair of rails stretching ahead of me became almost hypnotic. I shook my head. If I weren't careful, I would fall asleep. I channeled a boost into my head to stimulate my brain or something. It worked once before, and it worked now. My eyes flew open.

The night passed on as I kept moving. At this rate, I would be passing the Asylum in a couple of hours. Suddenly, I remembered Rick. I pulled out the talker and flipped it on.

"Rick? Are you there?"

The talker crackled as it usually did, and then Rick's voice burst through: "Where have you been? Did you stop the messenger? What's going on?"

"Sorry I didn't call sooner. I'm on my way back. We stopped the messenger." I explained about the twenty-four hours and the rail rider. "I can't be sure, but I think I'll be near the Hub by dawn."

"All right, I'll head back that way myself. Caedan and the boys are still there. Together, we should be able to stop it."

I agreed and turned off the talker. I turned back to the monotony of riding the rails. Every so often, I had to slow for a turn through the hills, but otherwise, it was all the same. The night wore on, as did my mental boosts to stay awake. This practice of keeping myself awake could turn into a bad habit. But what choice did I have? Everything depended on my presence. The other guys were competent, but my cyb implant gave me huge advantages. I never asked to be this important; I never sought it out for myself. It just happened.

In the dark, I couldn't be totally sure how close I was getting to the Hub. I hoped I'd see lights in the distance, sometime before dawn broke. The Aurelian Sentinels couldn't see in the dark, after all.

Instead, my only warning came with a flash of gold armor in the rail rider's light. A Sentinel ran across the tracks up ahead. Fewmets! I threw the lever down to cut the speed and tried to yank the brake knob out. The rail rider came to an almost complete halt, and flipped forward. If I hadn't given my mind a boost a few seconds earlier, I would have gone with it. Instead, with my reaction time shortened, I boosted my legs and dove out of the rider in mid-air. I still landed hard on the ground and rolled. Behind me, the rail rider smashed into the tracks and rolled a few times itself.

Shouts sounded nearby, but I scrambled to my feet and ran. In a few seconds, I raced out of their range. I stopped to catch my breath, and then took out the talker. I was lucky it hadn't broken in my fall.

"Rick, I'm close, but I lost the rail rider and ran into some Sentinels. Are you nearby?"

A few moments later, he answered: "I'm with the others. Where are you, exactly?"

I looked around. "I have no idea. It's dark. I'm somewhere near the track from Viridia. That's all I know."

"All right. You'll need to cross it, and come west. We're near the Caesious track, so you'll also have the cross the one from Atramentous."

"Right, right."

Problem: I didn't know how to find west in the dark. But I still had a good idea of where the track from Viridia lay, so I could find it at least. I jogged in that direction and soon crossed it. Now things got a little more tricky. The Hub would be to my right now, so if I angled that way somewhat, I would eventually reach the other tracks, and not risk heading off to the south instead. At least, that's how it made sense in my brain.

As I jogged along, my vision grew clearer. Dawn was approaching. I stopped and put my hands on my knees, taking a break. After a moment's thought, I found a dry spot and sat down. I may as well wait for daylight now. We still had almost all day to find a way to stop the attack. I could afford to rest... as long as I didn't fall asleep.

My head jerked up. Had I started to doze? Everything looked much brighter.

The talker crackled. "Beryl, are you still there?"

"Took a break to catch my breath," I answered. "Moving your way now."

"Better hurry. They've stepped up activity in there. I'm not sure what's happening."

I sighed and got to my feet. "No rest for the exhausted," my father used to say. I had no idea what he meant back then, but it sure seemed appropriate now. I hurried to the nearest hill to get my bearings.

I spotted the Hub in the distance on my right. Good to know I hadn't wandered too far in the dark. The Atramentous rails were only a couple hundred yards away. Once I crossed those, I could swing more toward the north to reach the Caesious line. I set out, giving my legs a little boost to keep them going. I could rest when I was with the others.

Lovat spotted me first, of course. He appeared out of nowhere to guide me the rest of the way to the others. To my surprise, Lainey was waiting along with Caedan, Rick, and Peri. Seeing my look, Rick came to greet me. "I picked her up on my way back. Thought we might be able to make some use of that rifle of hers," he explained, glancing back at her. "And she wouldn't let me take it."

"All right. So, where do we stand?" I looked around. The guys had parked the two four-wheelers down in a ditch, hidden by some scrub brush. Caedan and Peri stood waiting, grim looks on their faces. Seeing them side-by-side, it struck me how much Peri had changed since his arrival. He'd gone from a skinny priest to a tough-looking, wiry warrior. He and Caedan had been working and training together for weeks now.

"Just before dawn, they suddenly got really busy in there," Caedan reported. "It's hard to tell what they're doing, but they've got that device on the tracks outside the building now."

"Take a look with those cyb eyes of yours," Rick said. "Maybe you can see something we can't."

I doubted that, since Rick held binoculars, but I did want to see. I followed them to the rim of a very short rise in the ground. We stretched out on the ground and looked toward the Hub.

With my regular vision, I could see figures moving around, but not much else. I activated my zoom vision and looked closer. I saw Aurelian Sentinels, many of them fully armored and carrying those enormous bladed weapons. They stood at equidistant points in a circle around the device. They were the security division. A number of others moved around with lighter armor and swords hanging from their belts. I wasn't sure if they were also security, or if they had another job. Their movements didn't appear to form any sort of pattern. Finally, I saw about a dozen other men and women, unarmored, working on the device, or examining different parts of it. Some carried clipboards or tools. The tech crew, no doubt.

Even with all the strength I could wield, Lainey's rifle, and the other guys, I did not see any way we could get anywhere near the device. The odds were definitely against us.

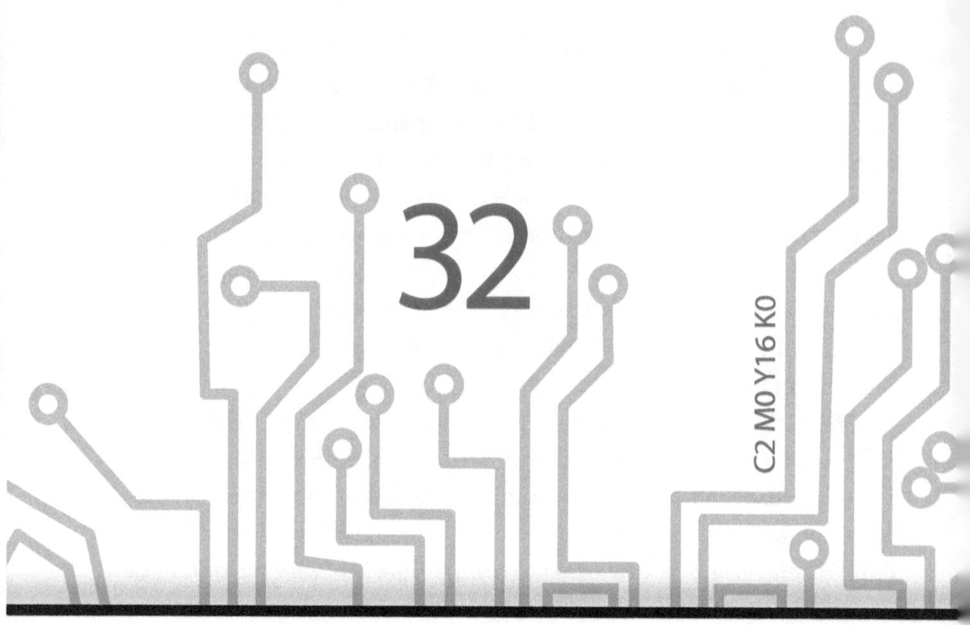

32

I looked closer at the device itself. At first glance, it looked like a giant version of one of Lainey's bullets suspended in a metal frame mounted on the tracks. The more I studied it, and technicians moved out of my way, I made out more details. When Caedan and I had first seen them, I had gotten a cylindrical impression. But now I could see tapering in the front, which gave it the bullet shape, but at the size of a train tanker car. The tapered front also had a number of antenna-like devices extending forward. All of it gleamed of metal: not gold, but something extremely solid. Chains connected it to the frame in multiple locations.

I checked out the frame and saw only strength. Huge metal beams formed an elongated rectangle around the device. Multiple stabilizing pieces criss-crossed it on every side except the front. All of it sat on top of something like a train flat car, but with an enlarged area near the back, presumably housing some kind of engine. Underneath, I saw double sets of wheels gripping the tracks on both sides. This would not be knocked off as easily as the rail rider. It was designed to hold on, no matter what.

"All right, I see it," I said. "I don't understand it, but I see it."

"That's an explosive device," Rick answered. "But larger than anything I've ever seen or heard of."

"It looks like one of Lainey's bullets." I glanced at her. She peered toward the device and shrugged. "It's big and scary looking, but what can it do?"

Rick held out his hands a few inches apart. "I've set off explosives this big and destroyed an entire building."

I looked back at it. If the size were an indication of the explosive power, I could believe it might take out most, if not all, of a city. "And it's going to target the blue dragon's power source, right?"

"That's the part we don't understand," Peri spoke up. "What will that do?"

"I can only guess," Rick said, "but I'm thinking that will make it far worse."

Maybe that's what the antennas in front were for: to detect the power source. I agreed with Peri: we had no idea what it might mean. If it released an opposite power, like we theorized, what would be the opposite of the blue dragon's lightning-like breath? Some kind of negative energy? In any case, I did not want to see it happen.

"I don't see how we can get to it while it's sitting there," I said.

"Maybe the rifle?" Rick asked, looking at Lainey.

She moved it into position and peered down its length. "It's metal," she said. "My shot would just ricochet off of it."

I rolled back and scrambled away. "Let's pull back." The others followed me back out of sight of the Hub. We stood in a circle. "All right. Ideas?"

"You can knock it off the tracks!" Lovat said.

I smiled at him. "I wish I could, pal, but even I'm not that strong."

"Maybe if we rammed it with one of the four-wheelers in the middle of a turn?" Caedan suggested.

"Possible, maybe. But we would lose the four-wheeler and probably whoever drove it. I'd rather this not be a suicide mission."

"You have to assume that if it gets knocked off the tracks, it's going to explode, anyway," Lainey said. "Anyone nearby would be killed."

"That complicates things. Rick, that sound right?"

He shrugged. "Probably. Any kind of violent action could set off many kinds of explosives."

There's more than one kind? Wow.

"How do we stop it without violence?" Caedan asked.

"We stop the engine," Peri said. "Let it glide to a halt. Then we can find a way to stop it from exploding."

"Okay, that makes sense. But how do we do that?"

"We'd have to get on board."

I nodded. "There's no way we can get to it right now. So we'll have to try after it starts down the tracks. I'm assuming it won't have guards riding along, unless the dragon has people willing to die for him."

"Never underestimate the commitment of those caught up in religious belief," Rick said. "It's a possibility."

Maybe, but it wouldn't be as many guards, at least. "So we follow along with the four-wheelers. I can jump onto it while it's moving, but I might need help, even if there are guards."

"You could throw me onto it!" Lovat suggested.

"I could," I admitted, eyeing him. I hated to put him into that kind of dangerous situation, but…

"No. You throw me," Peri declared.

I looked at him in surprise. "I guess maybe I could, but why?"

"It's my city. And I know engines better than anyone here."

"I know a lot," Caedan offered.

"Yes, but you're a better driver of the four-wheeler," Peri argued. "And I weigh less than you."

He made good points. "Fine. Caedan drives Peri and me. Rick takes Lainey and Lovat. Let's be ready. As soon as that thing starts moving, we move." I let my shoulders slump. "And while we're waiting, I need to rest."

"There's a sheltered spot over by the four-wheelers," Caedan said, pointing. "We've taken turns sleeping."

"Thanks." I started to go, but noticed Lainey staring off toward the Hub. "Is something wrong, Lainey?"

"This doesn't make sense," she said.

"What doesn't?"

She turned to look at me, her head cocked a little to the side. "Auric sent messages to the other dragons, right? Why don't they just come tear this place apart? How is it a threat?" She gestured toward the Hub. "Any one of the dragons could destroy all of that place in a few minutes, from what I've seen. Why don't they?"

We all looked at each other. "That's… a good question," I said.

"Is this all some kind of trick?" Caedan looked at me. "He challenged you to stop him. Is this all about you?"

"No, no. That makes no sense." I took several steps toward the Hub.

"They were setting this up before we ever met anyone from Auric."

"It's what they want," Rick said softly. "It always is."

"What do you mean?" I turned back to him.

"The dragons don't want a war. They never did." He pointed back toward Viridia. "We forced them into it. They want things to stay the way they've always been. This gives them an out."

"What do you mean?" Peri asked.

"The dragons will let this happen. They'll let another city be destroyed, make peace, and tell each other: 'we had to do it. Auric forced us. Nothing we could do.'"

"But they could! They could stop it!" Peri looked more agitated than I'd ever seen him.

Rick shrugged. "This is the way they think. They're comfortable with the way things have always been. They're upset about the death of Caesious, but they don't really want to change things." He pointed at me. "They were close to ending it all with the peace summit, but you ruined that for them. This is their next attempt."

"They'll sacrifice an entire city of people just so they can go back to the way things were?" Peri ranted.

I wanted to say I was shocked, but… I wasn't. "All along, we've been saying the dragons think of us as nothing," I said. "We're only worthwhile in the way we serve them. The people of Caesious aren't doing anything for the dragons right now. That makes them worthless."

Peri stomped away, fists clenched. Lainey wore an expression of deep sadness. She turned away also. Caedan quietly smacked his fist into his palm a few times. Lovat looked from one to the other of us.

"Lovat, go keep an eye on the Hub," I said. "Take the binoculars. Let us know the minute they start trying to move that thing."

He obeyed, and I made my way to the sheltered spot Caedan spoke of. I stretched out on the ground, closed my eyes, and sought for sleep. It defied my efforts to find it for at least half an hour. Despite my body's exhaustion, my brain kept coming back to the last conversation. I pondered the dragons' evil until I finally found sleep and insisted it take me with it.

I think I slept for about an hour. The sun hadn't moved very far when Caedan woke me with a shake. "Lovat says they're doing something,"

he reported.

"No way it's been twenty-four hours," I griped.

We gathered back at our overlook. I zoomed in on the device sitting outside the Hub. The Sentinels were all pulling back from it. The tech crew moved away as well, one by one, until only one man remained next to the device. He did something I couldn't see, then jumped to the ground. The device started moving.

"This is it," I said. "Mount up. We have a city to save."

33

As planned, Caedan drove one four-wheeler with Peri behind him. I climbed behind Peri. "You sure about this?" I asked him again.

"I've never been more sure of anything," he answered. "Let's do it."

Rick pulled the other four-wheeler out, with Lainey and Lovat behind him. He nodded to Caedan and we set out toward the tracks.

As we drew near, the device moved past us, picking up speed. We turned parallel and chased along beside it.

"No guards," Caedan yelled over the engine noises. "So they're not suicidal."

"Get as close to it as you can!" I shouted.

Caedan gunned the engine and zoomed up next to the device. The tracks and the slope around them made getting close difficult. If Caedan moved in too near, he risked overbalancing the four-wheeler and flipping it. The device was already moving faster than I anticipated, and getting faster.

Peri flipped himself around, both legs on the side nearest the rails. I braced myself and grabbed the back of his shirt with one hand and his belt with the other. "Ready?"

He released his grip and reached out. "Ready!"

I sent massive boosts to both arms and hurled Peri toward the device. He flailed through the air, and for a moment, I thought he would fly right over it and smash to the ground on the other side. But he caught hold of the top part of the frame and stopped his momentum. He flipped over it, but hooked his legs over the furthest bar on the frame and brought himself to a stop.

Caedan swerved back and forth to regain the four-wheeler's balance after the sudden shift in weight. I flipped my leg over and gathered myself for a jump.

"I'm going all out!" Caedan yelled. "If it gets any faster, I won't be able to keep up!"

"Follow as you can!" I told him, and leaped.

I landed on the side of the device and caught hold, under much more control than Peri. Then again, no one had thrown me. Peri grinned at me and swung down onto the flatbed.

A big turn in the rails came up. The device took it at full speed. The explosive rocked on its chains, but the frame and flatcar didn't tilt at all. We were never going to be able to knock this thing off the rails if it could do that.

I dropped down next to Peri, but held on to the frame to steady myself. "What now?" I asked him over the wind.

"I need to try to get into the engine." He pointed at the sealed off section at the back of the flatbed. He checked to make sure another swerve wasn't coming up, then crawled down to that end. I moved nearby to support him with whatever he needed me to do.

I checked on the four-wheelers. Caedan had been right. They couldn't keep up and were already a dozen or more yards back and losing ground on us every moment. I waved to let them know we were at work, then bent down to see what Peri could do.

Peri pointed to a metal panel. "This is bolted down. Can you get it off?"

I repositioned myself and tried to get a grip on the side of the panel. Rick's cybernetic hand sure would come in handy right now. Ha. Handy. I'm so funny in my own head. I managed to get a tiny grip on either side of the panel and yanked on it. The metal edges bent upward, but didn't come off. I shifted around to the other sides and tried again. This time, one corner of the panel popped loose. I got my hand under the corner, boosted it again, and ripped the whole thing off.

Peri moved in to look. I lifted my head to check our status. The four-wheelers were now over a hundred yards behind us. With the twists and turns, hills and trees, I would lose sight of them in seconds. But it wasn't like they didn't know where we were going.

I had no way of judging how fast we were traveling, or how much distance we covered. I knew a regular train traveling from the Hub to the city of Caesious would take a couple of hours or more. I would hope we had at least that long.

"This is bad!" Peri called. I bent back down to be near his head. He pointed to some thick wires leading from the back of the engine up to the device itself. "I don't even fully understand this engine, and these things are wired to the explosive for some reason."

"Should I pull them loose?"

"No!" He shook his head violently. "We don't know what will happen! I'm worried that if the engine quits, the explosive goes off!"

"We have some time!" I told him. "See what you can figure out."

He nodded and resumed looking over the engine. He pulled a screwdriver from his back pocket and nudged around a few places. I let him look and kept my mouth shut. I had no idea how these things worked. Yet I had a nagging feeling in the back of my mind. I also couldn't be sure, but it felt like we were still accelerating.

"Where's the fuel?" I asked. "Can we drain it out somehow? Rip it open?"

"It's underneath the car. I don't see how we can get to it!" He shook his head again. "This engine is unlike anything I've seen before."

"It's Loden's engine." That was the nagging feeling.

"What?"

"One like his, anyway. He called it the fastest train engine ever." Somehow, Auric's engineers had duplicated it. Did they have Loden's notes? No, that didn't make sense. They must have discovered it on their own, the same way he did.

"It's worse," Peri said, leaning in so I could hear him. "These wires... I think I've figured it out." He reached up and touched the back end of the explosive device. It did taper outward at the very end, forming a nozzle of some kind. "There's another engine inside this thing, I think. When the flatcar stops, or crashes into the train station at Caesious, these wires activate the engine in the device." He looked at its shape. "I think it flies out and aims for the power source, wherever that is."

I looked it over and considered his theory. It made sense. The power source wouldn't be at the train station, obviously, and that's where this track ended. The device had to keep moving, and it would have to go up before it could come down. Fewmets. How could we stop this thing?

"Can you find a way to keep the engine running, but not turning the wheels?" I asked.

Peri wrinkled his brow. "I don't think so, but I'll take a look." He got down with the engine again and stuck both hands inside the assembly.

I said we had plenty of time, but I was getting worried. If the engine was anything like Loden's, it could reach faster speeds than we'd anticipated. We might not have two hours. We might not have even one!

I inched along the flatcar to the front. The wind tore at my clothes, reminding me of the day months ago when I rode Loden's train to its appointment with the blue dragon. Now this one had an appointment with the blue city, and we needed to stop it, not help it.

I climbed up and examined the chains holding the device to the frame. If necessary, I thought I might be able to break one of them, but what good would that do? I suppose it might unbalance the thing enough to cause a wreck on a big turn, but it might not. If I broke both chains up here, it might drop the tip of the explosive down onto the flatcar. For all I knew, doing so might set the whole thing off. And with the way things were going, I might have to do it, and try to jump clear. I'd save that idea for a last ditch effort, with the city in sight.

I moved back to Peri and found him prying a panel off from the back of the explosive device. He'd gotten one side curved up with his screwdriver, so I reached in with my left hand and yanked it off the rest of the way. Sliced my third finger in the process. I instinctively put pressure against it with my thumb, but it bled a lot.

Peri stared at the innards of the device, then looked at me. "I don't know what to do, Beryl."

34

Peri looked back at the open panel. He pointed with the screwdriver. "I have no idea what any of these wires and things do. If I mess with any of it, I could set the whole thing off!"

His face showed his desperation and I couldn't argue with him. We were in a horrible situation. Thousands of lives in the balance. Reminding him of that wouldn't help. He needed encouragement, not more desperation. I reached out and grabbed his shoulder and looked him in the eyes.

"You can do this, Peri. I brought you here because you're the best one for the job. I believe in you." It seemed like the kind of speech a leader should give.

The muscles in Peri's face hardened and his jaw set. He gave a curt nod and turned back to the panel. "How much time do you think we have?"

I looked around. I didn't know this area at all. The only time I'd traveled through it was by train. "I don't know," I said. "Just do what you can."

Trees rushed past as we zoomed through a grove or wood. Caedan and Rick would still be pursuing us, but Caedan knew this area better. He'd be cutting across country to avoid some of the wide loops the tracks took. But he couldn't possibly catch up with this thing, as fast as it flew along now. We'd get no help from them. If Peri couldn't stop this thing…

I tried to give him the time he needed. I moved all the way around the flatcar, every step an effort with the wind tearing at me. I looked for anything, anything at all that might give me an idea. I found nothing.

I looked ahead. How would I know when we were getting near the city? The tallest building, the tower of Caesious, had been knocked down by Incarnadine. I knew there were other tall buildings, but I hadn't seen them from the train until we were almost there. We would have no warning before we reached the city.

I came back to Peri. "Anything?"

He pointed with the screwdriver. "I'm almost certain that part right there will set off the explosives." He pointed another direction. "And over here is that second engine I was talking about." He shook his head. "But I don't know what I can do about either of them."

"We can't give up!" I looked ahead again. "We'll find a way!"

"I can only think of one way." He didn't shout, and I almost didn't hear him.

"What's that?"

He looked at me with apprehension in his eyes. "If anything happens, Beryl, tell Caedan... tell him he was the best friend I could have ever hoped for."

"Tell him yourself," I shot back. "What do we need to do?"

He nodded, as if coming to a decision, then took a deep breath. "All right. I need you on the outside of the frame here." He pointed.

I obliged and swung around to the outside, holding on against the rushing wind. "What now?"

He handed me the screwdriver. "You'll need this." I took it and shifted my weight while holding on with my left hand.

He pointed up. "Do you see where the chain connects the device to the frame up there?"

I looked up. "Yeah, I see it. You want me to try to disconnect it?" I shifted my weight again to climb up.

"I'm sorry, Beryl." That's when he shoved me. If I'd had only a moment longer to send a boost into my hand. Or if my hand hadn't already been a little slick with blood from the sliced finger. Or...

I fell. I triggered boosts and tried to roll into a ball, but I still hit the ground at a tremendous speed. I flailed about as I tumbled over and over. With a pop, my right shoulder disconnected again. Strangely, it didn't hurt anywhere near as much as everything else.

"Peri!" I screamed once I could speak again. I scrambled to my feet, ignoring the pain and my limp right arm. I boosted my legs and raced after the train. I could catch him. I knew I could. If I pushed hard enough, used enough boosts, I could do it.

I could see the train, taking a bend to the right, far ahead of me. I triggered the boost to my eyes and zoomed in. Peri stood in the same spot, his head bowed. Then he lifted it, squared his shoulders, and reached into the open panel on the explosive device.

The brightest light I'd ever seen blinded me completely. In the same moment, something like a wall of heat and force struck every inch of my body. I left the ground, flying backward. I smelled burnt flesh. I could taste it, along with the coppery flavor of blood. I heard nothing, but my ears felt like ice picks jammed into both of them at once.

I hit the ground again, far harder than when I'd fallen from the train. I'm sure I felt something else crack somewhere. I still couldn't see a thing. I bounced like a child's ball before coming to a stop. Something else hit next to me. My hand brushed against it and burned.

I screamed Peri's name, over and over, until my throat choked up from dust and blood. My consciousness faded out, only to rush back all at once from the pain throughout my body.

My vision cleared up in a hurry, though everything still looked washed out for a few minutes. Right next to me, a twisted piece of railroad track rose into the air, embedded at least a foot into the ground. A few inches closer, and it would have embedded through me. I turned and looked out over an apocalyptic scene.

I lay at the very rim of a new crater, or so it looked to me. Dark smoke and clouds of dust obscured almost everything. I caught glimpses of fire, shattered trees, a few pieces of train tracks. Nothing remained of the device. Or Peri. I choked again, rolled onto my side and spit out what I could.

My clothes were in tatters, but at least I wasn't naked. I lay there, resting on my left arm, until I heard the sounds of the four-wheelers approaching. I lifted my head up to see them coming to a stop a few feet away. Caedan, Rick, Lovat, and Lainey dismounted and rushed to me.

"Beryl!" Lovat shouted first. He stopped next to me, unsure what to do.

Lainey bent down. "Are you all right?"

I nodded and pantomimed water. She pulled out her canteen and handed it to me. I couldn't open it with one hand, so she twisted the cap and poured the water into my mouth. I rinsed out the gunk and spit it out, then drank eagerly.

Rick and Caedan stared out over the devastation. I couldn't tell if they were in awe or horror or both.

Caedan turned solemn eyes on me. "Peri?"

"He did it," I said, my voice cracking. "It was the only way. He… he shoved me off and then did it." I didn't know what else to say.

"He saved our city," Caedan said. "He's a hero."

I nodded, thinking about the young priest. He'd come to us only as the servant to the high priest, Mazarine, but he soon proved his worth in more ways. He helped us with the engines on the four-wheelers and the Sky Claimer, and then he'd participated in the riot at Incarnadine. He'd even been training in fighting with Caedan. Out of all the new recruits since the original gang, he'd been the most… promising. And now he was gone.

"Peri's dead?" Lovat asked, his voice trembling.

Lainey put a hand on his shoulder. "He died to save others," she told him.

"The power it took to do this…" Rick mumbled.

Lainey turned back to look me over. "You have burns all over the place. Some of them look pretty bad. Your hand is bleeding."

"Just a cut on my finger." I was actually amazed I had taken so little hurt. I'd been channeling boosts at the moment of the explosion; maybe that helped somehow.

"And why are you always getting your clothes torn off?"

"Because I know how much you like it," I said. Or didn't. I actually didn't even think of that response until about half an hour later. Why am I like this?

"We'd better get out of here," Rick said, turning back to the four-wheelers. "That blast would have been seen and heard for miles. Someone will be coming to check it out, possibly a dragon or two."

"I need a little help, Rick," I called.

He swiveled back. "What is it?"

I pointed at my right shoulder. "Can you guys pop this back in again?"

As Lainey and Caedan helped me to my feet, Rick walked over and looked me over. "They say it gets easier," he observed. "Let's see." Before I could prepare, he grabbed my right arm, then smacked my shoulder with the palm heel of his cybernetic hand. The arm popped back into the joint before I could even scream.

"Owwww!"

"You're welcome. Let's get going."

With Caedan's help, I got back on the four-wheeler. As he revved up the engine, I took one last look at the destruction. And I remembered: Auric had four more of these devices.

We drove due east for a while, until I told Caedan I couldn't go any longer. He found a place to stop next to a narrow creek. He and Rick drove the four-wheelers up under some nearby trees, while the rest of us found rest next to the creek. Lainey brought the medical kit from one of the four-wheelers and set about bandaging the worst of my injuries.

"We don't have enough bandages," she pointed out.

"A common problem when he's around," Rick said, joining us. "Beryl seems to have a habit of surviving disasters. You'd think he'd have more scars."

"Yeah." I wasn't in a mood to trade quips. "Where's Caedan?"

Rick flicked his eyes back to his right. "He wanted some time alone."

I nodded. He'd grown closer to Peri more than any of us. They'd even known each other in Caesious when they'd both served the high priest.

Lovat shifted next to me and leaned against my side. I winced from the pain. Lainey opened her mouth to say something to him, but I shook my head and put my arm around the boy. I didn't think he and Peri had been very close, but it's never easy to lose someone you know, especially at that age. How old was Lovat now, anyway? Ten? Eleven? I tried to shield him from the worst parts of our lives, but he still saw more than a kid his age should ever see. Then again, he'd grown up on the streets of Viridia. He'd seen bad stuff from the moment he was old enough to understand. It was a wonder he still had any innocence remaining at all.

After a few moments of silence, Rick spoke up again. "Well, Auric dared you to stop him, and we did. What was that supposed to mean again?"

I snorted. "He said if I succeeded, he might tell me more 'truths' to broaden my perspective."

"So what? Are you going to report back to him?"

"Why would I do that?" At the same time, I did consider what it would mean. If I could gain another promise of safe travels to talk with the golden dragon again, maybe he would tell me something more worthwhile this time. I was tired of the hints, and books missing pages, and all the other mysteries.

"I say we head straight for Viridia," Rick suggested. "Where was that power source again?"

I let my head rest against the ground. Lovat wriggled a little beside me, agitating a few of my burns. "What would we do if we found it?" I asked.

"Destroy it! And then he'll be vulnerable. One more dragon down. Isn't that our goal?"

"Yeah." I glanced up as Caedan joined us. He sat down a few feet away, but said nothing.

Rick paced back and forth. "Maybe Auric wants you to do that. Maybe he wants all the other dragons out of the way, and all of The Circle just for him."

"We can't kill Viridia," I said, closing my eyes. "We don't have a weapon strong enough."

"If we destroy his source, it'll be like starving him," Rick argued. "He'll grow weaker and weaker."

"Yeah. We'll get there." His words bounced around inside my head, but I couldn't think clearly about them. All I could think about was Peri's face as he shoved me from the flatcar. And his last words.

I opened my eyes. "Caedan."

"Yeah?"

"Peri said to tell you…" I swallowed. "…that you were the best friend he could have ever hoped for."

Caedan didn't answer. I turned my head to see him, knees pulled up to his chest, arms folded over them, face hidden. I'd never seen him like this, even after we killed the dragon he'd been raised to worship.

"All I'm saying—" Rick began.

"Have you no heart?" Lainey snapped. "Your friends are exhausted, physically and emotionally. Your other friend died! Give them some time to rest and grieve." She shook her head in frustration. "And maybe do the same yourself."

"Sorry," Rick said. "It's just… it's my nature. Sorry guys." He walked away.

I closed my eyes again.

"You're not going to die too, are you?" Lovat whispered.

How could I answer that? "I'm going to do the best I can not to die," I told him. "And I'm pretty hard to kill, you know."

He nodded. I could feel his hair brushing against my burns. It wasn't pleasant, but after a minute or two, he grew still. I followed after him in sleep.

Caedan shook me awake a couple of hours later. "Just thought you should know: one of the red dragons checked out the, um, explosion site. It only circled a couple of times, then flew away. We couldn't tell which one it was from here."

I nodded, and sat up. Pain erupted across my body again, from the burns, but also from bruised muscles making their presence known. I groaned. "My life is pain."

"At least you're alive," Caedan said.

"Caedan…" I groaned. "Peri and I tried everything we could think of. He chose what happened. I tried to stop him."

He shook his head. "I know. Peri had a way of, of… getting his way. But it took a while for that part of him to come out."

"When he first showed up, he was just, you know, Mazarine's servant," I recalled.

"Once he grasped the idea that he didn't have to do everything the high priest said any more, it changed everything." Caedan chuckled. "You should have seen Mazarine's face the first time Peri told him no."

"I can imagine!" I laughed too. Even living out in the open like we did, the high priest had great difficulty losing his pompousness. Peri, on the other hand, shed his priestly ways almost as fast as he lost the robes.

"You'd been training him, right?" I asked.

Caedan shrugged. "Yeah. He wanted to learn, to find other ways to be useful to the cause. Besides, I needed the workouts too. You were gone, and Rick was busy…"

"I'm sorry, man. Our lives have been just… crazy."

"Yeah…" Caedan took a deep breath. "You know, when you first kidnapped me and introduced me to your… team or whatever, I thought you were crazy. But I stuck around because I was having fun. And then you killed Caesious, and it flipped my world."

"Caedan…"

He held up a hand. "Just wait. It took me a while to put it all together in my head, but once I did, I was fully on board with you. Kill the dragons. Free the humans. All of that. I want you to know that."

"I do. But thanks."

"Yeah. Except… I also woke you up to let you know I'm leaving."

"You're what?"

"I'm going back to Caesious. I need to find Peri's family, and tell them what happened."

"He had family?"

"Parents. A little sister. A few other relatives." Caedan looked away.

"Oh." I felt stupid. Why hadn't I ever gotten to know Peri well enough to know this information? I needed to do better. I made a mental note to talk with the other newer recruits about their families. I should probably start with Jaden.

"So I don't know how long I'll be gone," Caedan went on. "A couple of weeks, most likely. And who knows? Maybe I'll bring a whole group of blue-marked recruits for the team when I come back." He smiled, but it didn't look real.

I got to my feet, muscles protesting. Ignoring the pain, I gave Caedan a hug. "You'll be missed," I said. "Do what you have to do. Be safe. And come back." I swallowed. "I need you, man."

He nodded his head too many times, and sucked in his lower lip before looking away again. "Can't let Mazarine Chalybeous be the only representative from our city."

"I'm amazed you can still remember and pronounce his name."

Caedan snorted. He adjusted his backpack, waved to the others, and started walking.

"You don't want to take one of the four-wheelers?" I called.

He waved back. "You need them more than I do!"

"Come back soon, Caedan Teal!"

He waved one more time and kept walking. I watched him until a fold in the earth took him out of my sight.

Rick joined me. "You gonna be all right?"

"I have to be." I turned to see Lainey and Lovat watching. "Let's get back to the Asylum."

"I still think we should head straight for Viridia."

I held out my arms. "Can I at least get a change of clothes?"

He laughed. "Yeah. Yeah. I guess we've waited this long. Let's get things together back home. But then we're going after that dragon."

"I'm with you. Just… give me a little time, okay? We've lost a lot here." I glanced back in the direction Caedan walked.

"We also won, you know."

I sighed. "Then why doesn't it feel like it?"

Our return to the Achromatic Asylum the next day, without two of our company, created a lot of long faces. I gathered everyone else together and told them what happened. Kelly sobbed. Bice shook his head and mumbled some things to himself. Even Mazarine looked a little bit down. Dusk appeared the least moved, but she'd barely known Peri. And of course, I couldn't tell what emotions Protogonus Blue might be feeling.

Kelly went to Rick, and drew him into the cave. Maybe now she'd finally tell him her news. I hoped Rick wasn't an idiot about it. Don took Lovat somewhere. Lainey went off to be with her cat.

As for me, I wandered around the Asylum until I came, without thinking about it, to Peri's "room." I stared down at the makeshift bed, and the pillow made from his old priest robes. This was all he left behind. No, that wasn't true. He left behind a city of several hundred thousand people, alive today because of him.

"Beryl, will you be all right?"

I turned to face Bice, and I knew he could see the dampness in my eyes. Stupid cybernetic eyes. Why did they tear up so much? Why did they tear up at all? "Where is he, Bice? Tell me he's not gone forever."

Bice bowed his head for a moment. "I don't know. I don't know the answers. I only know what isn't true." He looked up and smiled through his own tears. "There are no chromatic hells where enemies of the dragons spend eternity. The dragons have no power beyond this life."

"Then who does?"

Bice stepped forward and put his hand on my shoulder. "Whoever it is, whatever gods there may be… when Peri's spirit appears before them, I only know this: he gave his life to save others. There is no greater love. I believe he will be judged on that, regardless of whatever else he did in this life."

I nodded. It was some comfort. But the not knowing made me sadder than I wanted to think about. I needed something else to distract me.

"Anything happen here while we were gone?"

"Nothing much. Kelly and Don returned. He and I have taken it on ourselves to do some walking patrols when the four-wheelers aren't here." He jogged in place a bit. "It's good exercise."

"Good thinking. We can't assume the patrols will stop. The green and black are still looking for us." I considered for a moment. "Nothing from the gold direction, I'm guessing?"

"Nothing that we've seen, anyway."

"Good. Mazarine cause any more trouble?"

Bice shook his head. "Nothing specific. I'm still watching him, though. Me and Pe—" He broke off. "I guess I need a new partner in that job too." He grimaced. "Now sit down and let me check your bandages."

"All right." I looked down at Peri's bed. "But… not here."

Bice understood. We found one of Don's crudely-built tables where Bice could check me over yet again. "Seems like you're always doing this," I observed. "I mean, you met me while I was in bandages."

"It's the least I can do." Bice removed some of my bandages, replacing them when needed. "Some of these burns probably destroyed nerve endings. Tell me: does this hurt?"

"Does what hurt?" I craned my neck to see what he was doing.

"That's what I thought. I was touching one of the wounds. You have no feeling there. In some ways, that's good. It keeps some of the pain away. But it could have long-term effects."

"Sometimes the pain shoots through me," I admitted. "Like electricity or something." I'd been trying to ignore those bursts when they happened, but it wasn't easy.

Bice nodded. "I've heard of severe burn victims experiencing that." He sighed. "Nothing much we can do about it here. Maybe your implant will help you deal with it. We just don't know how far it goes."

I sat up. "Yeah." I looked over some of my injuries. "At least I have skin and muscle to burn. I'm not completely cyb."

"No one said you were. You still eat and drink. I assume you produce waste." Bice chuckled. "You're human, Beryl. We've talked about this."

"I know. But since then, I've survived crashing into a mountain and being... blown up. It makes me question things, you know?"

"It's all right to question things. Just don't... don't let it cripple you. You're needed, Beryl. Your absence made that abundantly clear."

I hopped off the table. "Yeah, it's hard to think about that kind of thing too," I admitted. "I don't want to feel like everything depends on me."

"You've been thrust into this position," Bice said, looking me in the eyes. "I have to believe that's for a reason."

"Well, right now I need to thrust into bed." I closed my eyes. "Never mind. That sounded totally stupid."

Bice laughed, the biggest laugh I'd heard from him in... months, I guess. It was good to hear.

A few minutes later, I found a secluded spot and dozed off. I never seemed to be caught up on my sleep any more.

When I woke from the nap, Don stood beside me. "Hey," I greeted him as I stretched. "What's up?"

"Gold activity," he said. "At the fake headquarters."

I jerked to look at him. "What did you see?"

"Just movement. I didn't get close, since I was on foot and couldn't move fast if they saw me."

"All right. Let's get one of the four-wheelers and check it out."

I told Bice where we were going. At the four-wheeler, I remembered to check the fuel level. Good thing I did, since it was almost empty. As I filled it, I felt the absence of Peri and Caedan even more. They would have kept up with this. In fact, they would have checked over lots of details with the four-wheelers after the drive we took. The rest of us would have to step up with those jobs, if we wanted to keep these things running.

With Don behind me, I drove out toward the false base we'd created for Taizong Gold's visit. Why would Auric's forces be there? The draconic made it clear we hadn't fooled it. Were they looking for any clues we might have left behind to lead to our true location?

We saw no activity on our drive, so I took us to within a quarter mile from the false base. Don and I hiked the rest of the way. Without any large hills in this area, it would be hard for anyone to hide from us (one of the reasons we'd chosen it), but we saw no one. I climbed a tree and used my zoom vision in every direction. Nothing.

"Are you sure you saw them?" I asked, when I jumped down from the tree.

Don pointed at the gorge where the false base had been built. "They were right over there. I know it."

"They could be hiding inside, I guess." I frowned. Once again, actions from the gold city made no sense. This seemed to be a recurring theme. I could understand everything done by the other dragons, at least most of the time. They operated on obvious, very selfish motivations. But the gold dragon? I couldn't figure him out at all.

"All right. I'm going in. You stay back a bit," I told Don. "If you hear me yell, you hop on that four-wheeler and get out of here."

"Not without you."

I rolled my eyes. "If it's bad enough to stop me, then you can't help me on your own. Go get help and come back for me."

Don frowned, but gave a short nod.

I made my way down to the gorge. I considered tearing open the false roof and dropping in from above, but if there was a trap, that would put me right in the middle of it. Maybe not the best idea. Instead, I crept to the front entrance Don had built. It looked a lot like one of the entrances to the Asylum. From the direct point of view, it appeared as a cascade of dirt. Only when you moved in beside it could you see the openings leading into the hidden base.

I stopped beside the entrance, watching and listening. Still nothing. Why didn't I bring my sword? I picked up a large stick and gripped it like a club. It wasn't much of a weapon, but I felt a little more prepared for whatever I might find. I stepped into the base. A gleam of gold caught my eye and I swung the stick as hard as I could.

The stick shattered against one of the support beams for the roof. Nothing moved in response to my attack. No one yelled at me. The base was empty.

The gleam that caught my eye lay on the ground now. It appeared to be a golden tube. An empty pedestal showed where it had been sitting before my ferocious stick attack knocked it off.

I picked up the tube and found it sealed with a screw-off lid. I checked around the rest of the false base, including our fake "tunnel," but found nothing else to even indicate the presence of our visitors. I headed back out to Don.

"Nothing but this," I said, holding up the tube.

"What is it?"

I unscrewed the lid and removed it. Only then did it occur to me that it could be a trap of some kind. But nothing happened. I turned the tube up and a rolled piece of parchment slid out. I slid it back in and closed the tube.

"You aren't going to read it?"

"Not here," I said, glancing around. I couldn't shake the feeling we were being watched. "And we'll take a longer route home, just in case anyone's trying to follow us." Maybe I was being paranoid, but… like I said: I couldn't understand this dragon.

We took a circuitous drive back to the Asylum, making sure we traveled some wide open spaces to watch for followers, then zig-zagging through hills, skirting the edge of the Blasted Lands, and more. If anyone managed to follow us through all that, I'd love to know how they did it.

Once home, I did one last scan for pursuers, then took the tube straight to Bice. I set it on the table. "Looks like the gold dragon left us a message."

Bice took the parchment out and unrolled it. He brought one of our lanterns over for a better look. Rick and Kelly joined us. I explained the situation to them. While I talked, I tried to get some indication from their faces as to how their own conversation had gone. Kelly looked pleased, but I hadn't always been great at reading her emotions.

She moved behind Bice and looked over his shoulder. "Wow, that looks a lot like the message you created for Caesious," she observed.

"Yes," Bice said. "It's done in the same style, the ancient traditions of formal dragon communication."

"No virgin daughter, though," Rick pointed out. Kelly scowled at him.

"Read it, Bice," I said.

"To Beryl, once of Viridia, now seeking his own name," he read.

"Seeking my own name?"

"Shh. Let him read." Rick put a hand on my shoulder.

"'From Auric, first child of Chroma, creator of The Circle, and immortal god of gods. Greeting.'"

I snorted.

"'I find your choice most intriguing. Perhaps I did misjudge you. Or perhaps you are merely trying to impress me with what you believe I want to see. Regardless, you accomplished the task I set to you. Because of this, I will spare the city of Caesious. For now.'"

"For now?" Kelly exclaimed.

"'I am certain,'" Bice went on reading, "'that you are aware that your particular enhancements are of great interest to each of the gods. I confess that my advisors, on hearing of your capabilities, wanted only to capture you for study. But even were I so inclined, such action is no longer necessary.'"

A sick feeling rose into my mouth.

"'I possess spies within the other cities, as I'm sure each of them possess spies within mine. As it turns out, two of my fellow gods are on the verge of breakthroughs in cybernetic advancements with the brain. The one of greatest interest to you, I believe, is Viridia. In fact, both of these break-throughs seem to be happening because of notes each one of them obtained, notes that appear to be written by the very scientist who enhanced you. At least that is what my spy in Viridia believes, and I must agree.'"

I spun away, gagging, almost vomiting. They had Loden's notes? "How?" I screamed.

"Maybe… maybe Loden left some notes behind at his lab in the city," Rick suggested. "Not all of them, obviously, or they'd already have the discovery, not on the verge of it."

"That doesn't sound like Loden," Bice said.

I clenched my fists. No, it did not. Something was seriously wrong here.

Kelly put a hand on my shoulder. "Everyone makes mistakes, even Loden."

I shook my head. I didn't trust myself to answer.

"Is there more to the letter?" Rick asked.

"Yes," Bice answered. He resumed reading: "'Should you wish to investigate this for yourself, keep in mind the other bit of information I shared with you. I must admit: I am quite fascinated to see what you do with this information.' There's a long empty space in the letter here, and then: 'I will be in contact again at a later date.' That's all."

"I'm guessing the other bit of information is the location of Viridia's power source," Rick observed. "But I can't imagine how those two things connect."

I slammed my fist onto the table. "This is what we're going to do," I said through my teeth. A cold certainty had settled onto me. "We are going to Viridia. We will find one of these scientists. And we will get the truth about this out of him, no matter what it takes."

"Beryl—" Bice began.

"No! Don't tell me to take my time and think it over! This is Loden's greatest discovery we're talking about! I will not let them have it!" I threw a boost into my arm and slammed my fist down again, splintering the table. "You know what I can do. Do you want them enhancing the draconics this way? Or themselves? How powerful would a dragon be with the same power I have?" I shook my head as I straightened up. "No. No. We're putting an end to this now. Rick, are you with me?"

"You know I am. But we should investigate the power source too."

"We will. And then we find a way to finally put that green dragon down."

"Beryl!" Kelly snapped. "Auric is taunting you! He's playing on your biggest fears to manipulate you! Can't you see that?"

"I don't care." And I didn't. At this point, nothing they could say would change my mind. "Don, tell Lovat I need him for a mission. Rick, get a four-wheeler fueled and ready. And Kelly, I need something from you too."

"What now?" she asked, frustration in her voice.

"I need Mason Forest's address."

Her eyes widened a little, but she nodded. "Don't… don't hurt him, Beryl. He's still a human, caught up in all of this like we were."

"Then he won't mind telling me what I need to know." I stalked off to the workshop to find my sword and anything else we might need.

Dusk looked up from her studies as I stormed in. "What's going on?"

"You can stop looking for Loden's notes about me," I snarled. "Apparently, the dragons have them."

Her mouth fell open, but she said nothing.

Bice caught up with me. "Beryl, you will listen to me! No one here knew Loden better than I did. This does not make any sense!"

"So what? You think the gold dragon is making stuff up just to mess with me?"

"I don't know! But I also know—I know!—that Loden wouldn't have left behind any notes about you in Viridia! He wouldn't do that!"

"Then how would they have his notes?"

"We don't know that they do!" Bice stopped and took a breath. "All we have is the word of Auric, and you've said yourself that he doesn't seem to make any sense. How does he even know about Loden? Kelly's right. He's trying to manipulate you."

"Then it's working." I found my sword and strapped it on. I looked around the workshop. "Have you found anything else that can help us kill a dragon?" I demanded from Dusk.

"Um, uh, no. Nothing like that. I—"

"Then what good are you?" I stomped out of the workshop with Bice still in pursuit.

"Beryl, take it easy. You—"

I whirled back around and Bice stumbled to a stop. We were alone in the cave. "Listen to me," I hissed in a low voice. "There are only three possibilities here. Think about it. One is that Loden left some notes behind, which is not like him at all. You're right. The second is that the gold dragon is lying. But how would he even know to make up this lie? I never told him about Loden." I stopped, taking in a series of rapid breaths. "And the third possibility… someone took Loden's notes and gave them to our enemies. You want to know why I'm so angry, Bice? This is why. We have a traitor."

38

I looked back down the tunnel toward the workshop. "My primary suspect is Miss Glasses back there. Has she left the Asylum at all since she arrived?"

Bice glanced back. "No, not that I know of. No. Definitely not long enough to travel to one of the cities and back."

"If not her, then who? I can't—" I stopped and gathered control over myself again. "You're suspicious of Mazarine. But he's never been allowed in here, right?"

"No, never. Even when you were gone and he was supporting Rick's attacks."

"What about the draconic?"

"Blue? I can't imagine him doing something—"

"Has it been back here, Bice?"

"No. Never."

I slammed my fist against the rock wall, not caring about the pain. "The only people left are the ones I love and trust!"

"Maybe we don't have a traitor. We don't know—"

"I just listed the possibilities!" I interrupted him. "Which one makes the most sense?"

His shoulders slumped. "None of them do. Look, Beryl, just because something looks like a logic puzzle, doesn't mean it is a logic puzzle."

"What? What does that even mean?"

"You said there are only three possibilities." He held up three fingers. "But that's based solely on your viewpoint and opinions. There's a distinct possibility that you may just be wrong."

"Then give me another possibility," I pleaded. "Tell me I'm wrong."

"I know this is hard to hear." Bice spoke the next sentence one word at a time: "Sometimes, we just don't know."

"Then I'm going to Viridia to find out." I walked the rest of the way out of the tunnel. Lainey met us, rifle in hand. "No, you're not going!" I snapped. In that moment, I realized: Lainey had been in the workshop. What did I really know about her?

"Oh?" she said. "Then you have another way to see whether the dragon is in his lair or not?"

"What do you mean?"

Glacier bounded up next to Lainey and came to a sudden stop. Her saber teeth were already becoming more distinct from the rest. How long before that thing became dangerous?

"I know a spot on the mountain nearest Viridia," Lainey explained. "From there, with binoculars, I can see into the dragon's building."

"The Emerald Ascendancy?"

She shrugged. "Whatever you call it. The ledge lets me see into it. Give me one of your 'talkers,' and I can keep you updated on its movements."

I couldn't argue with that, even if I didn't know if I could trust her. "All right. We'll circle around to the back of the city and drop you off." I called to Rick: "Change of plans! We'll take both four-wheelers."

"At least you can listen to some advice," Bice grumbled.

"I'm not a complete idiot, old man. We're doing this, but we'll do it as smart as we can."

Lainey headed toward the four-wheelers. Bice stood nearby, unsure whether to keep trying to talk to me or not. Kelly came up and handed me a note. "Here's Mason's address. Be careful, Beryl."

I nodded and stepped closer. Putting my anger aside for the moment, I whispered, "Did you tell him?"

Kelly's face brightened. "I did. And… he's happy, Beryl. He seemed really excited!"

"Well, there's some good news, at least." I glanced toward the four-wheelers. "Stay safe, Kelly. I'm sure the two of you will have a lot more to discuss once we get back."

I made sure we had a pair of talkers. Lovat insisted on riding with me, so Lainey climbed on behind Rick. I watched in amusement as she positioned Glacier on a flat surface behind her. She put a couple of straps over the cub to hold her in place while she yowled in complaint. "I don't see why the cat needs to come along," Rick grumbled.

"Because I'll be up in the mountain alone, and I want company," Lainey answered, getting back into position. "Let's go!"

I took hold of the four-wheeler's controls and felt the loss of Caedan again. He'd be back; I had no doubt about it. But in the meantime, we would have to make do.

Driving through the lands of The Circle with the wind in my face helped cool me down somewhat. I knew we would have to take a circuitous route all the way around Viridia to drop Lainey off near the mountains. Then we could move in from that side of the city. I'd shown Mason's address to Lovat, and he knew he could find it. When it came to the streets of Viridia, no one understood them like Lovat.

Rick called for a stop only a couple of miles out. He got on the talker and walked off by himself. "Said he forgot to tell Kelly something," Lainey explained. We waited until he finished, then set out again.

I knew the location of the green dragon's power source. Rick seemed to think we could destroy it, or something. I liked the idea of it, but wasn't sure of the practicality. We didn't know how big the actual power source was, how to destroy it, or what destroying it would do, exactly. All the same, we could check it out, and if the opportunity presented itself, we would take it. Anything that helped bring down the green dragon was good news to me.

But before that, we needed to deal with two other problems, and both of them were probably at the Emerald Ascendancy. We'd gotten in there once, but as part of one of the public tours. Stacy said those weren't happening and security had been cranked up. I didn't know how we could get in now. I had one vague idea, but again: the practicality might not work out.

First, we needed to find out more about what might be happening with the body of Troilus Green. And second, find out how much the Viridian scientists knew about my implant... and where they got the information. The more I thought about it, the more dread gnawed at me. If someone had given them Loden's notes, and those notes came from his workshop in the Asylum, it could only be one of our core team. The only people who'd had access to the workshop were Bice, Rick, Kelly, Don, Lovat, and Caedan. I couldn't imagine any of them betraying us like that. And Lainey. But she'd only been inside a few moments. Surely she couldn't have found the notes just like that, could she?

And now we also had Dusk. Rick vouched for her, but I didn't know her. How would she have done it, though? First, she would have had to find the notes, something Bice failed to do for weeks. Then, she would have had to get them to the city, but according to Bice, she hadn't left the Asylum. Could she be working with someone else? Mazarine? But he never left, either. While I drove, I concocted multiple schemes of ways Dusk could have transported the notes. Maybe she had a Viridian Guard ally, who hid somewhere near our base, waiting for her to bring him information. Maybe she even used something like the self-inflating balloon we'd used to get the Books of Lore from the Flame. Maybe she used the rail lines somehow. The schemes grew more and more outlandish the longer I tried to imagine them.

But what other answer could there be? Loden left notes behind in Viridia? I couldn't fathom that. Loden wasn't that stupid. Could the gold dragon have made it all up? How? Why?

Nothing made sense.

After a while, Lovat started asking me questions, diverting my attention from the seriousness of our situation. He asked lots of questions about what I could do, how high I could jump, what it felt like, and so on. Once he tired of that subject, he moved on to anything else he could think of. He said Lainey wasn't an orphan since she had a father, but how could she not have a chromark? I tried to explain what little I knew, but it didn't help.

"How big will Glacier get?" he wanted to know. I glanced at the other four-wheeler. The cub was already more than twice the size she'd been when Lainey adopted her.

"Bigger than you," I said. "Maybe bigger than me."

"Then she can help us fight the dragons," Lovat concluded.

I couldn't argue with that.

Rick signaled another halt. "We've seen patrols in this area a lot lately," he explained when I pulled up beside him. "We'll need to take it slow and scan around every once in a while." He pointed at his eyes and then me.

I nodded and turned away. With a thought, I sent a boost to my cybernetic eyes and zoomed in on the landscape ahead of us. I looked back and forth, scanning in every direction, as far as I can see. "No movement," I reported. I was about to return my eyes to normal, when I glanced up in the sky. A dark shape moved against the clouds.

"Dragon!"

39

"Which one?" Rick yelled, staring up in the same direction I watched.

"Can't tell yet, but does it matter? Let's get out of sight!"

Lainey pointed to some trees, three half-dead-looking firs. They weren't much, but at least we wouldn't be moving spots out in the open. We raced the four-wheelers there and parked right up next to the trees. We all scrambled off and did what we could to hide ourselves. With a nudge from me, Lovat climbed up onto the first big branch of one of the trees. The rest of us stayed close to their trunks and watched the skies.

I zoomed in on the spot where I'd seen it. After a few moments of scanning, I located it again. "It's the black dragon," I reported.

"Atramentous? Out here? That's strange." Rick squinted, trying to see it for himself.

"He's allies with the green dragon, so it's not so strange to me," I said.

"Yeah, but… none of the dragons leave the cities very much lately. Besides…" He turned to look at Lainey. "Didn't you say the black dragon fought with Incarnadine?"

"Black and red fought, yes. It was crazy!"

I looked again at the flying dragon. Now that I could pay attention, I noticed some oddities about his flight. He looked a little wobbly from time to time. I told the others.

Rick nodded. "He's stretching his wings, testing them after getting injured in the fight. He probably feels safe enough out here closer to Viridia, and far away from the red cities."

I continued to watch the dragon. "Too bad we couldn't take advantage of their injuries somehow."

"If we keep the war going, they'll end up hurting each other more," Rick predicted. "That's when we move."

"Sure." But how? We still didn't have anything that could even hurt a dragon. But they did. A crazy thought popped into my head. What if we could get one of those explosive devices from Auric? Even a dragon wouldn't be able to survive one of those. But obtaining one, and delivering it to a dragon might be even crazier than trying to kill a dragon without it.

"Still there?" Lainey asked.

"It's moving away," I said. "I think it'll be out of range in a few minutes." Sure enough, the dragon flew on toward the southwest. It seemed to shimmer and vanish as it reached the range of my vision. I blinked to get my vision back to normal. The angle of the sun created weird lighting while zooming. It took me a moment to clear my eyes. Only then did we climb back on the four-wheelers and continue on our way.

Nothing else of interest happened the rest of the day. We camped in an abandoned barn we'd used before. The only complaints about the accommodations came from Glacier, but Lainey quieted her before it became annoying.

The next morning, we set out soon after sunrise. Soon after, we entered lands I didn't recognize. I'd never circled around the east side of Viridia to come in from the southeast. Rick knew the way, and it wasn't hard to keep the city on our right. As the day lengthened, we had to slow down and watch our path a lot more. We crossed areas where people traveled. Viridia possessed an extensive number of mines at the foot of the mountains, where Don had once worked. A major road connected the city to the mines. I had to scan both directions with care before we dared cross it.

Once past the road, we picked up speed. Now we covered territory where few people, if anyone, ever wandered. This area, a narrow strip of land between the city of Viridia and the mountains, was too uneven and rocky for agriculture. At Lainey's instruction, we veered off and moved even closer to the mountains. Eventually, we reached a spot where the four-wheelers could no longer travel. Lainey hopped off and set Glacier on the ground.

"Is the range going to be all right?" she asked, holding up the talker.

I looked up at the mountain, then back toward the city. With a quick zoom, I could see the city itself. The sun had almost disappeared, but the lights of the city gleamed clear. "I don't think it's over three miles," I said. "We might have a weak connection, but I hope it works. I'll try to contact you just before we enter the city." I looked around. "In fact, we should just leave one of the four-wheelers here. It'll be easier to hide one instead of two."

"All right." She started hiking up. After a moment's hesitation, Glacier bounded after her.

"You sure you don't want to wait until the morning?" I called.

"No, thanks. I'll be good." She kept going.

Rick shook his head. "I can't figure that one out sometimes," he observed. "All business one minute, and emotional female the next."

"She's unique," I said. "Like all us humans."

"I like her!" Lovat chimed in.

Rick got off his four-wheeler and looked up again. "We won't be able to drive much longer," he said. "This close to the city, we don't dare use the headlights. Maybe we should leave both vehicles here and hike it."

I considered the suggestion. It would only take us about an hour to reach the city if we kept up a good pace. Mason should be arriving home any time now, if I guessed right at his work schedule.

"What about rest tonight? Are we going to sleep in Mason's apartment?"

"Why not?" Rick shrugged. "It'll keep him from running to the Guard."

I laughed. We'd come a long way from the beginning of all this. Back then, I'd met Mason in a diner, with Kelly there to persuade him. Now we'd be kicking in his door and making him help us. Well, maybe not kicking in the door. We might need to shut it again.

We ate the last of the food we'd brought along. After this, we'd need to snag something in the city. Lovat, I knew, was a champion at that particular skill.

By the time we reached the edge of Viridia, the sun had vanished behind the mountains. I checked in with Lainey and was pleased to discover the talkers worked well enough. She'd found a spot to spend the night about halfway to her intended perch. She sounded cheerful, I guess. We agreed to check on each other in the morning and signed off.

Lovat took the lead. We followed him through numerous back alleys, squeezing through gaps between buildings, crossing larger streets in the darkest spots, and steadily making our way to our destination. It proved much more difficult than a few months ago. The Viridian Guard patrolled the streets in regular patterns.

I will admit, I felt a touch of envy when we arrived at Mason's apartment complex. Working for the dragon himself paid well. I'd already known that, of course, but it still annoyed me. No one I knew ever lived this well. Except maybe Loden, I suppose. Or Stacy. How much did actors get paid, anyway?

To my surprise, Mason's apartment was on the second floor. I'd expected the first. Rick looked up and down the hallway, then wrenched the door handle open with his cyb hand. The three of us entered the apartment and closed the door behind us.

I told Lovat to stay by the door and led the way into Mason's living room. "Nice place," Rick observed. "Where's the geek?"

At he said it, Mason walked out of the bathroom, zipping up his pants. The skinny scientist looked up and saw us through his huge glasses. "Hey, what—aw, no! Not you guys again!"

Rick grinned and flexed his hands. "Yep, it's us again." He took a threatening step toward Mason.

The scientist held up both hands and stepped back. "Come on, what do you want from me now? I can't help you get into the Ascendancy again! They've locked everything down!" He stole a glance toward his bedroom.

I boosted my legs and jumped across the room between him and the bedroom door. "Mostly, we want information," I told him. "But things are different now. You're right about that." I gestured at Rick. "For one thing, we're a lot more desperate."

"And we don't care much about people in our way," Rick added, losing the grin.

To emphasize the point, I drew my sword. Mason's eyes grew even larger behind his glasses. He stumbled over to his couch and sat down hard. "Wh-what do you want to know? My clearance isn't very high, so I, I don't know a whole lot."

Rick took hold of a fancy lamp with his cyb hand and squeezed. It crumpled under his grip. "Now see, Mason, I don't think that's true. I think you're selling yourself short."

I moved behind the couch. "For starters, tell us what they're doing with the body of Troilus Green," I ordered.

"The body?"

"Yes, the body. Its remains."

"Oh, you think it's dead?"

I froze. I must have heard him wrong. "What did you say?"

He glanced nervously back at me. "You think Troilus Green is dead?"

I lowered my sword onto the couch where Mason could see it. "I put this sword down its throat," I said, emphasizing each word. "I'm pretty sure it was dead."

"That was you?" How big could his eyes get, anyway?

"If you don't want him to demonstrate how he did it, tell us what we want to know," Rick warned.

"Okay, okay." He fiddled with his hands like he didn't know what to do with them. "Draconics are extraordinarily hard to kill, especially one like Troilus Green, who'd had so much cybernetic augmentation."

"Go on."

"They brought it back to us. I don't know how that worked. But it isn't dead. Not completely, anyway." He shrugged a couple of times, or it might have just been a nervous twitch. "It looks dead, at least to most people. But the top guys seem pretty sure they'll be able to revive it, given enough time."

So all of Protogonus Blue's nonsense about Viridia merging with the draconic's mind turned out to be pointless, anyway. He wouldn't have to. He just had to wait until his "child" woke up. Unbelievable. Cold anger flooded through my veins again. I looked up and saw Lovat watching me from the door. It's a good thing he was there watching, I told myself. Otherwise, I don't know what I would have done. I might have crossed some lines.

"Guess you should have made sure it was dead," Rick said.

I scowled at him. After stabbing it, I had left the body in the train that crashed into Caesious. How much more sure could I get?

"Y-you're not going to be able to get to it," Mason stuttered. "I'm not even allowed anywhere near the level where the draconics work. Even if I got you into my section, you couldn't get there."

"We'll talk about that later," I growled. "We want more information. How much do you know about the cybernetic research in the Ascendancy?"

"Well, like I told you before, I'm just a low level tech worker. I'm not privy to the advanced stuff." Mason seemed to be getting a little bolder.

I spotted a display shelf on the wall with some Dragon Action toys posed on it. "Oh, here's your collection," I said, walking over to it. I picked up a Viridian Guard figure. "Is this one valuable?"

"Oh, come on," Mason pleaded. "I'll tell you whatever I can!"

"Then do it," Rick said.

"All right, all right. I know this much: the cyberneticists are giddy right now. They're on the verge of a major breakthrough of some kind."

"What kind of breakthrough?" I put the figure back on the shelf.

"I don't know exactly. Something to do with the brain itself, I heard." His face brightened behind his glasses. "Can you imagine what that would mean? I mean, the implications are incredible!"

"No," I said, looking at Rick with a straight face. "Walk us through it."

"Well, I mean, the brain has enormous potential. It controls everything else in the body, right?" Mason's whole body moved when he talked while excited. I almost thought he might be having a seizure of some kind. "Up until now, our cyb enhancements have been replacing body parts, like um, your friend's hand there. Some of the draconics have some better stuff. They tell me it's totally hue, but aren't very specific on the details. I'm thinking internal organs.

"But the brain, now! That's a game changer! If it's done right, then it can almost act like the entire body is cyb!"

"How so?" Rick asked.

"The brain can basically convince the other body parts they can do almost anything. If done right, a cyb implant in the brain could make someone stronger and faster than anyone else… and probably more! I mean, subject to the limits the human body is capable of, of course."

"And what would this mean to the dragon?" I asked, trying to keep my voice level.

Mason waved his hands even further. "How do you take an immortal god and make it even more immortal and powerful? I don't know, but this would be it!"

I came back and leaned in close to Mason. "This is the most important question." I looked him in the eyes. "Where did the techs get the notes for this breakthrough?"

"Notes?"

I slammed my sword down through the couch cushion. "Who gave them the information for this?"

"I don't know what you mean!" He stared at the blade piercing his couch.

I yanked the sword out and went back to the shelf. "Oh, look. You've got figures from the other cities here. That one's out of date." I pointed at an Aurelian Sentinel. "Their armor is much more streamlined. Now this one…" I picked up a Cerulean Corps figure.

Mason whimpered. "I'm telling you all I know!"

I held up the blue action figure. "This one is probably going up in value, what with the death of Caesious."

"No, come on! I don't know where the information came from! I thought they discovered it on their own!"

"So you never heard about some notes from an unusual source? A spy report, maybe?" I wiggled the figure back and forth. It reminded me of Caedan.

"They don't tell me where the discoveries come from!" Mason reached out a hand toward the figure. "I don't know anything about spies. You'd have to talk to someone from the Guard or something!"

"Or something…" Rick tapped his fingers against the wall in sequence. "Other than the Viridian Guard, Mason, who would be the most likely to know the answers to our questions?"

"Um, well, I guess one of the higher level techs."

"Great. Where can we find one?"

"In the Emerald Ascendancy."

I wiggled the figure again. "Don't get smart with me now, Mason. Does one of them live in this building, maybe?"

"No! I mean… they used to. But they're locked down now. All the high level people are being kept in the Ascendancy." He glanced back and forth between us. "You have to believe me! They aren't allowed to come home any more. They have quarters on the same floor as their labs."

I looked at Rick. "I suppose that might be true."

"He doesn't have a lot of reasons to lie. Do you, Mason?"

"No! Why would I lie to you? I don't even know what you guys are doing!" He waved at me. "He's got a bleaking sword, for the love of Viridia! Who has a sword?"

"I do," I said. "And it's more fun than your toys." Although I had to admit, this figure was pretty cool. He even had a baton, like Caedan used. And was that a projectile weapon on his belt? I lifted the figure's arm to look closer. And the entire torso fell off.

"Aw, man!" Mason jumped off the couch. "The o-ring broke!"

"O-ring?"

He scrambled to pick up the fallen half of the figure. "The little rubber band that holds the figure together. Sometimes they break."

I looked at Rick and he shook his head in disgust. "I think we're done here," he said.

Mason looked up from the floor. "You're leaving?"

"Nope. Just going to get ready for bed. Rick, do you want the couch?"

"I don't know. Let me check out the bedroom." Rick wandered down the hall.

"You're staying here?" The last word from Mason was almost a screech.

"Just for the night. We need sleep too, you know."

Rick came back. "On second thought, Mason should sleep comfortably in his own bed tonight. That way, he won't be tempted to sneak out and report us."

Mason got to his feet and set the broken figure pieces on the shelf. He seemed to gather himself, then turned back to face us. "Look, whatever you guys are mixed up in, I'm not a part of it, okay? I haven't told you anything you couldn't find out by talking to anyone else. Fine. You want to sleep here? Go right ahead." He hurried toward his bedroom.

"Good talk," I called. "If we think of any more questions, we'll ask in the morning."

Rick shook his head. "I've tried to get info out of lots of different people over the past few years, but I've got to admit: I've never done it by threatening a guy's toys before."

"Action figures," I corrected him. "Hey Lovat, come here and check these out."

While Lovat looked over the action figures, we discussed our next move.

"By all accounts, we can't get into the Ascendancy," I said. "Unless…"

"Unless what?"

"Remember the tunnel I followed out of the dragon's lair? If Viridia's not at home, we could follow it, and maybe get into the Ascendancy from there."

"From the spot where you found all the trees and stuff?"

"Yeah." I smiled. "And that spot? That's the green dragon's power source."

41

Rick blinked. "The trees?"

"That spot. Remember the whole thing about opposition?"

"And since Viridia's power involves poison…"

"…His power source is a place overflowing with life."

Rick sat down on the couch with a plop. "Why didn't I see that before? It's so obvious!"

"It's been staring us in the face our whole lives," I said, pointing toward a window. "Everything in Viridia is covered in concrete. I always thought it was because the dragon had no sense of style. But it's actually because without it, the plant life would run wild here."

Rick started laughing.

"What?"

He pointed at me. "Remember our first base? In that old church?"

"Yeah?"

"You! You kept trying to fix the toilet." Rick kept laughing. "And found it was clogged up with roots!"

Holy—well, I didn't think much of anything was holy any more, but… wow. Even the stupid toilet problem had been a clue to the reality of Viridia. How messed up was that?

Speaking of toilets, I needed to use one. And what a luxury that was, after living in the Asylum for so long!

"Let's get some sleep," I suggested, coming back into the living room. "We're going to have a busy day tomorrow."

"No matter what happens, it's going to be crazy." Rick paused. "Beryl… thanks."

"For what?"

"For letting me be a part of all this. No matter what happens tomorrow, I want you to know that. I appreciate it."

I shrugged. "We're friends. What are friends for, if not trying to overthrow ancient dragon gods?"

Rick chuckled again and stretched out on the couch. "One of us should probably sleep near the door," he pointed out. "Sorry you missed out on the couch."

"Ouch. So much for friendship."

"Hey, you can have the couch in the next geek we question."

Lovat curled up in an easy chair. I yanked a pillow away from Rick on the couch and positioned myself on the floor blocking the exit. Even without anything else, it was still more comfortable than how I'd been living the last few months. Sleep came soon, despite all my anxieties.

I woke once during the night to discover that one of Mason's toys lit up. I think it was a Viridian Guard truck. I pulled my shirt off and tossed it over the light to hide it, then went back to sleep.

Mason stumbled into the bathroom before dawn. How early did he go to work, anyway? His noise woke Lovat and me. Rick slept on. I considered throwing a pillow at him, but decided to leave him alone this time.

Now that it came to it, I had to admit I wasn't in a hurry. If our plan worked, we'd be entering the dragon's lair. The last time I did that, I barely survived. We could hurry through, and I was confident Rick and I could open that crazy door which led back into the Ascendancy, but… it wouldn't be pleasant. We would need to leave Lovat behind. Maybe I could send him to join Lainey.

Rick woke before too long, and we readied ourselves while Mason went through his morning routine. By the time he was ready to leave, so were we.

"You probably won't see us again," I told him. "But then again, that's what I thought the last time."

"But don't forget," Rick added, "if you tell anyone about us, they'll assume you gave us information and you'll be in big trouble with the draconics."

"As if my life isn't crazy enough," Mason grumbled. He opened his front door, then stared at the handle. "What did you guys do to my door? I'll have to get this handle replaced!"

"Sorry. I'd pay you if I had anything."

He shook his head and set off down the hall. I looked at Rick and Lovat. "Ready?"

"I've been waiting for this a long time," Rick said. "Let's get moving!"

"Right." I turned to Lovat. "Do you remember where you found me when I was sick, and had the dragon's tooth?"

"Sure."

"That's where we need to go."

"Hue." He set off without waiting to see if we followed. Rick and I scrambled to keep up.

Moving without being seen in the early morning proved to be substantially more difficult than at night. In retrospect, we should have left before dawn. Actually, in retrospect… well, a lot of things look different when you look back at them. So many choices shape our lives.

What if I'd never met with the gold dragon? What if I'd stopped Peri and still saved Caesious? What if Caedan had been with us on this trip? Or I'd brought someone else along, like Don, or even Kelly? So many choices, so many paths we travel… The "what ifs" extended all the way back to that day I first met Rick and everything started. I guess my mind went in this direction since Lovat had to stop repeatedly and decide to go left or right, based on our destination and the current foot traffic in the city. More than once, we almost ran into people, just like I'd run into Rick that day.

After about an hour, Lovat stopped in a particularly dark alley. "You was here," he informed me, pointing at a filthy spot on the ground. Beautiful.

"All right." I walked to the end of the alley and looked out. I could see the edge of the city off to the right. "This way."

We left the city. The openness of the ground made me nervous. I kept glancing back at the city, expecting to see a Viridian Guard patrol pursuing us. But none showed up.

"How far?" Rick asked.

I pointed ahead. "I think about two miles." I used my zoom vision and spotted the dark green on the horizon. "Yeah, looks about right." I returned my vision to normal and looked around. "We're moving closer to the mountains, but maybe off to the south…west of where Lainey's hiding. Let's check on her."

"Good morning," Lainey answered when I tried the talker. "Get any sleep?"

"Can't complain," I said. "You?"

"Glacier and I are fine. The green dragon is busy this morning."

"Oh?" I perked up and glanced at Rick.

"Yeah. Hang on. Let me look again." I heard some rustling and a growl from Glacier. "Yeah, he's inside the big building, but not going down into the lair."

"Huh. That's different."

"He's been sitting in one spot since the sun rose," she said. "He seems really focused on something inside the building. I think he's watching people do stuff."

I had an idea what that meant, and didn't like it. "Okay, let us know if he changes."

"Sure thing. Where are you now?"

"We're southwest of you, out in the open, heading toward the dragon's power source. You might be able to see it from there. There's a lot of trees."

"Oh?" I heard her moving around again. "Let me see… Oh. Yeah, I see it. Can't see you, though. These binoculars aren't that powerful."

"Close enough. Talk to you after we're there."

"Okay."

We signed off. I noticed Rick had moved quite a few paces ahead, and I jogged a little to catch up. Lovat, meanwhile, wandered all over the place, as he usually did. Without an alley, the boy never could walk in a straight line.

"What's your hurry?" I asked Rick when I caught up to him.

"Just anxious to get this done. What did Lainey have to say?"

I filled him in. In under an hour, with the morning sun rising higher, we climbed the hill that led to our destination. I double-checked with Lainey again to make sure the dragon hadn't moved.

As we crested the hill, I marveled again at the enormous trees. Though we'd gotten used to seeing trees out in the open, nothing compared to these. The height, the beauty of the bright green growth… I'd been half-dead with poison the last time and been in awe. Now… awe didn't even begin to cover it.

This was the opposition power to the green dragon's poison, no question about it. Life, green life, shone from everything in sight: grass, ferns, bushes, weeds, and the trees themselves. We wandered through the beauty for a few minutes, silent in our wonder. I wanted to stay here forever.

"Can we move the Asylum here?" Lovat spoke my own thoughts.

"Maybe after everything's over," I said. Wouldn't that be something? To set up our home in the middle of the dragon's power source?

A moment later, we spotted the gaping cave entrance leading down into the dragon's lair. Though the cave itself provided a dark blotch amidst the green, I could see how the green persisted, trying to grow down into it. Vines and branches reached in toward the darkness, and tons of their remains lay trodden on the ground, crushed by the dragon's passage.

I'd returned to the one place I'd felt the most peace in my entire life.

And then my entire life fell completely apart.

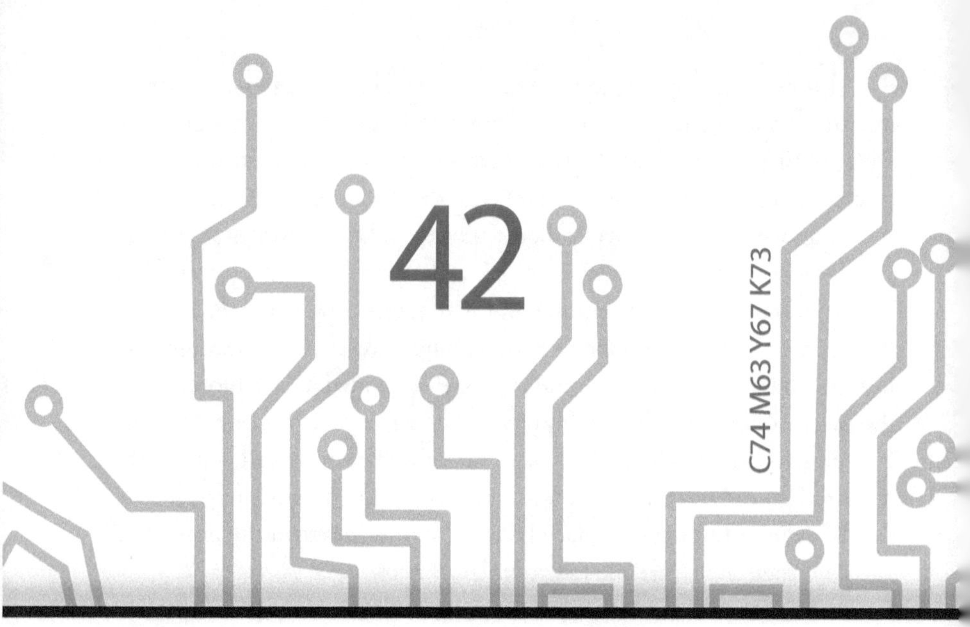

42

"I despaired of this day ever happening," Rick said in an odd voice.

I looked over at him. "What do you mean?"

He let his backpack slip off and fall into the dirt. He fell to his knees and pulled off his gloves. He thrust his left hand into the dirt, digging in with his fingers. "I've waited for so, so long." He closed his eyes and his head went back, as if in ecstasy. "The source… it's all I needed…"

Out of the corner of my eye, I noticed Lovat climbing one of the trees. I'm amazed he found a branch low enough to get hold, but he was already about six feet in the air.

"Rick? What's going on?" I stepped toward him and pointed at the cavern. "That's the way to the lair. The green dragon is out. Let's find the door into the Ascendancy. Come on."

He lowered his head, inhaling deep. "Oh, Beryl, my friend. If you only knew. There's so much I could tell you now. This is where it all ends. Or rather, begins."

"If I only knew what?"

"Where do I start?" He pulled his hand out of the dirt, and unzipped his backpack. "Let's begin here." He removed a stack of papers and held them out to me. "Oh, and you'll need the other stuff in this pack too." He tossed it on the ground by my feet.

I took the papers and looked over them. It took me a moment. "These are the missing pages from the Book of Lore!"

"Yes," Rick said, thrusting both hands down into the dirt now. He seemed to be trying to get them as deep as possible. "I tore them out when I was bringing the books back to the Asylum. Bice might never have figured out enough from them, but I needed to be sure. And anyway, they're pure propaganda. That's not exactly how it happened."

I flipped the pages over, and saw a lot about the dragons and the destruction of the rebellious city… and my eyes stopped on one sentence: "We had to do it. The loss of the city was regrettable, but our brother had to be stopped." Brother?

"What does this mean?" My hand shook. To keep from dropping the pages, I picked up Rick's pack and stuffed them back into it.

Rick gazed at me with such a strange look. I could read immense pride and delight… but also sadness in those ancient-looking eyes of his. A cold chill ran over me.

"Trusting me was the best thing you could have done, Beryl, to accomplish your goals," he said very slowly. "But trusting me was also the worst thing you could have done over all. Our goals overlapped, yes. But mine went so much further."

"I don't understand." I glanced up at Lovat, who stared down at us from the tree, eyes growing wide.

"Get mad at me."

"What?"

"There's something you always do when you're mad at me, and I want to hear it."

"What are you talking about?"

He rolled his eyes. "Fine. I'll make you mad at me. You want the truth about Loden's notes? I took them."

"What?" This could not be happening.

"I took Loden's notes. The ones about you and your implants. Fascinating reading, even if I don't understand all the jargon." Rick dug his hands deeper into the earth.

"Where are they? How could you—"

"When I let myself get captured, I gave some of them to the Viridian Guard. Then I had to let myself get captured by the Crimson Elite, so I could give them some too. Couldn't let one side have all the info, you know."

My brain refused to grasp this. Rick, my best friend, was telling me he'd betrayed us. I could not accept it. I couldn't.

"No? That didn't make you angry enough? Do I need to talk about Kelly?"

"Shut up, Onyx. Just… shut up." I wanted to clench my fists. I wanted to rant and scream. But I still couldn't believe it.

"There it is…" Rick breathed. He shook his head with a smile. "All these months. You've called me that so many times. I really appreciated that. It made me feel almost… normal." He paused. "I've gotten so used to being Richard Onyx for so long, I almost forgot what it was like… to be me."

Something painful settled in the pit of my stomach. A tremble ran down my shoulders to my hands. He couldn't possibly mean the horrible thing that popped into my head at his words. It couldn't be.

Rick pulled a handful of dirt up in front of his face, still smiling. "I've waited so very, very long for this moment. You can't even imagine. All these years. So many attempts." He waved at the trees. "I suspected when you told me about this place, you know. It had to be Viridia's source, right? What else could it be? But I couldn't come then. Your friend Loden had such a beautiful plan and we needed to see it through. After that… I'll admit we got kind of busy, and you never did tell me where this place was."

"Why? Why did you want to find this spot?" I thought I already knew, but I couldn't accept it.

He plunged his hand back down into the dirt. "Ahhhh. There it is." Again, the look of ecstasy filled his face. "I tried so hard in Atramentous, you know. It was the one city I could move around in freely at first, thanks to this stupid mark. I actually went to some of the other cities and then back again. Each time, I got close… but never close enough. Then I came to Viridia. And then…" He looked at me. "Then there was Beryl. And you changed everything."

I leaped back as black flame erupted from the ground right in front of me, and all around Rick in a circle. The tongues of fire swirled around each other, forming an orb around him. I could just make him out through it all. I had seen this same effect a few days ago… except it had been gold then.

The talker squawked at me from the back of my belt. Lainey's voice came through: "Something's happening! The dragon just dove down into his lair!"

Rick grew, his body growing larger by the second. And with each iteration of growth, he tore at the ground with larger hands… hands that transformed into claws, one real and one cybernetic. The orb of black fire grew too, forcing me further back. Lovat scrambled down out of the tree and ran to my side. Together, we moved backward, our eyes transfixed by Rick's transformation. Lovat held me tight. I kept one hand around him and held on to Rick's backpack with the other.

"Beryl!" Lainey's voice shouted. "Did you hear me? The dragon is coming!"

Rick's face elongated. His mouth split open into jaws lined with horrible teeth. Glowing liquid spilled out of his mouth, flowing to the ground and eating into it. His eyes… he looked through the black flames at me, and his eyes looked the same as they always did. I'd always had the vague impression that Rick's eyes looked older than he did. I just… never thought they were a thousand years old.

Black scales rippled across every inch of Rick's body. He twitched and drove his now huge claws down deeper into the earth. A muscle appeared to roll across his back before it exploded upward. Bat-like wings erupted from the split muscle and spread out and out as he continued to grow. He rose up on his hind legs and threw out his forelimbs, smashing through some of the gigantic trees like they were toothpicks.

The black flames rushed outward and dissipated all at once. A wave of heat struck us. I closed my eyes for only a moment, then opened them to stare up at the creature before us.

"Black dragon?" Lovat whispered. "Rick?"

No. Not Rick. My best friend Rick was no more. In fact, he'd never existed. Instead, we gazed up at…

Onyx.

The black dragon. The one everyone believed to be dead.

He lifted his enormous head and roared a challenge into the sky.

Not dead. Very much alive.

"Beryl! Answer me! Viridia is coming!"

43

The green dragon exploded from the cavern with a snarl. It came to an abrupt halt, staring at the newly formed black dragon.

Rick—Onyx, that is—turned to face him. "Hello, brother. Did you miss me?" His voice still sounded so much like Rick, full of the same attitude and swagger, yet so much deeper and enormous.

"You're dead!" I'd heard Viridia's voice before, yet the rumble of his bass flooded through me. The smell of decay washed over us at the same time.

Lovat clung to me, but we were beneath the green dragon's notice now. He focused all his attention on Onyx, spreading his own wings—the left one gleaming—to match the black dragon's. Side-by-side, the two dragons appeared equal in size, though Onyx didn't have quite the same bulk. He appeared sleeker, faster. And yet both of them towered above us, filling our vision with their enormity.

"Beryl?" Lainey's voice wavered over the talker. She sounded genuinely worried. "Where did the black dragon come from? Are you there? What's happening?"

I couldn't answer her. I didn't know what to say.

Onyx, the black dragon, lifted his right hand, the cybernetic one, and flexed the claws. "Obviously, I'm alive. Come now, brother. Has age diminished your vision that much?"

The green dragon moved to his right, circling Onyx. "We made sure. We hit the city with everything."

"Yes, it was quite devastating. I didn't think you'd do it, right up until the moment that you did."

"We destroyed your source!"

Onyx nodded. "And if I'd stayed in dragon form, I would have been destroyed with it. But in human form, I could escape down into the room I'd prepared for just such an eventuality." He spread his wings even wider. "Sadly, I did not anticipate being trapped in human form all these years. It's been quite… restrictive."

"You killed Caesious!" Viridia almost charged him with the realization. His wings flared, and he tore at the earth with his claws.

"Well, I had help with that." Onyx chuckled. "We always underestimated the humans, you know. They are capable of so much more than I ever expected. Walking among them for so long has changed my perspective."

"What do you want?" Poison, glowing green and smoking, seeped from the green dragon's jaws.

Holding on to Lovat, I backed further and further away. This was going to get immensely destructive. We did not want to be here. But I couldn't leave. Not yet.

"Rick dragon," Lovat whispered. "How?"

"I don't know," I murmured. I still couldn't believe… I just couldn't.

"That's it," Lainey's voice said. "I'm coming to find you."

"I want what we've always wanted," Onyx boomed, stepped to his right while continuing to face the green dragon. "Worship. Power."

"You lost it all. There is nothing left for you now," Viridia snarled. "Leave The Circle, or we will kill you again."

Onyx lifted a claw just like Rick lifting a finger to say something. "You know, I've learned a little more about what's on the other side now, and… I don't think I will. And with all of you already fighting each other, you aren't in any condition to kill me."

"This is my source of power. You cannot possibly think to best me here."

"Best you? Maybe not. But I can keep you busy while someone else takes care of your source." With that, Onyx launched himself directly at Viridia, spewing acidic fire. The green dragon shot into the air, roaring with pain and anger, and responded with his own poison breath.

I yanked Lovat down and shielded him. The dragons threw acid and poison back and forth at each other, and weren't paying attention to where it fell. "Down the hill!" I yelled. Lovat threw himself over the edge and rolled. With a glance back at the horrifying spectacle above us, I dove after him. I reached the base of the hill and looked up only to see the green dragon's tail smash through one of the enormous pine trees and send half of it tumbling down toward us.

Lovat and I scrambled out of the way, splashing through the tiny stream I'd discovered the first time I'd been here. The tree crashed into the spot we'd just been, sending up a shower of needles and dirt. We found another clear space between two more giant trees and looked back up at the battle.

When I fought Troilus Green, I thought it was the most vicious creature in the world. I was wrong. The dragons made the draconic seem like an angry toddler. They tore and bit at each other with a ferocity impossible to describe. Poison and acid rained down from the sky, occasionally mixed with dragon blood. Onyx's cybernetic claws seemed to do more damage than the dragon's real ones. And while both dragons ripped gashes in each other's wings, Viridia's cybernetic wing remained undamaged. No wonder they all pursued cyb technology so fervently.

"What we do?" Lovat whimpered.

"We stay out of their way," I said. "Until we can get out of here, anyway."

The dragons entwined with each other, tearing with their claws. Unable to fly at the same time, they plunged toward the ground. At the last minute, they separated. As the enormous form of Onyx shot over us, the wind from his wings stirred up a maelstrom of dust and pine needles.

"Berrrllll," he growled, before turning to speed back toward the green dragon.

Was he saying my name? Why? I couldn't do anything in this fight, and even if I could, would I want to? I hated the green dragon more than anything. I always had. But Rick… Rick… I still couldn't say it in my head. This was a nightmare. I would wake up on Mason's floor soon. Or maybe the Viridian Guard captured us in his apartment and injected us with some kind of drug that was making me see all of this. My theories got wilder and wilder as my brain clung to its denial.

A massive blow from Onyx sent the green dragon spiraling back toward the city. The black dragon circled back at once. As it flew over us again, this time I heard him clearly: "Backpack. Destroy." And then the green dragon smashed into him, and they both tumbled out of the sky somewhere toward the mountains.

"The backpack!" Lovat exclaimed, holding it up.

I grabbed it and ripped the zipper open. Beyond the pages from the Book of Lore, I saw the usual traveling supplies, and two other things. The first one I pulled out was the strange drill device Dusk found in Loden's workshop. The other…

"What that?" Lovat asked. His speech had dropped back into his old patterns, I noticed. Under these circumstances, I didn't feel like talking right, either.

I turned the second device over in my hands. I guessed almost immediately, but at first I couldn't be sure. It consisted of several long blocks of a material I didn't recognize, all fastened together with wire. Two more larger wires led from the ends of the blocks into a small panel with a single switch and a knob.

"It's an explosive device," I said. It had to be. Rick talked about using them, and I think he used one in Incarnadine. But I didn't know he had more. What could we have used this for? We could have blown up the railroad tracks to stop Auric's attack! Peri would still be alive. The injustice of it solidified my roiling emotions. The confusion, pain, disbelief, and sadness all melted away, leaving behind the one thing I had always been able to hold on to: my anger.

"Why?" Lovat picked up the drill device.

I looked up as the green dragon swept overhead again, much higher now. Onyx chased after him. He had almost reached his foe's tail when the green dragon folded his wings in and dropped. Onyx sped past him, but Viridia reached up as he did and scored long gashes across Onyx's belly. The screams of both dragons assaulted our ears.

"He wants me to destroy Viridia's power source," I realized.

44

Somehow, the green dragon got Onyx's tail in his mouth. The battle did not seem to be going well for my former friend.

"Former friend." I'd never had a friend as close as Rick before. I shared everything with him. I—

Lovat found the activation switch for the drill. "Whoa." He stumbled back and dropped it, turning it back off in the process.

"Careful!" I picked it back up and looked it over. Dusk was right: what could you do with this thing other than drill a straight, small hole? I looked at the explosive device. It would easily drop down into such a hole. I had no doubts about Rick's intentions. He wanted me to do it, though. And if I did, he would kill the green dragon.

Wasn't that what I wanted? My entire life's purpose? I hated the dragon with everything in me. But Rick's betrayal…

I took a deep breath. What were my options? I could do as Rick wanted. Or not. And if I didn't, the green dragon would probably win this fight, judging from the way it was going. I would never see Rick again, and would lose the best chance we'd probably ever get at killing Viridia.

Fewmets. Rick knew I couldn't walk away.

"Arrrgh!" I put my hand into the back of the drill where I found a handle with just one button. Pressing and holding the button activated the drill itself. I expected the motion of the device to be difficult to handle, but it moved smoothly and didn't jerk my arm around. I walked back to the hill we'd tumbled down and aimed the drill into a steep slope. It bit into the dirt, tossing it aside as it pulled me forward.

After a few seconds, I struck rock. Now the drill jerked at me, but it kept going. I was up to my elbow already. How deep should I go?

Hearing the splash of liquid above, I let go of the drill and leaped backward just in time. A shower of the green dragon's venom splattered across the side of the hill. I recognized the bitter odor, taking me back to the day I almost died here, filled with the dragon's poison myself.

"Lovat! Are you all right?" I spun around and found him several feet back, getting up out of the stream where he'd fallen in his haste to escape the rain.

"Yah. I'm good."

I turned back to the hole I'd been drilling. It couldn't be deep enough yet, especially not with the drill device still lodged inside. I reached inside and found the handle. The whole thing had turned a little to one side when I let it go. I pressed the button and got it spinning again. I had to boost my arm to twist the drill back into place; even so, my wrist ached from the effort.

After a few seconds, I pulled the drill back to drag out some of the debris. Was this rock itself the dragon's source? Or was it something deeper inside? If Bice were here, he might be able to tap into it. We should have brought him along. We should have done so many things different. My brain raced through these thoughts, always diverting itself from thinking about the big fact: my best friend was one of the dragons I'd sworn to kill.

I cursed Onyx up and down, with every imprecation I could think of. I may have taught Lovat some new words. Actually, growing up on the street, he probably knew more of that kind of language than I did.

I activated the drill again and kept digging. The dragons' battle shifted away from us, giving us a few moments of safety. Lovat scrambled back up the hill to take a look.

"Where are they?" I yelled. The drill hit a harder bit of rock and had trouble moving again. I tried shifting it a little to the right or left.

"Vir'dia fell on top of a building!" Lovat called. "Now up again!"

Oh no. The nearest buildings to us were mostly empty or warehouses, but if the fight moved further into the city, homes and apartments could be in jeopardy. More lives than our own were now at stake.

"Beryl?" Lainey's voice came over the talker again. "I'm almost at the four-wheelers. About to head your way."

I fumbled for the talker with my left hand, and dropped it. I stopped the drill and caught the talker before it rolled down into the water. "Lainey? Lainey! Stay where you are! We'll come to you!"

"You're alive! What about the others?"

"Lovat's safe for the moment." I glanced back at the sky as a shadow passed over again. "No time! Gotta go!"

I tossed the talker on top of Rick's backpack and resumed my work with the drill. "Lovat! Where'd the dragons go?"

"Rick fell on the mountain," he reported. "Vir'dia fell on top of him."

Maybe that gave us more time. I couldn't reach any further into the side of the hill; I was up to my shoulder. Was that deep enough? How would I even know? I pulled the drill back out and used it to clear out more space around the hole, making the opening wider. Once I'd done that, I thrust my hand back in. I could drill for maybe a couple more inches. That would have to be enough.

"Coming back!" Lovat shouted. He scurried down the hill beside me, keeping his eyes upward. Both dragons sped over us, one after the other. I couldn't tell which one was chasing and which was being chased.

Enough. I needed to—What? The drill suddenly shot out of my hand, deeper into the hole, all by itself. At the same time, I felt a rush of cool air sweep over my arm, followed by a tingling feeling. I yanked my arm back out of the hole and stared.

Light shone from the hole, a warbling, shaky kind of light. Along with it came the cool air, diluted by the warmer air around us, but I could still feel it.

"Tastes funny," Lovat said.

I licked my lips. He was right. The air itself tasted… metallic. It reminded me of something, but I couldn't place it.

A loud roar from nearby reminded me of our situation.

I picked up the explosive device. I hoped the knob set the timer. Otherwise, all I'd blow up would be myself.

"Lovat, head to the edge of the green here," I told him. "When you see me coming, run toward the mountains as fast as you can. I'll be running with you."

He looked at the light sputtering from the hole and nodded. As soon as he was out of sight, I turned the knob. It clicked as it turned. I wondered if each click meant a second, a minute, or something else entirely. Either way, it came to a stop after seven clicks.

I looked up to see both dragons circling each other high above, snapping and clawing, though making fewer connections than before. "I hate you, Onyx," I snarled. I looked down at the explosive. "But I hate Viridia more, I guess." I pushed the button and chunked the device into the hole.

Seven clicks. Seven minutes, I hoped. I grabbed up Rick's pack and the talker, then ran after Lovat. He saw me coming and took off, as instructed. I caught up with him, racing away from the trees and stream and cave and all that beauty. Dragons destroyed beauty. It was their nature. Yet I'm the one responsible for it now. What did that make me?

Too slow. "Get on my back!" I yelled to Lovat. I stopped and bent down long enough for him to scramble on, then I took off. I channeled as much boost energy as I could into my legs. I think I ran faster than I'd ever done before, except maybe when I ran after Peri.

I'd never been good at keeping track of time in my head. I tried counting seconds, but the pace of my feet pounding the earth threw me off. And I didn't even know for sure how much time we had; seven minutes was a guess.

My eyes saw movement ahead. Lainey on one of the four-wheelers! She'd ignored my order and come to check on us. I waved at her to turn around. I didn't have the breath to yell. She saw how fast I was moving and understood. She pulled the four-wheeler into a complete u-turn and raced beside me.

Viridia's power source exploded.

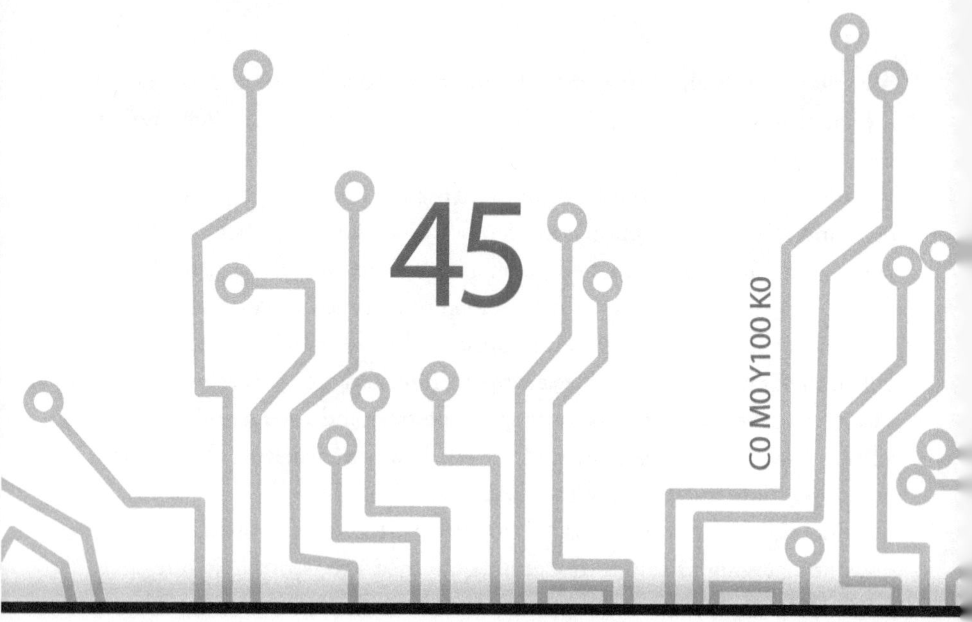

45

I sensed it before it happened. I stopped my boosts and dove for the ground. My hands plowed into the earth and my right wrist twisted a little further in the wrong direction, sending sharp pain all the way up my arm. Lovat rolled free.

Light erupted behind us, illuminating the mountains. I never heard the sound. A wave of force rushed over me. Lainey cried out. Lovat screamed. Rocks bounced off my back.

And then the same kind of air Lovat and I had tasted before swept over us. Cool air, not at all like the enormous heat of the explosion that killed Peri. And now the tingling feeling flowed over my entire body. My twisted wrist straightened out and felt better at once. In fact, I felt great.

I rolled over and sat up. Beside me, Lovat clambered to his feet. "Tickles," he said.

I looked to the other side. The four-wheeler lay on its side, except now it only had three wheels. A few other parts lay scattered about. Lainey lay facedown several yards ahead. Glacier sat beside her as if nothing had happened.

I scrambled to my feet and ran to her side. "Lainey!" As I reached for her, she pushed herself up and spat dirt out of her mouth. "That was…" She paused, shook her head, then rolled over to look up at me. "I don't understand."

"Are you all right?"

"I feel great!"

I reached out. She took my hand and jumped to her feet.

"I thought I was dead!" She patted herself in various places. "I flew off the four-wheeler and hit the ground. It hurt worse than anything… but now I'm fine." Her eyebrows twitched and her mouth hung partially open. "What was that?"

I turned around. "The dragon's source," I said. "We blew it up."

I stared at the results of the explosion. Nothing remained of the trees and everything green. The crater that took their place looked very different from the crater on the rail to Caesious. This one looked like the earth had vomited something out, leaving behind an empty throat and stomach. A gross analogy, but it was all I could think of. A hazy smoke drifted all around, interspersed with flashes of light, each one like a tiny explosive going off in the air.

I took a step toward the devastation.

Fifty feet in front of me, the green dragon slammed into the earth, its wing almost coming down on my head. The force of the impact threw me off my feet. I landed on my rear and watched open-mouthed as Onyx descended in a rush, landing on top of the other dragon.

"The others…" The green dragon's voice no longer sounded intimidating. In fact, it sounded weaker by the word. "…they won't let you…"

"No one can stop me now," Onyx snarled. "Everyone's given me exactly what I need." The dragon shot a look at me. Could a dragon smirk?

"I… can't…" Viridia whispered. Then his head fell back and his eyes glazed over. But he wasn't dead; I could see his chest moving, and his claws continued to swipe at Onyx. What was going on?

"What are you doing?" Onyx demanded. He swiveled his head back toward the city. "Oh, I see…"

Onyx slammed his front feet down on the green dragon. The green wing rose up in front of me, blocking my vision as Onyx's head came down. A horrifying tearing and crunching sound followed. The green wing, all I could see, jerked spasmodically. A hand touched my shoulder. I almost leaped to my feet before realizing it was Lainey.

The wing spasmed one last time, then settled slowly to the ground. Onyx jerked his head and something tumbled through the air toward me. With a final thump, the severed head of Viridia, the green dragon, landed on top of its own wing, facing me.

My eyes locked on to the open and staring eyes of the dragon I'd hated for so many years. From the moment of my baby sister's death, my entire life had focused on this and only this. Everything I'd wanted and everything I'd worked toward now lay on the dirt in front of me. I knew that face as well as I knew my own: from toys to paintings to statues, I'd seen it every day of my life, and the one terrifying time in person. The green scales. The massive white teeth. The two horns curving back from the top of the head, the right one banded in silver. Only one thing was missing: the dragon's eyes always glowed red. Now they held no glow at all.

Viridia was dead.

But I felt no elation, no sense of fulfillment, nothing celebratory at all. My eyes tore away from the dead dragon's and looked up at the face of the live dragon: my best friend, who'd betrayed me in every way possible. The green dragon's blood didn't just drip—it almost poured from his jaws.

"Well?" Onyx said. "Isn't this your dream?"

I got to my feet. Lainey tried to assist me, but I shrugged her off. My hands shook, and my eyes returned to the severed head. I could take three steps and be inside its mouth. So close. So final.

"What's happening?" Lainey asked quietly.

I lifted a shaking finger to point at Onyx. "Why?" My voice shook almost as much as my hands.

Onyx turned his head as if he hadn't heard me.

"Why?" This time I screamed the word with such force, a surge of pain blossomed in my throat.

Onyx scratched at the scales on his neck. "Because this is who I am, Beryl. I am a dragon. I am a god. Your assistance in returning me to my true form is appreciated."

"You're not a god," I snarled. I clenched my fists to control the shaking.

Lainey gasped beside me. "Is that… Rick?"

In the distance, I heard alarms sounding in the city. What would things be like once they discovered their god was dead?

"In respect of our friendship, I will forgive your blasphemy," Onyx said, waving his claw. He snorted. "I already have worshippers, anyway. All part of the plan, you know. I'm sorry things had to turn out this way for your plans, though. There will be one dragon left at the end, the one true god of The Circle." He lowered his head. "And that god is Onyx."

I didn't know what to say. I had so many questions, but my anger overrode them all. I wanted to charge forward, attack this dragon, even though I knew it would kill me.

"Yes, I used you, Beryl. I used many, many people along the way. But you were the best." Onyx glanced toward the city, then back. "You so desperately wanted a new family to replace the one you lost, it made you easy to manipulate. And when I saw you in action that first day, and realized what it meant about cybernetics, well… I had to stick with you."

He made a weird sound in his throat. Maybe it was laughter. "The one thing I didn't anticipate was how much Auric would spill to you. He always has been a little strange. Never can quite figure him out. Anyway, that accelerated my plans. I hadn't meant to reveal myself this early."

Early? What did he mean?

"I'm also genuinely sorry about Kelly. Maybe you can have her back when I'm done with her." His eyes turned to Lainey. "Though if this one had come along earlier…" His tongue ran along the edge of his teeth.

Only then did I realize the implications for Kelly. I thought I'd felt sick before, but now… I wavered and almost fell.

Onyx took one more look toward the city. "I have to be going now. I really did like you, Beryl. I'm sorry things had to go this way. But my plans come first." He gathered himself up like a cat. With a massive thrust of his wings, he took to the air and swept away.

I fell to my knees and vomited. Lainey stayed beside me, her hand still on my shoulder. I felt another, smaller hand touch my other shoulder. Lovat.

But neither of them brought me any comfort. All along, I'd been afraid for my friends, believing the worst thing that could happen in this war of ours would be if they were captured or killed by the dragons. But this was worse, far worse.

And nothing could make it any better.

46

"Vir'dian Guard on the way," Lovat reported, some ten minutes or so later.

I hadn't moved from my spot in front of the dragon's head. The smell of my own vomit mixed with the decay the green dragon always brought with him. In death, the effect magnified. Already, I could see the grass withering around the body, spreading outward. My hands dug into the corrupted earth, like Rick's hands had sought out the power source.

"All right, Beryl, that's enough," Lainey said, coming back to me. "Get up. We need to get out of here."

"Why?" I murmured. "Everything's... wrong."

"Because Lovat needs you," she answered. She knelt and grabbed my arm. "Yes, it's horrible. I can't even begin to understand how you're feeling. But he needs you. And I need you. And you have other friends depending on you."

I let her help me to my feet. I took a last look at the head of Viridia, letting it burn into my memory. Then I turned to follow her.

We abandoned the four-wheeler. Maybe if we had enough time, or if Caedan or Peri were here, we could have fixed it. Or maybe not. It looked pretty bad. With Lainey leading the way, we hurried toward the mountains and the location of the second four-wheeler.

When we reached the rocky area, safe from other eyes, I took a look back. I zoomed my vision at the body of the green dragon. A squad or two of Viridian Guard had arrived. Some of them lay on the ground, overcome with despair or some other emotion. Others just stood, unable to do anything else. A pair of them examined the four-wheeler. That would create a nice mystery for them. Two others had actually come part of the way after us, though they seemed reluctant to continue the chase. They appeared to be arguing with each other.

Lovat took my hand. "How is Rick dragon?" he asked.

I shook my head. "I don't know, buddy. I guess he always was one."

"How?"

I bowed my head and tried not to snap at him. "I just don't know."

"Let's keep moving," Lainey said.

The afternoon wore on. When had the sun crossed the sky so far? Even little details like that were hurting my brain. The whole world seemed wrong. I hiked along, an ache in my gut like nothing I'd felt, except when Loden died. But Rick wasn't dead. This was worse.

I didn't know what to do next. I saw no path forward. If Lovat hadn't been with me, needing me, I think I would have just curled up alone and died. As things stood, I opened my mouth several times, about to ask Lainey to take him back and leave me behind. But I never did.

"I hope you're able to drive," Lainey said when we found the four-wheeler. "I'm not confident enough to do it myself."

I nodded and climbed on. I drove almost without thought. Lovat held on beside while Lainey rode behind, along with the cub. We retraced our path between the city and mountains, eventually reaching the road to the mines again. We had to stop, hide, and wait for the road to clear. Dozens of men were hastening back toward the city. All of them appeared agitated, talking to one another and moving as fast as they could in such a crowd. Word must have spread.

I should have been ecstatic. The people of Viridia were free of the dragon! But the circumstances kept me from enjoying the moment. These men would return to a city in chaos, no doubt. Would the draconics and Guard be able to maintain order? Would Atramentous try to extend his rule over this city like the red dragons had done over Caesious? My mind briefly touched on these thoughts, but couldn't explore them. That took too much effort.

The shadows lengthened as we finally crossed the road. Night would soon be on us.

"We'll need to stop soon," Lainey observed.

I grunted

"Driving in the dark will be dangerous," she pointed out. "The Viridian Guard will be everywhere. We should be hiding."

I nodded. We didn't have time to make it to the barn we often used. Instead, I directed the four-wheeler off to the east until we found a complex series of ravines. We drove down inside one, hid the four-wheeler, then walked on a bit until we found a good spot for sleeping. We were all used to it and needed little time to spread out the sleeping bags and prepare for bed.

I didn't sleep at all. Lovat, exhausted after the physical and emotional exertion of the day, fell asleep almost at once. Lainey whispered with the cub a bit before also dozing off. I lay awake and alone, staring up at the stars.

Every day from the moment I met Rick rehearsed through my mind. I searched for clues to his true nature, things I must have missed. Things we all missed, to be fair to myself. Things he said, the way he acted… I could see some of it in retrospect, but how could I have known from such scant clues? How could I have guessed?

I should have! I should have known. Like a fool, I went along with everything he wanted. What was it he said to me? I so desperately wanted a new family to replace the one I lost? It made me easy to manipulate. I was too trusting.

No, not trusting. Just… afraid to lose anything again. I was so happy to have friends—happy to have a best friend!—that I compromised to keep him happy. I would have done anything to hold on to the friendship.

He'd been working his own plans from the very beginning. He must have given some of Loden's notes to the Guard when they captured him… and that was before we even left the city! How did he get Loden's notes that early? I had been blind to his actions even then!

A cloud passed in front of the stars. Or was it a cloud? Maybe Rick was returning to finish us off, realizing he couldn't leave us behind or we would… what? What would we do? I had nothing now. We had been struggling since Loden died, and now with Rick gone… what was the point of our rebellion now? The green dragon was dead, but now we had another black one!

And Kelly. Chromatic hells. Her baby was a draconic. She could die from it. We still had time to deal with that, at least. But it was all my fault. I should have fought harder to hold on to her, not let her slip away to Rick's seduction. Was that a dragon power? Seduction of human women? Ugh, I didn't want to think about that. Kelly would need me now. That's all that mattered.

The cloud moved on, letting the stars re-appear. No dragon attack, at least for now.

We would have to leave the Asylum. Rick knew… well, he knew everything. We would have to find a new hiding place. Maybe Lainey could help. We could go back to her father, maybe. Could I get a message to Auric? If I told him all about Onyx, maybe he could do something. They did it before, apparently.

I wish I had a god to cry out to, like Bice believed. Divine help would come in handy about now. "Please," I whispered toward the stars. "Please…" I didn't even know what to ask. I didn't know what I wanted any more.

Revenge against Rick? Part of me screamed for that, wanting payback for the betrayal. Yet… how? He was a dragon! And he'd just murdered another dragon right in front of me. With my help.

I felt a little bit of satisfaction ease in at the thought. I did help kill the green dragon. Just like I helped kill the blue one. Maybe I was really lucky, like Kelly said. Well, that and my cyb implant.

Oh, fewmets. What did Rick mean to do with that? He'd deliberately given the notes to two different cities' scientists, so they could make progress on it. If he got the information he needed from them, he could get the same kind of procedure done to himself. A dragon with my capabilities. He'd tear the other dragons to shreds. Nothing could stop him.

Maybe I did sleep a little. I don't know. I don't remember sleeping. I only know that morning found me staring at the growing light, awake and still circling the same thoughts of betrayal and my own stupidity, over and over and over…

47

As the morning light grew, Lainey and Lovat slept on. I pulled Rick's backpack to me and withdrew the pages torn from the Cerulean Book of Lore. I figured I should probably read them.

The writer of the book talked about how Onyx grew too antagonistic in his heresies, sending "missionaries" to the other cities to encourage humans to worship him as the highest of the dragon gods. He also boldly spoke of traveling outside The Circle, something the other dragons opposed. Even Amaranth, who'd supported it at first, now agreed Onyx was going too far. His ambitions seemed to be dominion over all of The Circle, and even outside it.

The dragons could not tolerate it. They repeatedly insisted that he stop, sending messages in every way. Amaranth even confronted him face-to-face and demanded he cease his actions. When she returned from that meeting, she summoned the other dragons and told them of Onyx's plans.

I flipped from one page to the other, then back. What had she told them? The writer wasn't clear about that. Whatever she said, it was enough to galvanize even Auric into joining the attack. They came together at once and destroyed Onyx's power source. Then they laid waste to the city, creating the Blasted Lands. They never found Onyx's body, of course, but they assumed he'd died in the explosion of his source.

But he lived. Protogonus Blue's story of a "lone draconic" turned out to be partially true, except it wasn't a draconic. It was the dragon himself all along.

"Learn anything?" Lainey asked.

I jerked and crumpled one of the pages. I didn't even realize she was awake. She stood beside me, looking down, silhouetted by the rising sun. I couldn't complain about the view.

"It's all bad," I told her. I stuffed the pages back into the pack.

"What do we do now?"

"We get back to the Asylum as quick as we can," I said. "We need to get everyone together and… and leave. I don't know where yet."

She nodded as I climbed out of the sleeping bag. I felt exhausted, mentally, emotionally, and physically. I sent a boost running through my entire body to perk me up. If we got moving now, we could be back at the Asylum before dark. My stomach growled, reminding me we were out of food. Unless we could find some fruit or something, we wouldn't eat until tonight, either. All the more reason to get moving.

I checked the fuel level on the four-wheeler and added the rest of the spare can. We were running out of everything. Once the others climbed on, I gunned the engine and made a beeline for the Achromatic Asylum.

How many times had I traveled this route now? I tried to figure it out in my head, but gave up. I'd been walking for most of them. Used a train a couple of times, and rode or drove a four-wheeler at least twice. No, that wasn't right. One of the four-wheeler trips came from the Asylum, but then went to Incarnadine. Did I count that one?

"Stupid," I muttered to myself. The whole mental exercise was just an attempt to distract me from the ache inside and the fuzziness in my head. Lack of sleep combined with emotional trauma did not make a good combination.

"I don't think you're stupid," Lainey leaned in close and said in my ear. The sudden warmth gave me a pleasant feeling all over. Maybe… maybe life could go on. Maybe it wasn't the end of the world. Yet.

"Still feel that way," I said over my shoulder. I did feel that way, but I kind of just wanted her to talk into my ear again.

"Why? Because Rick deceived you? He deceived everyone, from what I could tell. You have some smart people on your team, and none of them knew."

"But you saw something," I realized. "You said he wanted

something else."

"I could tell he had other motives, but that's a far cry from realizing he's a dragon in disguise!"

Even so, I felt new respect for the girl riding behind me. She had keen insights. I remembered the emotions she'd drawn out of me back in Auric, how she'd gotten me to tell her my story. She told me I was valuable, whether I succeeded in my mission or not. I wasn't sure I could believe that now, not with a failure so deep.

We stopped only to stretch and relieve ourselves from time to time. Glacier the cub complained the most about being stuck on the vehicle for so long, but I kept pushing. The day passed without further event.

We had no warning that anything might be wrong back home. No smoke. No wandering patrols or dragons flying through the sky. Everything appeared quiet and normal.

Until I saw Jaden stumbling toward us almost half a mile from the Asylum.

Seeing us, he stopped and waited until we pulled up beside him. I climbed off, wiping the dust from my face. I opened my mouth to speak, and he punched me. The blow caught me by surprise and I stumbled back into the four-wheeler where Lainey caught me. Lovat hit the ground and ran toward Jaden, fists raised. Jaden held out his crutch to block him.

"Lovat, wait," I said, feeling my jaw. That hurt more than I would have expected. I looked at Jaden and waited for him to speak.

"I was starting to believe you," he said, glaring at me. "At first, it all sounded so utterly ridiculous. But then you… you were so sure. You ran all over the place, talking to the gold dragon, saving Caesious… you made it look like this whole crazy thing might actually be possible." He snorted. "I'm going back to Viridia."

I looked toward the Asylum. "Jaden, what's going on? Where is everyone else?"

"It could never last!" He swung his crutch at me, but couldn't reach me now. "Humans can't fight dragons! It was only a matter of time before it came crashing down!"

"What are you talking about?"

He pointed back the way he'd come. "Atramentous! He came! And that stupid priest and the girl in the cave were working for him!"

I'd heard enough. I took a step toward the Asylum.

"Where are the others?" Lainey asked.

"They're gone!" Jaden waved his free hand. "I'm the only one left!"

I ran. I boosted my legs and ran. Exhausted as I was, I couldn't move as fast as I'd like, but I pushed myself as hard as I could. It wasn't Atramentous; it was Onyx. It had to be. He'd mentioned already having worshippers. Bice's words about Mazarine came rushing back to me. And of course Dusk would be in on it. Why had we stopped? We should have driven straight through the night! We should have...

I stopped. Even with all that had happened, I was unprepared for the sight. The Asylum lay in ruins. All of Don's careful, meticulous work in disguising our base of operations had been torn asunder. Why, Rick? You couldn't leave me even this?

I swallowed and stumbled, almost falling before I channeled another boost to keep myself steady. I pushed my way into the debris, shoving aside the remains of one of our water barrels.

"Kelly!" I screamed. "Bice! Don! Kelly!"

The only sound I heard came from the four-wheeler pulling up behind me. Lainey hopped off, and helped Jaden down. I didn't even wonder how she'd convinced him to come back.

Lovat ran past me into the mess of our former home. "Don!" he yelled as loud as he could. "Don!"

We both climbed and scrambled our way through every bit of the ruins. We found nothing salvageable... and more importantly, we found no one.

Onyx. He'd taken everything else I cared about.

I almost collapsed then and there. But I had one last hope. The cave. The workshop. Maybe it was still there, and my friends were hiding inside.

Even with the devastation, I knew exactly where to locate the cave entrance. We found it blocked by a lot of dirt and debris. With Lovat's help, I cleared enough out of the way to crawl into the darkened cave. Lainey fetched a flashlight from the four-wheeler. I used it to look down the passage. Dust particles hung in the air, reflecting the light, and I could see rocks on the ground here and there.

"Kelly! Bice! Don!"

A low moan came from somewhere ahead. I gasped and rushed forward, watching my feet. I passed some of our belongings—cots, blankets and such—scattered on the floor.

A wall of rock brought me to a sudden halt. The roof had caved in, bringing down tons of rock and blocking the final few feet toward the workshop. Even with my enhanced strength, I might not be able to dig through all of it. Some of the rocks looked enormous. I was so stunned and horrified by the discovery that it took another moan for me to realize: Protogonus Blue lay half-buried beneath the rocks.

"Blue!" I knelt beside him. Lovat came up behind me, so I handed him the flashlight. I started to move some of the rocks covering the draconic.

"Don't… bother," Protogonus Blue managed to say with a cough. His head lay turned on its side, one eye looking up at me. "My spirit… will soon join that of my father in whatever awaits… beyond."

"No, come on. I can get you out." I boosted my arms and pulled another rock out of the way. "Lovat, leave the light and go fetch some water!" He obeyed me at once.

"No, you don't understand." Protogonus Blue reached out to me with one of his claws. I took hold of it without thinking. "My body… is crushed, Beryl Godslayer. I only held my spirit here until… I could speak with you… one last time."

"What about the others? Kelly, Bice, Don. Where are they?"

"Onyx." Protogonus Blue's voice grew weaker. "Onyx came. He… here all along."

"I know." I glanced over my shoulder. What was keeping Lovat? "It was Rick. He betrayed us."

"More… I did not see… did not comprehend…"

"Neither did I. The others. Where are they? Did he take them? Are they trapped in the workshop?"

"I tried to prevent… collapse," the draconic said. "Knew… you needed workshop." He coughed.

I looked up at all the rocks covering him. He'd tried to stop it?

"Lovat!" I yelled back down the tunnel. "Where's the water?"

I turned back to Protogonus Blue. "Hang on. I can still get you out. I know it." I felt stupid even saying it, but what else could I say?

He didn't answer me for a long time.

"Blue?"

He blinked. "I am… still here."

"Where is everyone?"

"Onyx… took the girl… his mate…"

My heart sank even further. Kelly. He had to mean Kelly. Rick took her. Of course he did. She was valuable to him, but only for the draconic child she carried.

"Bice? Don?"

He didn't respond. Hearing rocks displaced, I turned and saw Lainey coming up behind me with a canteen. "This is all we have," she said. "I sent Lovat to the stream to get some more." In the glow of the flashlight, I could see the sadness in her eyes as she knelt by the draconic and offered him some water. He accepted it, but Lainey had trouble getting much of it down his throat. Most spilled out on the cavern floor.

"Beryl…"

I almost didn't hear his whisper. "I'm still here," I told him, leaning in close to the reptilian snout.

"You… inspired me… Beryl… name of… many colors."

He coughed one more time. I watched his eye stop moving, staring straight out in the flashlight's dim glow. Protogonus Blue was dead. Only then did I realize I still held his hand.

"He's dead," I whispered.

Lainey stood, but didn't say anything.

I bowed my head. What now?

My best friend was one of the dragons I was trying to kill.

Peri and Protogonus Blue were dead.

Caedan was gone.

Kelly was taken against her will.

Bice and Don were missing, maybe dead.

"There's nothing left," I said. "Nothing."

Lainey sat down beside me and gently took my hand from the draconic's. She held it and looked at me. I looked back, but couldn't say anything else. My devastation was complete.

"I told you I would tell you what you wanted to know," she said, "once I'd learned everything I could." She glanced down at Protogonus Blue. "I think we've reached that point now."

She got to her feet and pulled at my hand. "Come on. It's time we went back to my father."

Beryl's story continues in

Onyx

For more information on the Dragontek Lore series,
and other upcoming books,
visit timfrankovich.com

Joining the mailing list is the best way to stay informed,
plus you get free stories!
(including Rick's story before he arrived in Viridia!)

If you enjoyed this book, please post a review
on Amazon, B&N, Goodreads, etc.
There's no better way to spread the word.

Acknowledgements

A couple of years ago, I joined an organization called the Apex Writing Group. I joined for the purpose of learning all I could about the craft and business of writing, both from dozens of special guests who appeared in our weekly Zoom meetings, and the founder of this group: David Wolverton (also known as David Farland, his other pen name). Dave was one of the giants of the fantasy genre, best known for his Runelords series. He'd been everywhere and done everything. Each time we met, I was further amazed at how much he'd involved himself in, throughout the years. From teaching Brandon Sanderson to advising Scholastic to take a chance on this book from the UK about a boy wizard named Harry, Dave did it all. It's hard to imagine anyone else having more of an effect on our genre in the past few decades.

As I write this, it's been only a few weeks since Dave passed away from an accident. Those of us in the Apex group (along with everyone else) were stunned when the news hit. We'd been speaking with and learning from Dave every week, sometimes multiple times a week.

His loss is profound. I've dedicated this book to him, because it's my next book to come out, but in a way, every book I write now has been influenced by David Wolverton. And that, I suppose, is the best way to honor him.

As always, I am exceedingly grateful for my beta readers Stephen Tallman and Allen Perkins.

Beryl's insane adventures have a long way to go. Stay tuned. There's more coming.

If you want to keep track of my progress on all my writing, you can connect on timfrankovich.com, my Facebook author page, Twitter, etc. But the best way, which keeps you informed and gives you exclusive previews, is to join the mailing list. Sign up on the website. (You'll get free stories too!)

Tim Frankovich has been exploring fantastic worlds since third grade, when he cut up a grocery sack and drew a Godzilla-meets-superheroes story. Since then, he's gotten a little bit better at the writing part (not so much with the drawing).

His goal as a writer is to transport readers to another world, make them care deeply about characters in dire situations, and guide them deeply into life itself.

At the moment, he is probably suitably conscious somewhere in Texas with his beloved wife, awesome four kids, and a fool of a pup named Pippin.